HUNTRESS

SCATTERED STARS: CONVICTION BOOK 5

HUNTRESS

SCATTERED STARS: CONVICTION BOOK 5

GLYNN STEWART

FAOLAN'S PEN PUBLISHING

faolanspen.com

This edition published in 2022 by:

Faolan's Pen Publishing Inc.

22 King St. S, Suite 300

Waterloo, Ontario

N2J 1N8 Canada

ISBN-13: 978-1-989674-25-3 (print)

A record of this book is available from Library and Archives Canada.

Printed in the United States of America

1 2 3 4 5 6 7 8 9 10

First edition

First printing: May 2022

Read more books from Glynn Stewart at faolanspen.com

1

THE HARDEST LESSON for any military commander to learn is when to let go.

For Admiral Kira "Basketball" Demirci, commanding officer, primary shareholder and Chief Executive Officer of the Memorial Force mercenary company, it was a lesson she was still only passable at.

The slightly built blonde woman had lost the coin toss with her second-in-command and largest minority shareholder, Commodore Kavitha Zoric, and the other woman had taken their primary capital ship and all of the destroyers off on the latest contract.

Someone had to stay in the Redward System to take delivery of Memorial Force's newest warship, after all, and either of them could command the supercarrier *Fortitude* to handle an Outer Rim brush war.

That left her on the flag deck of the cruiser *Deception*, watching the Redward Royal Fleet go through maneuvers above the fortresses that safeguarded their system. They were a far cry from the converted freighters and undersized cruisers the RRF had commanded when she'd arrived in the system years earlier.

"Hell of a difference, huh?"

She glanced over at her companion. Abdullah "Scimitar" Colombera was one of the few survivors of the original squadron she'd fled her home system with. They'd served in the Apollo System Defense Force's 303 Nova Combat Group during the war against their homeworld's enemies in Brisingr.

Their government had then sold them out to Brisingr as a secret condition of the deal that had ended that war, so they'd wound up out here. Redward was part of the Syntactic Cluster at the edge of the Rim, almost fifteen hundred light-years from Sol and over two hundred from Apollo.

"They're starting to look like a modern fleet now," she told Colombera.

There were three proper modern capital ships out there anchoring the whole fleet. Each was one hundred and twenty thousand cubic meters, partially designed by Kira's boyfriend Konrad Bueller, and they were the largest warships ever built in the Syntactic Cluster.

They fell short of the ships that had fought Apollo's war in several areas—but *size* wasn't one of them. Eventually, Kira had been promised a sister to the carrier *Royal Shield*, but that wasn't the ship she was in Redward to take possession of.

"They *are* a modern fleet now," Colombera replied, then snorted. "For the Rim, anyway. Go five hundred light-years Coreward..."

"And everything changes," Kira agreed. The zone from a thousand light-years away from Sol to fifteen hundred light-years away was the Rim. Still considered part of "civilized space" and mapped by the major astrography corporations, even her home system only counted as a seventh-rate power in the overall galaxy.

Redward had dragged itself and its partners kicking and screaming to eighth-rate status—and for all of the battles Kira Demirci had fought on their behalf, most of the help they'd received making that transition had actually been from her boyfriend.

She'd originally met the now-ex-Brisingr engineer when he'd

been a POW during the war. The universe moved in strange ways, and they'd met in the Syntactic Cluster again long after that war was done.

"Are they still pissed at us over the fighters?" Colombera asked, watching as a wing of nova fighters blinked out of existence on the sensors. It would be a minute or two before *Deception*'s scanners would locate the starfighters again. Most likely they'd only jumped a light-minute or so, but the scanners were still limited by the speed of light.

"Some of them are," Kira agreed, but she was smiling as she said it. "Helmet thinks it's fair play, though, and *he's* the only one whose opinion matters on that point. They screwed us on the new carrier, so we kept the new fighter designs we acquired."

The fighters in *Deception*'s hangars were more advanced than the ones she'd brought to Redward when she'd arrived. Redward's fighters were based on those Hoplite-IVs and contemporary planes.

Deception's squadrons now flew fighters based on the designs Memorial Force had acquired from the Navy of the Royal Crest when they'd procured *Fortitude.* If the RRF had prioritized building the full one-twenty-kilocubic carrier the way Kira felt they'd promised, she'd have sold them the designs.

As it was, the Crown Zharang of the Crest, the person who'd hired them to steal *Fortitude* from their own fleet as part of a complex coup against the totalitarian government of their country, had asked Kira not to. And she'd been feeling far more generous to the Zharang than to Redward.

"Are your fighters ready?" Kira asked Colombera. The younger Apollon wasn't part of *Deception*'s crew, after all. Like many of the Memorial Force officers currently living on *Deception* and Redward's Green Ward asteroid battle station, he'd been handpicked to take up a more senior role on their new ship.

"Seventy-two planes, with pilots, munitions, the works," Colombera confirmed. "Though I think some of Helmet's people are eyeing my planes a little *too* closely."

Admiral Teige "Helmet" Sagairt had skipped a few grades to reach his current rank, entirely by virtue of being the senior nova-fighter pilot in the entire RRF. He was now the commanding officer of the RRF Nova Fighter Corps and directly reported to the senior commanders of the system's military...including His Majesty, King Larry.

He might understand why Kira hadn't sold him the designs for the ships she built for her own use, but with twelve squadrons of those planes currently in an expensive private hangar on a semi-civilian station above his homeworld...she'd have been shocked if he *didn't* have people taking pictures and other scans.

"He wouldn't be doing his job if they weren't," she conceded. "And we wouldn't be doing *our* job if we made it too easy. We made some promises with regards to those planes, after all."

"We're doing what we can," Colombera agreed. "But the RRF *does* own Green Ward. Even if we're renting hangars in the civilian sections to store the fighters."

He shook his head.

"How long?" he finally asked.

"Davidović is already aboard," Kira told him. "Plus about thirty or forty chiefs and techs, plus Bueller. I expect to hear from them tomorrow with a go/no-go on the final commissioning date."

"I knew *that*," Scimitar replied. "I lent her the best people I have." He sighed theatrically. "Though I'll point out that we ran this Cluster dry of people who know which end of a star fighter the guns fire from a long time ago."

There had been less than twenty nova fighters in the Syntactic Cluster when Kira and her friends had arrived. They weren't *solely* responsible for Redward's sudden explosion in starfighter capability—that had taken unintentional assistance from several old enemies—but they'd certainly helped nurture it.

But there were very few people in the six habitable systems of the Cluster who Kira would trust to maintain a nova fighter—and most of them *already* worked for either the Redward Royal Fleet or Kira Demirci herself.

"We've been training techs almost as hard and fast as we've been training pilots," Kira reminded him. "And techs have a lower casualty rate."

That rate wasn't zero. The RRF had lost enough capital ships with their tech crews aboard over the last few years to prevent that—but they'd also lost over half of their existing pilot base when they'd finally kicked the inner-world meddlers of the Equilibrium Institute out of the Cluster.

"But we expect to have the new ship cleared for duty by the end of the week, with a formal commissioning party once we have everyone aboard," she noted. "My understanding is that Their Majesties are planning on making it a big deal at their expense, so I can all but guarantee the Redward side of things will run smoothly."

Her old subordinate chuckled. "No one wants to disappoint them, that's true. So, two weeks?"

"About that," she confirmed.

"And when do we get to start using the *name*?" Colombera asked. "*CVL-Four* is a bit...bland. Almost Brisingrian."

Deception was a Brisingr-built heavy cruiser and had delighted in the name *K79-L* in their service. The Brisingr Kaiserreich Navy, Kira's old enemies, didn't believe in ship names as a rule.

"Redward tradition is that it's bad luck to name a ship before she's finally commissioned," Kira told him. "So, when we take full possession and turn the lights on, we start calling her by name. Until then, she's just the hull number."

Even if everybody knew that Redward's fourth light carrier was going to be *Huntress*.

2

Kira was in her office when her headware informed her that Konrad Bueller had returned aboard *Deception.* The ubiquitous neural implants of modern humanity, in her experience, allowed people to make human mistakes faster and without the excuse of misremembered data.

They also acted as communicators and allowed her to keep working through the seemingly infinite datawork of running a mercenary organization that operated eight—soon to be *nine*—major nova warships until her boyfriend returned.

And to still make it to their shared quarters at the same time as he did to allow them to share dinner. It was a small luxury, one that she reveled in when they could make it work, and she grinned at her steward as she stepped into the room to find the young woman laying out the plates.

"I see we are becoming predictable, Jess," she told Jess Koch, the personal keeper she'd finally hired when the addition of *Fortitude* and three more destroyers to the fleet had finally overwhelmed any excuse she had of being able to take care of herself!

"I figure it won't last," Koch replied. "Commander Bueller will be here in about two minutes, though, and dinner is ready. Enjoy!"

One of the things that Kira adored about Koch was that the woman had an extremely solid sense of when to let the principals have time to themselves—hardly a surprise, given that she'd been recommended by Queen Sonia of Redward herself.

Jess Koch was an exceptionally well-trained bodyguard as well as a professional chef and administrator. Kira wasn't entirely clear on why she'd entered Kira's service after completing all the training to enter the Queen's...but she wasn't complaining.

Konrad Bueller stepped through the door almost exactly two minutes after Koch disappeared, the big engineer's face lighting up with a brilliant smile at the sight of dinner and Kira.

Probably not in that order, she admitted.

"Ah, my dear," he said. "I see you once again have escaped the computers at *exactly* the right moment."

"It's like we plan this or something," Kira said drily. "Eat, Konrad, then tell me how our ship is doing!"

He laughed, but he joined her in digging into Koch's excellent food. After a few minutes, they both leaned back and sipped their drinks. Here, at least, they were safe enough to drink wine.

It wasn't like anyone was going to try to attack Redward. Nova drives could only carry so much cubage with them, which strictly limited the size of nova *ships*. Sublight monitors and asteroid fortresses had no such limitations, which more than balanced out the nova vessels' greater maneuverability.

"*CVL-Four*," Konrad murmured, making a tossing gesture as he linked their headwares and created a virtual image of the carrier between them, "is doing just fine."

Kira could recognize the flattened box of their new carrier in her sleep at this point. She'd been staring at images of the *Bastion*-class carriers for eighteen months, after all. Redward had built three of them for the RRF and one for Memorial Force.

The ship was a hundred and ten meters long, twenty meters thick, and a tad under thirty-five meters wide. There were two heavy plasma-cannon turrets mounted on top of the hull and a second pair mounted on the bottom, but her main armament was the heavily armored hatches at the bow and stern—or, at least, the seventy-five nova fighters on the flight deck those hatches covered.

Less visible were the ship's eighteen lighter anti-fighter turrets, spaced along her two thinner surfaces. She was designed to carry her own fighters into action and defend herself against enemy fighters, not tangle with enemy capital ships on her own.

Redward had two *Baron*-class cruisers for every *Bastion*-class carrier they'd built and was following a similar ratio for the battle-cruisers and fleet carriers. Their carriers weren't designed to operate alone.

Kira had her own opinions on that matter and generally preferred *Fortitude*'s design—the big supercarrier had almost as many heavy plasma cannon as *Deception* and could operate independently if needed.

"Any concerns in the testing?" she asked. "Marija is still sending everyone off the ship at the end of the night, so..."

"An abundance of caution, nothing else," Bueller told her. "She still thinks like regular Navy—it's a flaw we suffer from as a mercenary organization, I suspect."

Marija Davidović, designated to become *CVL-4*'s new Captain shortly, had been an RRF officer seconded to Memorial Force at one point. The trip into the Mid Rim to pick up *Fortitude* had awakened a degree of wanderlust the woman hadn't realized she had, and she'd transferred permanently.

Now Kira was giving the woman the carrier command she wouldn't have earned in the RRF for another few years—because Davidović could do the job. Everyone benefited.

"We're *all* a bit too former-military, sometimes," Kira conceded. "Even you."

"I wasn't exempting myself from the assessment, no," Bueller agreed. "But I've gone over *CVL-Four*'s systems from stem to stern. She's up to speed and up to snuff." He shrugged and smiled.

"I'll be back over there tomorrow, helping Davidović run the tests and exercises, though," he continued. "Just because the hardware looks good doesn't mean it will all work well.

"That said, I'd make sure you have your dress uniform laid out for the Queen's party. The ship won't be delaying it!"

Kira chuckled.

"I'm not sure even the shipbuilders in this system want to disappoint Queen Sonia," she observed. "I certainly don't!"

She wouldn't go so far as to call the Queen of Redward a *friend*, but Sonia made a point of mentoring a lot of the women and enbies around her. The Queen had found Kira an asset of value in her schemes and maneuvering—and she'd made being so quite lucrative for Kira in turn.

"There are many terrifying women in my life I would choose not to disappoint," her lover pointed out with a chuckle. "I'm still not entirely sure why you are here and Kavitha is with *Fortitude*.

"The *last* time we let you get bored, after all, you took a set of destroyers out on anti-piracy patrol."

Kira shook her head at him.

"I *am* getting older and more mature; I'll have you know," she insisted. "But...well, we flipped a coin and I lost. One of us had to go to Obsidian. One of us had to stay here with *Deception* and commission *CVL-Four*."

"Lucky Kavitha," Bueller noted, then smiled broadly. "Lucky me, too."

Kira laughed at him.

"Do you know what she said to me before she left, love?" she asked, the memory hitting her as her boyfriend attempted his best leer. It was a pretty laughable attempt—despite being the same fortyish as Kira, Konrad Bueller was surprisingly easy to embarrass.

He hesitated.

"Knowing our good Commodore..." He sighed. "I don't know, and I'm not sure I *want* to know. But you're going to tell me anyway."

Kira nodded and grinned.

"My beloved and oh-so-professional second-in-command informed me that the high end of the time estimate for the mission was a bit over nine months, and that I should take advantage of that," Kira told him. "Because I wasn't going to have any *other* quiet times to get knocked up anytime soon!"

Konrad joined her in her laugh as she fondly reached across the table to take his hand.

"I *presume*," he finally said, very carefully, "that if you were considering that suggestion, you'd give me a bit more warning."

She squeezed his hand.

"The thought crosses my mind occasionally," she admitted. "But there's never a good time, and where would we even *keep* a kid?" She shook her head. "Not opposed to the idea—in general *or* with you specifically—it just has a lot of logistical issues right now."

"Mmm." Konrad squeezed her hand in turn. "I'm in much the same place, I'll admit. Plus, if we had a kid, my family would *explode* if we didn't bring them home...and I'm not flying you to Brisingr."

"No offense, my love, but there is no force in the universe powerful enough to get me to even return to our home sector, let alone *your* homeworld," Kira admitted, a cold shadow passing over her amused emotions and rare moment of maternal contemplation.

Her lover's home system, after all, had sent assassins all the way to the Syntactic Cluster to try and kill her. His Kaiser was on the very short list of people Kira would potentially consider killing in cold blood.

He squeezed her hand again and smiled at her as she met his gaze.

"Hey, we're here and we're focused on today, all right?" he told her. "We're not going back there and we're not dealing with my bloody-handed distant cousin, all right?"

"I know," she told him, letting herself focus on the warmth of his skin against hers. “We’ve got more than enough work without going within a hundred light-years of home.”

Even if she occasionally missed the rocky fields and wandering sheep of her home village in the hills above New Athens.

3

The crowd gathered on the Green Ward observation deck *ooh*ed appreciatively as the nova fighters flashed past in lockstep formation. Running lights gleamed on the three-squadron formation of Wolverines, all eighteen starfighters shining like beacons in the night.

The running lights were necessary because the spacecrafts' reactionless Harrington coils produced no light when running. *Heat*, yes, Kira knew, but no light. The dispersal webs woven into modern armor to handle plasma fire had begun with systems to handle the heat from Harrington coils.

Memorial Force's Admiral stood silently next to the observation deck's massive windows, feeling like an undersized gargoyle watching the crowd gathered for the ceremony collectively inhale again as the second set of squadrons made their pass.

Apollo's nominal pacifism and anti-militarism had limited the amount of pageantry involved in most of their military activities. The Kingdom of Redward, on the other hand, had no such false imagery of itself.

She waited for the flybys to complete. There would be five of them, three of two squadrons apiece and two of three squadrons, showing off all seventy-two of the carrier's new fighters as they made their formal transfer from the Green Ward hangars to the still officially unnamed *CVL-4*.

"I still wish you'd let us buy at least the bomber design," a voice murmured to her.

She looked over to see that she'd been joined in her spot by the window by a slim man with brilliant copper hair. He wore a similar dress uniform to hers—a decorated long jacket over a military shipsuit—but his jacket was the dark blue of the RRF to the dark teal of her Memorial Force uniform.

And, of course, he had three stars on his collar to her two. Kira might have accepted the *Admiral* title, but Teige "Helmet" Sagairt was one of RRF's dozen or so full Admirals.

"I promised the Panosyans I wouldn't," she told him. "And they played almost completely straight with us."

Sagairt didn't even wince. He just shrugged.

"If you change your mind, let me know," he said. "Feels like that should make up for at least some of the retainer you lost."

"*Fortitude* has brought us enough work to make up for that," Kira said calmly.

Redward had paid Memorial Force a hefty retainer up until they'd first left the Syntactic Cluster on the mission that had acquired *Fortitude*. Part of the reason she'd given that retainer up, though, was that it had already been becoming politically untenable for King Larry to keep paying it.

"It should. Not many hundred-and-fifty-kilocubic carriers this far out," Helmet replied. "Even *Royal Shield* couldn't take *Fortitude* assuming equally skilled fighter groups."

The bombers that had started their conversation made their own flyby and Kira nodded silently.

Royal Shield was the new one-hundred-twenty-kilocubic carrier the RRF was putting through its paces as they spoke. She carried four dual plasma-cannon turrets to *Fortitude*'s five and only one hundred and eight nova fighters to *Fortitude*'s hundred and fifty.

But no one pretended that Memorial Force *wouldn't* leap to Redward's defense if they were around when the system came under attack—not least because Kira Demirci and the rest of her senior staff trusted King Larry to make good on a reasonable price afterward.

Eventually. Even if they were still grumpy about the carrier slip.

"Her Majesty is almost here," Helmet told her after watching the bomber. "She sent her regrets for missing the beginning of the ceremony. Larry sends even *more* regrets—he got locked up in a committee meeting at the Hóngsè Chéngbao and won't be free today."

Kira nodded. The Hóngsè Chéngbao was the physical seat of Redward's Parliament, and while King Larry wielded a great deal of day-to-day power in the government of Redward, he also very definitively answered to the elected representatives of his people.

"This is just...parading so far," she said. "I can delay the next piece for a few minutes if Her Majesty is late."

"That might be helpful," Sagairt conceded. "Sonia wants to make sure everyone sees her support for you and your people."

"It's appreciated," Kira said. "Even the guests are mostly here because of *her*, after all."

"That's not entirely fair," he replied. "At least half of the people here are RRF, either from the nova ships or from Green Ward itself. *We're* here because we respect and value Memorial Force. Very few members of the Fleet don't understand where we'd be without you."

Kira chuckled.

"And even some of the politicians and industrialists and foreign dignitaries understand the same, I guess," she said. "But at least forty percent of the people in this room are here because the King and Queen of Redward were supposed to be here."

"And they will be a tad disappointed that King Larry can't make it, but they'll survive," Sagairt told her. "And the rest of us are here for you."

He smiled.

"Who's throwing the traditional champagne bottle, anyway? Sonia?"

"Your Commander Bradley's little girl," Kira said. "A sign of remaining connections, I suppose."

"Mmm." Sagairt nodded. "By which you mean Neha is throwing the champagne bottle, given that Jessica isn't quite three."

Neha Bradley was now a squadron commander with the RRF—but she'd once been blackmailed into acting as a spy for the Equilibrium Institute conspiracy that had tried to undermine Redward. Once she'd come clean, Kira had taken her into Memorial Force, and she'd eventually transferred back to the RRF.

But, like so much of the system's military infrastructure, Commander Bradley had been shaped by Memorial Force. It was a subtle reminder, Kira figured—but it was a reminder nonetheless.

Redward and the Syntactic Cluster *owed* her people, and she didn't want them to forget!

FINDING a shipsuit sized for a toddler hadn't been as difficult as Kira had initially assumed. The nature of the nova drive resulted in a *lot* of small, cheap ships traveling the laneways—and the vast majority of the default ten- to twenty-kilocubic freighters doing that were family-owned.

Those families couldn't afford to stop moving just because they'd had a baby, so there was an entire market for shipsuits that allowed small children to move around, gave their parents some degree of control over what they could access, *and* were size-adjustable to handle the rapid growth spurts of kids of all ages.

Despite her general neutral feelings on kids, even Kira had to admit that Jessica Bradley was *adorable* as she stood on the skiff jetting out toward *CVL-4*. The child's mother was holding her in the uncertain gravity, fully wrapped in her own RRF shipsuit with barely-visible safety cables connecting the two vac-suits.

"Gentlefolk," Kira said calmly. She crossed from the side of the window to stand on the dais in front of the view, turning a gentle smile on her audience.

She traded a firm nod with Queen Sonia, the elegantly tall monarch now standing at the back of the room. Several people had already tried to pin the Queen down for conversation, only to be brushed aside.

Right now, the Queen was there for the show.

"I *hope* everyone here knows who I am, but I accept the reality that some of you are here for the buffet and some of you are here because you knew the Queen would be here," she told them. "My name is Admiral Kira Demirci, and I am the commanding officer, CEO and primary shareholder of Memorial Force.

"We have operated out of the Redward System for as long as we have existed, and a significant plurality of our personnel are drawn from Redward or the rest of the Syntactic Cluster.

"This is a significant moment for all of us, though," she continued. "Five years ago, the only carriers in Redward's possession were crude freighter conversions."

One of those conversions had, in fact, been given to Memorial Force after their previous carrier had been destroyed in Redward's service.

"Today, Redward has not only built four carriers for their own service but has also built a carrier for what is arguably an export sale. While I think we all recognize that Memorial Force and the Kingdom of Redward have a special relationship, it is still true that very few powers in this universe *ever* export capital ships.

"But here we are." She waved behind her, where *CVL-4* was slowly drawing into view at minimum power. The carrier was flanked on all sides by a skeletal sphere of Scimitar's fighters. *Most* of the nova craft were now aboard the carrier, but Colombera had left a dozen of his planes in space to provide safety beacons for her safe travel.

"Gentlefolk of the Kingdom of Redward, this ship will serve

Memorial Force, yes. But Memorial Force will *always* be the friend of Kingdom and Cluster alike. You have my word."

Anyone who was stupid enough to try to hire Memorial Force to operate against Redward or the Syntactic Cluster Free Trade Zone that King Larry had built with blood, tears and sacrifice deserved the rude awakening Kira would give them.

"And so today, Memorial Force takes possession of Redward Industrial Shipbuilding's hull *CVL-Four*," Kira concluded. "Em Bradley?"

"We're ready," Neha Bradley said over the com.

"Carry on."

The open-canopied skiff slid closer to the carrier on its Harrington coils, and Bradley lifted up her daughter with the oversized champagne bottle in her hands. The little girl hefted the bottle up to the edge of the skiff's gravity field, then tossed it gently at her mother's instruction.

The bottle left the child's hands and drifted slowly across space toward the carrier. Behind it, the skiff slowly pulled away to make sure its systems didn't interfere with the process.

A three-year-old's arms didn't impart that much velocity to a two-kilogram ceremonial bottle of what Kira knew to be absolutely *terrible* sparkling wine, but the skiff had brought the Bradleys within ten meters of the hull.

It only took a few seconds for the bottle to cross that void and hit the hull. Jessica Bradley might not have thrown the bottle with enough force to break it, but it didn't matter. A tiny explosive charge in the middle of the bottle detected the impact and went off.

Glass disintegrated into fine powder and faux champagne went spraying and fizzing across the carrier's hull. A moment later, the running lights lit up as one, illuminating the thick playing-card shape of the starship—and the name painted on her hull.

"Gentlefolk, I give you the Memorial Force carrier *Huntress*," Kira told her audience. "A mercenary ship, yes, but also a force for justice and decency in this universe.

"Like *Fortitude* before her, and *Conviction* before her, *Huntress* will stand against the darkness and the fire of mankind's worst," she continued. "We have stood with Redward before, and we will stand with others in the future, but I can promise you this: no carrier under my command will ever stand with those who would conquer or harm the innocent."

That got her a round of applause, especially once it was clear that was the extent of her speech. With a nod to her audience, Kira stepped down from the dais and went hunting for the buffet.

Now that she'd *given* the speech, she needed a drink.

KIRA BARELY MANAGED to eat a brownie and grab a beer before a pair of perfectly turned-out women appeared out of the crowd. Their simple black suits might as well have been uniforms, and the presence of two members of the Queen's private security detail created an instant bubble of space.

Both women moved with the slightly *off* grace of heavily boosted individuals, augmented with either biotech, nanotech or cybertech to be more than human. In Kira's experience, once people were in battle armor, boosts made no difference—but she could see the value for a bodyguard.

"You know, Melissa, Cora, I don't know if we necessarily need to intimidate everyone else away from the buffet before I grab a glass of wine," Queen Sonia Stewart said drily as she stepped up behind the two bodyguards.

Kira snorted as the Queen approached the buffet—and Kira herself.

"One of them has to scan the wine for you, anyway," she told the monarch. "They may as well be intimidating and save you time in line."

"Perhaps."

As Kira and Sonia spoke, one of the two women was doing

exactly that—running a scanner wand over the wine and the trays of pastries. Once the scan was complete, the woman snagged a glass of wine for Sonia and a plate of brownies for the bodyguards themselves.

If the confections being passed around Sonia's guardians slowed their reactions or attention to detail one iota, Kira didn't notice it. Holding her bottle of beer, she followed the Queen's unspoken command and joined her back by the window.

"I'm glad we're able to begin paying back the vast debt my system owes your organization," the monarch told her. "And don't give me any crap about being paid, Kira. We both know Estanza, Zoric and you have all gone far beyond what contract truly required."

John Estanza had commanded *Conviction*, the carrier that Kira had brought her people out there to join. A mentor and a friend, he'd died fighting the Equilibrium Institute to preserve the Syntactic Cluster's freedom to choose their own future.

The Institute wanted to mold all of humanity into a single path, a path they were prepared to enforce with fire and blood. John Estanza had once flown for them—but he'd died stopping them out there.

One debt paid, Kira supposed.

"We'll be here at least until the other carrier is commissioned," she told Sonia. "Your help along the way has been invaluable."

Sonia, after all, had put her in touch with Jade Panosyan, the heir to the Royal Crest and the person who'd used Memorial's theft of *Fortitude* to effect regime change in that system.

While the Queen of Redward played the socialite, trophy wife and mother—and played those roles *well*—she was also the secret head of Redward's combined intelligence and covert operations apparatus. Her fingers and eyes spread throughout the entire Syntactic Cluster and beyond.

"Larry and I fully recognize the sacrifices and efforts you have made on our behalf," Sonia repeated. "The debt we owe you and your people—and John Estanza's memory—can *never* be repaid, Kira.

Mere money and matériel cannot clear an account balance built of honor and blood."

Kira nodded silently. There wasn't really a response she could make to that beyond recognition. She and Sonia both knew the Queen was right.

"Larry is, well, about as angry as my Santa Claus wannabe of a husband gets that he couldn't be here," Sonia continued. "We thought the whole situation with the bill to fund the south continent's canal system was resolved and in hand, but..." She shrugged.

"Politics," Kira replied. "The last thing you could ever get me to do is run a planet! A dozen or so mercenary ships is more than enough."

"It has its rewards—and I don't mean the perks," the Queen said. "Thanks to us and the millions of others who've worked with us, I believe Larry and I will leave both our system and our neighbors better off than we found them.

"Not many can say that at all—let alone on the scale that Larry and I can. You're up there, though," she noted. "Mercenary fleet or no. Between here, the Crest, half a dozen other Rim brush fires...you and Memorial Force are making a difference."

Kira chuckled softly.

"You're not just buttering me up for giggles," she said. "What's going on?"

Sonia sighed.

"You're right," she admitted. "But I also want to remind you that nothing I just said was a lie or even particularly exaggerated. The Equilibrium Institute has to regret the day you and John Estanza ever met."

"I hope so," Kira said levelly. "Have we found another patsy of theirs?"

"Not that I know of," Sonia said. "But I have been making quiet conversation with an economic delegation that could use some military muscle they don't have. I think you may even know the Samuels System better than I do."

Kira nodded slowly.

"I know *of* the Samuels System," she conceded. "They were a strategic concern for Apollo—but they're about as far as you can be and still register as a strategic concern. One of two systems that act as a choke point between the Apollo-Brisingr Sector and a few others and the Outer Rim—them and...Colossus, I think?"

"Exactly. They have a delegation here, negotiating some trade deals with a few of our local corporations," Sonia explained. "They drifted into my circles of context a little *too* smoothly for me to think it was unintended, but they seem aboveboard for that.

"I want you to talk to them," she said. "No weight on it from my side—if nothing else, I know most of your capital ships are in Obsidian right now—but I think everyone would benefit from that conversation."

Kira chuckled again. Putting people in the same room to have a conversation sounded like a small thing, but she'd come to realize it was an extraordinarily powerful tool. A tool that Sonia Stewart wielded with the same grace and precision and skill Kira wielded a nova-fighter group with.

"I'll talk to them," she agreed. "I've never gone wrong following your suggestions before. I'm guessing they're here?"

The Queen chuckled.

"They are," she agreed. "Em Doretta Macey is the senior delegate. Officially she's just a trade attaché, but I have my suspicions."

"Oh?" Kira asked.

"That's part of why I'm putting you in touch with her at all," Sonia said. "Unless I misread the situation, Kira, Em Macey's entire purpose out here is to meet you."

4

KIRA MADE her way across the party with the ease of long practice, greeting acquaintances and friends as she approached Doretta Macey and her party.

The Samuels delegation was presumably larger than the four middle-aged women forming a solid block in one corner, quietly chatting with a man Kira knew ran a midsized shipping line out of Redward. If nothing else, none of the women had the body language that said they were in charge of security, which meant Macey and her companions were relying on Kira's security for this event.

If any of them had ever met Memorial Force's ground-force commander, they would have known that was a safe reliance. Milani might never leave their body armor, but they were among the top two or three small-force infantry tacticians Kira had ever met.

Kira might be wearing an armor vest underneath her dress uniform and have a blaster tucked into a concealed holster, but that was at Milani's insistence, not from any lack of faith in the mercenary.

Macey was aware enough to see Kira approaching and give swift whispered instructions to her companions. The other Samuels envoys slipped away, moving the conversations away from Doretta Macey and clearing a small bubble of privacy for her and Kira.

It was an impressive and clearly practiced maneuver, one that spoke to the recurring role of these women as negotiators and diplomats for their star system.

Macey watched Kira approach impassively, giving the mercenary a chance to examine her. She wore a conservative navy-blue pantsuit, with her silvering blond hair tied back into a tight bun. Blue eyes surveyed Kira in turn as the diplomat pursed her lips like she'd eaten something sour.

"Em Doretta Macey?" Kira asked as she stepped inside the circle Macey's companions had created.

"Mrs.," Doretta corrected softly. "I know it's archaic, Admiral, but most of the people of Samuels put a weight on marriage. *Em* is reserved for the unmarried among us."

"I see," Kira said. That was the sort of thing most people would include in their headware beacons—the small identity tag transmitted by their implants. Hers, for example, contained her rank, pronouns and name.

That Mrs. Macey *didn't* include it in her beacon—which simply gave her name and pronouns—suggested she was intentionally using it to set people on the wrong foot when they met her. In an age where it was easy to get everything right when addressing people, it was disconcerting to get someone's preferred address *wrong*.

"A mutual friend told me you were looking for me," Kira continued after a momentary pause. "Since you've gone to so much effort to track me down, all the way from Samuels, I figured I should at least see what you have to say."

"Oh, I didn't come all this way to see you," Macey replied. "We're here purely as an economic delegation, dealing with the new Syntactic Cluster Free Trade Zone. I'm led to understand your organization may be able to help us resolve a problem back home, though."

Kira smiled thinly.

"Mrs. Macey, I don't play games," she said quietly. "We both know that the Syntactic Cluster is too far away from Samuels to be of major economic interest to your world. We both know that anything Samuels would need here would be as easily negotiated in Ypres as Redward—and that every conversation you and your people have had since you arrived has been directed at making contact with Queen Sonia as an avenue to make contact with me.

"You've come a very long way to talk to me, and I'll give you the favor of hearing you out—but not unless we are entirely honest with each other.

"Frankly, my people don't need work that badly."

She started to turn to leave, but Macey held up her hand and returned the thin smile.

"I could argue that is egotistical of you," she told Kira. "Or question how you draw that analysis. But I suppose it doesn't matter. I need your help."

"All right," Kira said. "You managed to get yourself an invite to this party *and* convince Queen Sonia that I should speak to you. So, speak."

"Is this really the place?" Macey asked, glancing around at the party.

"I'm not planning on *negotiating* here, Mrs. Macey," Kira replied with a chuckle. "But it's as good a place as any for you to make your pitch, don't you think?"

"Fair enough. Water, Admiral?"

One of the servers had arrived with a tray of glasses that were distinctly lacking in champagne or other alcoholic beverages. The tall flutes only held clear water, and Macey took two of them with a nod to the waiter.

"Certainly." Kira took the drink.

"None of my team drink alcohol," Macey explained. "This young man has been extremely accommodating."

The "young man" in question—one of Milani's ground-force

troopers and part of the security arrangements—grinned at Kira and inclined his head.

"Carry on," she told him. "Tag the rest of the team—Mrs. Macey and I will need to talk semi-privately for a bit."

"Yes, sir."

Macey watched the waiter walk away with a sharp look.

"Security?" she asked, surprised.

"Every waiter here is either one of my mercenaries or a Redward Army Commando tasked to protect Queen Sonia," Kira told her. "Did you expect differently?"

"We are not...so focused on defense, I suppose, on Samuels," Macey admitted. "The dominant culture on our world remains the Interstellar Society of Friends—Quakers, you may know us as."

Kira didn't know them by *either* name off the top of her head, but her headware brought up the information rapidly. The key point was that the Quakers were almost uniformly anti-war if not outright pacifist.

"Pacifists," she murmured aloud.

"And most of the population of my system that are not Quakers are Baha'i or Buddhist or, well, other groups that lend themselves strongly to pacifism and a refusal of violence," Macey confirmed. "We don't generally have security to this level."

"I am the commanding officer of a mercenary fleet, in a system that has spent most of the five years I've been here in one war or another," Kira pointed out. "I am *not* a pacifist, and I have real enemies. So does Queen Sonia."

"I understand that intellectually," Macey conceded. "We maintain our own defense forces, after all. But it is still an oddity to encounter in the wild, so to speak."

"You didn't travel a hundred and fifty light-years to be surprised that I have guards and guns, Mrs. Macey," Kira said. "What do you need?"

Macey took a sip of her water and nodded slowly.

"You used to be with the Apollo military, yes? So, you are familiar with Samuels and Colossus?" she asked.

"I was and I am, but only vaguely," Kira admitted. "Not much more than the astrographic location and its implications for Apollo, plus whatever is in the Encyclopedia Galactica."

The EG was a charity project maintained by the same loose coalition of corporations that updated the trade-route maps of "civilized space." Like the maps, it was a subscription service that had a constantly updated location in every star system that a ship would upload updates to and download updates from when they arrived.

The trade-route maps told civilian ships where to jump. The Encyclopedia Galactica gave them a *very* high-level idea of what would be there when they arrived.

Macey sighed.

"That's enough to know that Samuels and Colossus are two sides of the same coin," she said. "The only two inhabited worlds in a roughly thirty-light-year cube. A ship can go around it, but for a significant chunk of the Rim, if you are going outward or going inward, you are passing through either Colossus or Samuels to discharge static.

"For a century, we have competed for that business. Colossus takes one fewer nova on most routes, so we have traditionally offered lower discharge toll rates and better amenities."

Kira nodded.

A nova ship could make six long-distance novas, with a usual max of around six light-years per nova, before they needed to stop somewhere and discharge tachyon and electrostatic buildup into a convenient gravity well.

The process took a full day, so even though inhabited systems charged a toll to do so, ships would usually discharge in "civilization" to have access to supplies and entertainment while they were stuck in place.

"And now?" she prodded Macey.

"For most of the last century, that competition has been relatively good-natured and polite," the Samuels woman told her. "As polite as any competition that is critical to the economies of the star systems involved can be, anyway.

"However, about twenty years ago, a more...nationalistic tone began to rise in Colossus politics," she noted. "We didn't take it overly seriously at first. All democracies go through phases, and our relationship with Colossus has always been solid."

She shook her head.

"But over twenty years, the Colossus Rising Party has gone from third-party status, to junior coalition member, to majority ruling party," she told Kira. "The CRP has held control of the system for about ten years now, to one degree or another, and remains stunningly popular.

"Of course, my feelings on the Rising Party are highly suspect," Macey admitted. "Much of their foreign policy goals and selling points to their membership have been based around *removing* Samuels as an economic threat to Colossus.

"We are an external threat that they have successfully mobilized a large portion of their population against. While we are a purely economic competitor to Colossus, they appear to be considering... non-economic methods of resolution."

"The usual 'continuation of politics by other means,' I assume?" Kira asked, then took a long drink of water. The story wasn't unfamiliar. In a slightly different format and structure, it was how Apollo and Brisingr had come to blows.

"War," Macey said bluntly. "We are...reasonably secure in the defenses of Samuels itself, but our military officers tell me that we lack the ability to secure the key trade routes through the zone we share with Colossus."

"If they have a nova-capable fleet, they would be able to blockade you and prevent you receiving customers, yes," Kira agreed. That was how war was fought in their era, after all. Any reasonably advanced star system usually had half a dozen or more asteroid fortresses that outmassed the largest nova ships a thousand to one.

"They didn't use to," Macey said quietly. "There was a semi-formal agreement between our governments to reduce that risk. Both of our systems can build nova ships and regularly build nova freighters, but we have both traditionally restricted our nova combatants to a pure nova-fighter force."

That spoke to the sophistication of the two systems' military technology as well. If they could build nova fighters at all, they could easily build real nova warships. Fighters had advantages but were also a *specialty* tool. By only building fighters, well...

Kira could see that being a problem. There was a *reason* that nova fighters were usually deployed by carrier, after all. They could make the same six-light-year nova as a ship with a class one nova drive, but their cooldown was almost thirty-six hours instead of the larger ship's twenty.

The price the class two drive paid for its short cooldown for short-range novas was a long cooldown for long-range jumps. Nova fighters could patrol the trade routes around a star system—but only by giving up their main tactical advantage.

"And now?" Kira asked.

"They have recently acquired a flotilla of decommissioned Brisingr Kaiserreich Navy warships of pre-war vintage," Macey told her. "While we believe the ships to have been properly disarmed, it will not be difficult for Colossus's yards to refit them to be combat-ready.

"They can definitely do so more quickly than we can build new ships on our own," the woman concluded. "They will shortly be in position to impose the exact type of blockade you warned of, and according to our military officers, we will not be able to stop them."

"I see." Kira finished her glass of water as she considered. "And you want to hire Memorial Force to either prevent or break said blockade, plus a potential counter-force mission to eliminate their new fleet while you build a proper defensive force of your own?"

"That...about sums it up, yes," Macey said slowly. "I dislike violence, Admiral Demirci. I dislike organized violence even more.

But I must, pragmatically, recognize that there is a threat to the world and the people I love and serve.

"So, yes. We want to hire your Memorial Force to protect the Samuels System."

"All right," Kira told her. "My people will be in contact this evening to arrange an appointment tomorrow."

Macey blinked at her. "Admiral?"

"You've made your pitch," Kira said. "I am prepared to at least consider the mission. Tomorrow, I want you to bring every piece of information you have on Colossus's military production capabilities and these ships they've acquired.

"Then you and I will negotiate over what this contract is going to look like. As you said, this is not the place for negotiations—and you are not the only person here I need to meet before the party is done!"

5

DORETTA MACEY COULD NOT HAVE LOOKED *MORE* uncomfortable as Milani escorted her into the conference room aboard *Deception* the next afternoon. Milani had that effect on people, often.

They wore jet-black powered combat armor that covered them from head to toe, concealing any and every aspect of their identity. Weaving threateningly across that armor was an active holographic pattern of a bright red dragon—one that was very definitely *watching* the Samuels representative.

Macey looked even more concerned as Milani walked into the room with her and took one of the two empty chairs at the table, bringing the number of mercenaries in the room to five.

Kira, of course, sat at the far side of the oval table and gestured Macey to the seat opposite her. The table was a gift from Queen Sonia, a hand-built construction of local hardwood with a varnish that would stand up to blaster fire—and the artisan had happily demonstrated with a sample that that statement was *not* hyperbole.

In most lighting, the table was jet-black. The conference room's lights, however, had been carefully tuned to bring out the deep iridescent green that offset Kira and her people's dark-teal uniforms.

Around the table were her two capital-ship commanders—Marija Davidović for the newly commissioned *Huntress* and Akuchi Mwangi for *Deception*—and her partner, Konrad Bueller, sat to her immediate right.

Milani took up the seat just past Mwangi, and Kira smiled as the Samuels representative eyed the dragon-armored merc but finally took her seat.

"I did expect to be meeting just you, Admiral," Macey admitted.

"While I am the CEO, CO and primary shareholder, Memorial Force is a corporate entity as well a military unit," Kira told the woman. "These officers are the ones who will be tasked with carrying out the mission if we take your contract, so I prefer to involve them in the discussions."

Not present in the room because he didn't like strangers was the mercenary company's purser Yanis Vaduva. Vaduva was listening in and had a link to Kira's headware for when he had something to contribute, but he didn't need to meet with Macey in person to be involved.

Kira gestured around the table, indicating *Huntress*'s hawk-faced Captain first.

"This is Captain Marija Davidović, *Huntress*'s Captain." Her gesture passed to the gaunt Black man just past Davidović. "Captain Akuchi Mwangi commands this cruiser, *Deception*. Milani, you've already met. They are responsible for all ground-force operations of Memorial Force."

And Kira's own personal security, a responsibility they took seriously enough that they'd sent a subordinate to command the mercenary commando sections aboard *Fortitude* and the supercarrier's escorts.

"Lastly, Commander Konrad Bueller is the executive officer and chief engineer of *Deception*, as well as our primary technical specialist.

"Everyone, this is Doretta Macey of the Samuels System, and she wants to hire us."

Macey nodded calmly and laid a datastick on the table.

"I have the information you requested," she noted. "The types and numbers of the ships Colossus purchased from Brisingr, plus best estimates of Colossus's ability to arm them. We are quite certain that Brisingr did fully demilitarize the ships before they turned them over."

"May I?" Bueller asked, gesturing at the datastick. "The BKN has been known to play games with the level of demilitarization they carry out. There are stages of decommissioning in their structures, after all."

Deception had formally been decommissioned and had been *supposed* to be partially demilitarized before entering service as a survey ship. In practice, thanks to the Equilibrium Institute, Konrad Bueller had arrived in the Syntactic Cluster on a fully operational heavy cruiser.

Macey slid the datastick over to him, but she eyed him oddly. She'd clearly recognized the accent.

"Forgive me, Commander, but are you one of *those* Buellers?" she asked softly.

Kira had never heard the question phrased quite that way, and she was wondering what she was missing for several seconds. Then her boyfriend grimaced and nodded.

"Yes, but given that Reinhardt seems quite solidly placed on his throne and I'm two hundred light-years away, it's hardly relevant, is it?" he asked.

"Konrad?" Kira asked slowly. She knew he was from a wealthy and political influential family, but Bueller wasn't that rare a last name.

"There is a main-line Bueller family on Brisingr that stand in the Succession," he admitted. "Technically, as an adult of that line between the age of thirty and seventy, I have the right to stand for election as Kaiser when Reinhardt dies or resigns." He snorted. "So do about nineteen hundred other people, last time I bothered to look at it...which was *before* I left Brisingr."

That was *not* something she'd known about her boyfriend. Given that they'd served on the opposite sides of a war both of them thought was stupid in hindsight, they generally didn't talk about home.

"Fair. I was simply curious," Macey admitted. "I was surprised to hear a Brisingr accent aboard Admiral Demirci's ship."

"This ship was a BKN heavy cruiser," Kira pointed out. "There are still a number of Brisingr expatriates aboard."

It was an open question whether or not any of them, including Konrad Bueller, could actually go home. While *Deception*'s operations hadn't been under the formal auspices of the BKN, many of the crew had still held active commissions or warrants in the BKN—and an argument could definitely be made that helping *anyone* steal and operate a Brisingr cruiser was treason.

"I see," Macey allowed. "That may be helpful in analyzing the data, I suppose. We do believe that the Kaiserreich is actively supporting Colossus in their current endeavors."

Kira wasn't surprised. She suspected, given her own experiences, that the *actual* backer was the Equilibrium Institute—but Equilibrium had their hooks deeply into Brisingr at this point. They believed that the stablest form of human civilization was areas of economic dependence on central military hegemons who kept order in their territory.

Without a massive tech imbalance, a star system was immune to external conquest, but someone like Brisingr—or, if she was being honest, Apollo—could use a nova-capable fleet to control which areas were and weren't safe for trade to move. That created zones of control—and it was the overlapping piece of those zones of control that Apollo and Brisingr had fought over.

And that her world had surrendered to Brisingr in the end, abandoning the euphemistically named "Friends of Apollo" to the tender mercies of their shared foe.

"How about you lay out what you understand Colossus to have in play and what the Samuels government is prepared to pay us to do?"

Kira told her. "You and I have gone over some of this, but I think my people will benefit in hearing it from you."

"Very well," Macey said. She produced a small portable holoprojector and laid it on the table, bringing up a local astrographic chart of two stars.

"Samuels and Colossus are eleven and a half light-years apart," she noted. "While it is theoretically possible to make the trip between the systems in two novas, there is no mapped nova stop halfway between.

"The standard trade routes tend to run through one system or the other," she continued. "That results in it taking three novas to travel from one system to the other.

"Our competition has traditionally been purely economic, but Colossus has grown more aggressive even in that sphere in the last decade. Now we have acquired intelligence that they have purchased eighteen obsolete BKN nova warships."

Macey waved toward the datastick Bueller was looking at.

"The details are in there, but my understanding is that they have two light carriers, two light cruisers, and fourteen destroyers and corvettes," she told them. "Combined with Colossus's existing fleet of nova fighters, our officers advise me that is more than sufficient to secure the trade lanes around both our systems and blockade Samuels indefinitely."

"Potentially," Kira agreed. "It depends on how they use them. Do you have any idea when and which ships will be online first?"

"I don't," Macey admitted. "My understanding was that we didn't expect to see more than a handful of destroyers for at least six months from when I left. Four months from now."

"*Deception* and *Huntress* can deal with any handful of destroyers," Kira noted. "Given that Colossus will be attempting to maintain a blockade, these two ships alone will be able to breach it at will.

"That would result in a rapid degradation of their forces and their ability to manage a full blockade."

Without more information—information she assumed was on the

datastick—Kira wasn't prepared to promise that her two capital ships could take on the massed flotilla that Colossus had acquired. The most likely divisions, though, would be either a cruiser or carrier with a handful of destroyers, or a cruiser-carrier pair.

Deception and *Huntress* were bigger and better armed than anything Brisingr would call a light cruiser or light carrier. Unless Brisingr had sent crews and pilots along with the hulls, her people were almost certainly better too.

"We were hoping to engage your full fleet, Admiral," Macey admitted.

"That depends on how long you want to wait," Kira said. "I don't expect *Fortitude* to return to Redward for at least eight to nine months. The entire fleet is also...not cheap to hire."

She understood Samuels to be a wealthy system, but if they were also trying to build a new nova fleet of their own for their long-term security...they potentially couldn't afford to engage the entire Memorial Force for an extended period.

Or maybe they could. Kira certainly wouldn't *object* in that case. The mercenary fleet's finances were still showing the lack of the four-million-kroner-per-month retainer they had once received from Redward.

It wouldn't have covered *Fortitude*'s operating expenses, but it had covered most of the day-to-day running expenses of the fleet before that. Now Kira had to keep the fleet in motion and active to make sure their bills were paid.

They were a long way from it being a *problem*, but it was now a *concern*—and a long-term security contract would help offset that.

"If we're only engaging these two capital ships..." Macey paused thoughtfully. "I might be stretching my authority to make any offer at all, but we do need the help."

"Pitch a plan and make an offer, Mrs. Macey," Kira suggested. "Otherwise, we're going around in circles."

"The basic contract would be to break any blockade established around Samuels," the delegate said. "Any further action would need to be a separate discussion with my government. To maintain a fleet in being and operate against the blockade for a period of, let's say, six months... I can offer seven million Apollon new drachmae."

Kira paused, pretending to think while she waited for Vaduva's commentary. She didn't really need the purser's advice to know she was being lowballed. When she'd arrived in Redward, one drachme had been a bit less than four kroner.

She was not under the impression that her home system's interstellar fiscal reputation had improved over the intervening years.

"Basic operating costs for *Huntress* and *Deception* are three point four million kroner per month," Vaduva's voice said crisply in her head. "New drachmae are currently trading at two point two kroner per drachmae as of the latest listing here in Redward. Even considering the local currency bias, we'd be *losing* money, taking that contract."

Kira let her smile become predatory.

"Please, Mrs. Macey, you did not come all this way to waste everyone's time," she pointed out. "Unless you can think of some reason why I would *spend* money to work for you...your offer doesn't even qualify as *insufficient*."

"You would, Admiral, be operating almost directly against Brisingr," Macey said softly.

"Mrs. Macey, I left Apollo a long time ago—and I left Apollo because the Council of Principals betrayed me," Kira said bluntly. "The enmities and conflicts of the past can stay in the past."

She suspected that her more *current* conflicts and enemies were involved in this mess, but that wasn't something she was going to admit. She certainly wasn't going to invest millions of *any* given currency in that chance.

"*Vaduva, what is Samuels's currency trading at versus kroner?*" she asked the purser silently.

"The Samuels pound is currently trading at two point one to the Redward kroner," Vaduva responded instantly.

"For a six-month contract, as you've specified, we are prepared to accept sixty million Samuels pounds," Kira said. That was roughly thirty million kroner or thirteen million new drachmae. Almost *twice* what Macey had offered—and a good ten percent higher than Kira might have asked for if the Samuels woman hadn't tried to lowball her.

She raised a hand before Macey could say a word.

"That is a *base rate*," she told the woman, "to provide a defensive fleet presence and patrol the trade-route stops around Samuels. If Colossus moves against Samuels and we engage in combat operations, an additional rate of one million pounds per day of combat, rounding up, will be included. This is to cover risks and expenses associated with active combat."

The Samuels woman was silent for a moment, making sure that Kira was done, before finally speaking.

"I don't believe that's in my budget," she said calmly. "There are almost certainly cheaper mercenary forces out there."

"You came here looking to hire a *supercarrier*, Mrs. Macey," Milani growled.

"Exactly," Kira said. "And you just tried to offer us a rate that wouldn't suffice to cover wear, tear and hydrogen. This is take-it-or-leave-it time. We will work for Samuels at that rate. Or you can find that cheaper squadron—because I promise you, Mrs. Macey, the only reason *Deception* is sitting at anchor is because I wanted a ship to watch over *Huntress* until she commissioned.

"Once it's known we're available for hire again, I don't think I'll be waiting more than a week or two for a new contract."

She met Macey's gaze. She wasn't unsympathetic to the plight of the woman's star system—if she thought Macey was feeding them a line, she wouldn't be considering the contract. Kira had learned that with a bit of care, she could both fight for just causes *and* make a great deal of money.

But she wasn't going to be pushed around, either.

"If it is that simple, then it is that simple," Macey said stiffly. "Have your legal team draft up the contract and send it to the office we are renting. We will engage your services at your required rate, Admiral Demirci."

"Good," Kira said. "And Mrs. Macey?"

"Yes?" the woman said grimly.

"That is the last time you and I will be on opposite sides," Kira told her gently. "Once that contract is signed, the defense of your people is my duty until it expires—Memorial Force does *nothing* by halves."

6

Kira's command staff regathered in the same conference room later that afternoon. This time, they were joined by the two Commanders, Nova Group, from the two ships.

Both Abdullah "Scimitar" Colombera and Mel "Nightmare" Cartman were members of Kira's old Apollo System Defense Force squadron. The other two survivors of the Three Oh Three were with *Fortitude*—Dinesha "Dawnlord" Patel commanded the supercarrier's nova group and Evgenia "Socrates" Michel now commanded *Persephone*, one of the escorting destroyers.

Vaduva joined them as well at this point, the ever-smiling purser settling into a chair and pouring himself a coffee without waiting for any of the stewards to offer.

This late in the ship's day, Kira was nursing a beer herself, and an artificial stupid robotic wet bar had rolled into the room. A trio of ship's stewards had laid out a meal of finger food, carefully kept away from the projectors concealed inside the table.

"The contract is solid, Yanis?" she asked Vaduva as she selected a meatier chicken wing.

"Standard boilerplate," the purser replied. "Pree and I have been over the template a hundred times at this point."

Priapus Simoneit had been an old friend of Kira's late Apollon commander. He was also one of Redward's top lawyers and had provided legal support to Kira and Memorial Force since its precursor, Memorial *Squadron* had been a subcontractor to John Estanza's Conviction Ltd.

"What about escalator clauses?" Mwangi asked. "*Deception* and *Huntress* can handle this little fleet of Colossus's easily if we're careful, but if Brisingr or Equilibrium is actively backing Colossus's play..."

"We could be looking at major backup arriving in short order," Davidović agreed grimly. "Baking in what it costs for us to call in *Fortitude* and the rest of the fleet makes sense."

"I agree, which is why that clause is in there," Vaduva said with a chuckle. "Twenty million pounds for the first month the rest of the fleet is in position, further rates to be negotiated at the time."

He shook his head.

"They have to activate that clause, of course, and I think Mrs. Macey's people didn't think it was likely," he observed. "I would prefer not to see it activated, seeing as how I will be aboard *Deception* myself."

Kira snorted at that and took a sip of her beer.

"Still sticking to my coattails, I see?"

The purser tended to stick with Memorial Force's senior management—mostly personified by Kira as majority shareholder—and had stayed behind in Redward when they'd sent the majority of their firepower off to Obsidian.

"I do not think that the early stages of construction of our next ship will require that much supervision, Admiral," Vaduva noted calmly. "So, yes."

"Konrad, did you get a chance to go over their data?" Mwangi asked. "You know Brisingr ships better than the rest of us."

"I think Kira would surprise you," Bueller replied. "But yes, I did.

The Samuels folks didn't have quite enough data to fully identify the classes involved themselves—but they had enough for me to run it against my databases and get us some types and weights."

He gestured, and the holograms of eighteen ships appeared above the table.

"Most of us are actually familiar with the most modern ships in the flotilla," he noted as four of the midsized vessels flashed. "D9C heavy destroyers. Given the rest of the ships in play, I'm guessing these four are some of the first units of the class built, but they are the most modern ships in the batch.

"Forty thousand cubic meters, decent gun armament, no fighters," Bueller laid out. "They also have four D5D destroyers of even older vintage. Those are twenty-seven kilocubic ships that even a Redward corvette might be able to take down in their design specs.

"The remainder of the escorts are six corvettes of the CV4 and CV3D classes," he told them. "Eighteen and sixteen kilocubics apiece. Like the D5Ds, they're old ships. Roughly comparable to Redward's tech when we first arrived."

The general rule was that for every ten light-years a system was from Earth, their general tech base—and *especially* their military technology—fell about a year and a half behind.

Right now, Redward was dragging the average military tech level of the Syntactic Cluster up around them, but they were still at least a decade behind Apollo and Brisingr. Almost two light-centuries farther from Earth than Kira's home sector, they had been *thirty* years behind when she'd arrived—and lacked key facilities for the production of the class two nova drives essential for nova fighters.

So, the corvettes were thirty years old—but the rest of the ships were newer. Still pre-war vintage, as Macey had said, but that could still allow for ships that were merely twelve to thirteen years old.

"What about the heavy ships?" she asked, eyeing the four blocky vessels at the heart of the virtual formation. Brisingr-built ships—like *Deception*—looked crude to her eyes, all flat surfaces and sharp corners.

Apollon ships smoothed those corners and curved those surfaces. It made the ships take longer to build, but also meant that they used slightly less material for a given cubage—and that they had less dead cubage rendered useless by geometry.

Brisingr settled for building slightly less effective ships faster and for the same price as Apollo. Given that the BKN had fought the ASDF to a standstill and pushed the Council of Principals to a near-surrender, she supposed the evidence spoke to which model was better.

"The cruisers are about what we were expecting," Bueller told them. "I-Fifty series, fifty-five thousand cubic meters, no organic fighter complement. Brisingr armed them with nine heavy guns in three triple turrets."

"What about Colossus?" Kira asked. "If they were fully disarmed, the locals have to build them new guns."

She had memories of the I50 cruisers when she thought about it, too. There was one of them on her own list of kills, whose silhouettes would be painted on her nova fighter's hull if Apollo had that tradition.

"I'll get to that," her lover replied. "First, though, the joker in our deck of castoffs."

The last two ships expanded and flashed.

"Mrs. Macey said the flotilla were all pre-war ships," Bueller noted. "In the case of the carriers, that would require some very careful hair-splitting. The N-Forty-Five series multi-function carriers were designed and laid down prior to the war, but none of them were commissioned until after the war began."

He shook his head.

"They weren't a great design. I believe the BKN built eight of them, and I believe the ASDF turned five of them into debris and corpses," he said quietly. "If they've sent two of them to Colossus, those are probably the last N-Forty-Five carriers in existence.

"For a war against a peer power, they suck," he stated. "To shuttle fighters around or maintain a blockade, however... They carry sixty nova fighters on a fifty kilocubic hull. They have limited self-defense weaponry, but their purpose is to put a crapton of nova fighters into a battlespace and then run like hell sublight and hope nobody catches them."

"It didn't work out for them in the war," Kira said quietly. "They ended up either being sitting ducks or holding back enough fighters for their own defense that the extra carrying capacity was irrelevant.

"But here, where they're expecting to mostly be handling nova fighters on long-jump cooldown or civilian ships, they are a problem." She shook her head. "If they get both of them in play, that lets them bring more fighters to a given battlespace than we can."

"So, we avoid going up against both carriers at once," Davidović said. "They're unlikely to keep them together until they know we're in play. Even then, we can dance around the bastards."

"Agreed," Kira said. "I'm not worried about our ability to handle them, though the N-Forty-Fives are definitely a wrinkle." She considered. "What can Colossus put aboard them, though?"

"So, that's where we come down to the 'What can Colossus do?' part of the question," Bueller replied. "And the answer is too bloody much."

The starships disappeared, replaced by a familiar and roughly triangular shape. Most nova fighters shared basically the same structure, after all. The proportions helped define what kind of fighter it was, and Kira quickly noted that the attack ship was a heavy fighter.

"Colossus only builds one type of nova fighter, the Liberator," the engineer said calmly. "They class her as an MFNC—multifunction nova combatant. I'd call her a fighter-bomber—heavy guns, overpowered engines, two torpedoes."

Kira nodded slowly.

"Big and expensive," she murmured. "But not enough so to give Colossus problems fitting them on a carrier."

"Almost," Bueller told her. "They'll have a harder time refitting the N-Forty-Fives to hold them than they would a more standard array of planes, but they're a damn good fighter. And that carries over to everything else Colossus can do."

"How bad?" Mwangi asked grimly.

"In BKN service, even the N-Forty-Fives would have had point-six-rated dispersion networks at best," Bueller noted. "Colossus can build point-six-five networks. If they spend the time to refit the defenses on all of the ships, they'll be measurably more survivable than their original specifications called for."

The rating of a dispersal network was an approximation of how much of the kinetic and thermal energy of a plasma burst would be safely grounded. *Deception* had a point-six-five network—but Redward was only up to building point-five networks.

The Colossus ships would be significantly more able to take hits than Kira's carrier. Of course, the main point was to *avoid* letting the carrier get hit.

"While their nova ships were limited to fighters and gunships, Colossus did build heavier plasma cannon for their defensive forts and monitors," Bueller continued. "Based off the information Samuels has on those guns, I expect that they'll be able to refit the ships to a standard roughly comparable with *Deception*, if not slightly better.

"Cubic for cubic, those ships are going to be capable of going toe-to-toe with *Deception* herself," he concluded. "Of course, *Deception* is ninety-six thousand cubic meters versus the fifty to fifty-five kilocubics for their heaviest ships."

"Between *Deception* and *Huntress* and the fighter wings, I'm still confident in our ability to take them all," Kira repeated. "But we needed to know what we're up against. The ships may be small, but by the time Colossus is done with them, they will functionally be frontline BKN units—or, at least, to the standard the BKN would bring them up to to keep in the front line."

"Does Macey know that?" Milani asked. "Might explain why she's so twitchy."

"Her home system's major external economic driver is now under active threat by their nearest neighbor," Kira said. "*I'd* be twitchy in her place."

"So, what now?" Davidović asked.

"We wait until Pree and the Samuels team have finalized the contract, then we check in with our new employer," Kira told them all. "For us...I suggest everyone make sure their departments and crews have everything they need.

"I don't expect to be in Redward for more than a few days now."

7

DECEPTION'S FLIGHT deck was silent in the calm before the storm.

Kira knew that the metaphor was exaggerating a bit. They were leaving Redward shortly, but it was a four-week journey to Samuels. Only a week less than the journey all the way to Apollo, a place she would probably never see again.

Her brother probably regretted that. She knew damn well that his wife didn't—she'd never got along with the woman, but then Kira was a starfighter pilot and her brother was a shepherd.

Their worlds hadn't really collided in a long time, even before she'd fled her home system one step ahead of Brisingr assassins.

She snorted and ran her hand along the side of *her* nova fighter. The Wolverine interceptor still felt strange to her. She'd flown a Hoplite-IV interceptor in the war against Brisingr and the first few years since arriving in Redward. The Wolverine, on the other hand, was the Navy of the Royal Crest's equivalent to the Hoplite-V.

Despite her attachment to the nova fighter that had carried her through her early years as a mercenary, she couldn't pass up the improved Harrington coils, the more powerful guns, the more efficient fusion reactor or the in-cockpit coffee maker of the more advanced fighter.

Her Wolverine was officially *Deception*-Alpha-Seven. The seventh fighter in a six-fighter squadron—and that said everything about Kira's position in the nova group. The nova fighter was stenciled with that hull number, her callsign, and her kill markers in Apollon three-dot style...but she'd never actually flown the craft in combat.

Kira's fingers rested on those three dots. Purple. Red. Orange. Purple marked thirty-two kills. Red marked sixteen. Orange marked four. Fifty-two kills, by the not-quite-simple metrics of a star system that espoused pacifism and lived pragmatism.

A stranger might see the three dots and assume that an Apollon pilot had only just made ace. In truth, though, the Apollo military had refused to let their pilots put *more* than three kill markers on their fighters—hence the color coding and the calculations of how many "kills" a sub-fighter or participation in a capital-ship kill was worth.

"What is it with fighter-pilot flag officers and hanging out on flight decks before the operation?" a voice asked behind her. "I'm told Estanza did it. I *know* Commodore Heller did it back on *Victorious*."

Kira smirked at Mel Cartman's words. The 303 Nova Combat Group had been the interceptor force assigned to *Victorious*, the fleet carrier anchoring Task Force *Victorious* at the end of the war.

Heller's Hellions, the news media had labeled them, as Commodore Heller had led a single carrier and four escorts through a series of minor but real victories during a phase of the war where Apollo hadn't had many victories at all. There'd been few real *defeats* in the final year of the war, but no victories. Just bloody draws the ASDF and their allies couldn't afford.

"It's weird," Kira admitted. "I know, intellectually, that I am a thousand times safer aboard *Deception* than I would ever be flying a fighter. I can even admit, most of the time, that I'm at *least* as effective in command of the entire fleet as I would be in a single plane.

"But I miss it."

"I'll admit, I like the fact that our structure means you *can't* promote me out of the cockpit," her old friend said brightly, joining Kira in leaning against the fighter.

A moment after reaching the Wolverine, Cartman produced two bottles of beer. She casually used the heat cowling over the fighter's port plasma cannon to pop the tops, then passed one to Kira.

"I think you just violated four different regulations," Kira noted—but she took the beer.

"Back home, sure. Here? Waldroup wrote the safety rules for our decks, and they rely on a solid sense of 'Don't be a moron,'" Cartman replied, taking a sip of the beer. "Homesick?"

"No? Yes?" Kira sighed. She was more honest with Cartman than with most people. The old Three Oh Three hands were special; everyone knew it. Zoric and Bueller had their own special statuses as well, but she'd known Mel Cartman, especially, for over a decade.

"It's hard to miss a place where the government decided you were expendable," she admitted. "I was thinking about my family and my old interceptor." She smiled wryly. "And yes, I know it's weird to put those in the same sentence."

"Your interceptor liked you better than your sister-in-law did," Cartman pointed out. "But yeah. I miss home sometimes. Though I realize that back home, I would probably have either washed out or been promoted to a desk by now."

"Or a bridge, which I tried," Kira reminded her. "Hell, I'll never tell Scimitar, but he *knows* he was third on the list to command *Huntress*'s nova group."

First on the list had been Ruben "Gizmo" Hersch, the senior of the surviving pilots from *Conviction*'s original group. Then Kira had offered it to Cartman—after Cartman had turned down command of the entire carrier.

"He knows you offered the group to me and Ruben," Cartman agreed. "Of course, I'm not sure anyone knows that you offered me the big seat."

"I didn't expect you to take it," Kira admitted. "I was surprised you stayed on *Deception*, though."

"I'm a shareholder, Kira," her friend reminded her. "I get paid much the same wherever I am in the squadron—and so long as Konrad Bueller is this ship's XO, *you* are using *Deception* as your flagship."

Kira waved a hand in the air.

"Touché," she admitted. "I didn't realize you were sticking around to watch my back, I'll admit."

"Someone has to keep you out of trouble," Cartman told her. "And keep your feet on the ground."

She rapped her beer bottle against the Wolverine.

"If I have my way, the only time you'll ever sit in this bird is for training," *Deception*'s Commander, Nova Group, told her boss. "Your job is to find contracts and put us all in the battlespace with a plan."

"And once the jamming goes up, I'm useless," Kira said quietly.

Multiphasic jamming was the reality of the battlespace. Complex and high-powered jammers combined with sensor-confusing baffles, the systems rendered everything except visual identification useless within an extended area—and rendered even visual ID difficult beyond maybe fifty thousand kilometers.

Capital ships could maintain laser coms with each other in the chaos at some distance, but fighters had to stay too mobile for that to be more than an intermittent connection. Since nova fighters carried the weight of the fighting in most of Kira's plans, that left her without command and control once the battle was joined.

"If you do your job right, you're *unnecessary* once the jamming goes up," Cartman countered. "And your track record is pretty solid on that front. You get us paid, boss, and we do the work."

Kira chuckled.

"I've never liked sending other people into battle for me," she admitted. "Sending Kavitha off to Obsidian with most of the fleet? It grates. Knowing that I have to do the same thing on a smaller scale in every battle..."

She shook her head and rested one hand on the fighter as she drank her beer.

"That would be why I still have my own plane, I guess," she admitted. "I know it's a luxury, but..."

"It's one we can afford," Cartman replied. "Better than we can afford one of our top half-dozen aces being grounded if we ever actually *need* you to get behind the stick again."

"I'm probably too rusty to be on that list anymore," Kira admitted. "But I appreciate the top-up to my ego."

"You'll always have a pilot's ego, boss. It's good for us all," the other woman said. "And I've got your back."

Kira grinned.

"And you staying on *Deception* has *nothing* to do with Akuchi Mwangi's cute butt," she said drily.

"I won't say that isn't a factor, though I have sadly determined that Mwangi isn't interested," Cartman admitted. "But hey! The horse may learn to sing."

Kira chuckled again and then clinked bottles with her friend.

"And so we go on."

8

"We've got eyes on our employer's ship," Isidora Soler reported.

The pale, raven-haired Tactical officer's report was theoretically meant solely for Akuchi Mwangi, but Kira had never quite got around to assembling a proper flag staff for *Deception* or Memorial Force. Thanks to virtual conferencing and the headware implants all of her people had, she managed by virtually merging the cruiser's small flag deck with the bridge.

Kira wasn't alone on the flag deck, but only Mel Cartman was actually present. Every other "person" around her was a holographic mirror of someone who was actually on the cruiser's bridge—and it was difficult to tell where the physical room she was in ended and the virtual mirror of the bridge began.

It worked for her, but even Cartman looked occasionally thrown off when she joined the Admiral on the flag deck.

"What are we looking at?" Mwangi asked.

"Pretty standard twenty-kilocubic diplomatic fast packet," Soler replied. "Not a yacht like our Crest friend had, but almost certainly comfortable on the inside. Scans suggest she can keep pace with us sublight."

The two mercenary capital ships slid into formation around Macey's transport. At twenty thousand cubic meters, the diplomatic ship was about twice the size of the smallest proper nova ship—but still on the small side for even the Rim.

"She's armed; I'm seeing both ventral and dorsal dual light turrets," Soler continued. "Hmm."

"I see your 'hmm' and raise you a 'that's interesting,'" Bueller added. Kira threw a glance at her lover's hologram and sent a mental questioning ping.

"I've got scans of her Jianhong radiation signature as we're spinning up for nova," the engineer told them. "That's not as covert as they think it is."

"Oh?" Mwangi asked. "We're novaing in a minute. Is this something I should worry about?"

"No, no, not *worry*," Bueller replied. "In fact, if we wait for the nova to finish, I'll be able to confirm what I'm looking at."

"Fine, fine, play wizard engineer of mystery if you wish," the Captain replied. "Wallis? We clear to nova?"

Lyssa Wallis was one of the newer members of *Deception*'s bridge crew—but, thankfully, experienced nova navigators were easier to come by than experienced nova-fighter pilots. The redheaded woman was triple-checking her calculations as Mwangi spoke.

"It's the standard trade route out to Ypres," she pointed out. "We've made this nova a hundred times. And yes, I've checked my calcs, *Huntress*'s calcs and *Springtime Chorus*'s calcs."

Mwangi chuckled. "Last fighters are coming aboard now. Nova on your mark."

"Novaing...now."

The world flashed around Kira. Wrapped in the armor of a starship, the only noticeable effect was the flash of her optical nerves getting confused. In a nova fighter, it could hit with waves of pain or nausea, though fighter pilots either got used to it or stopped being fighter pilots.

One way or another.

"Welcome to trade-route stop Y-Six-Seven-Five-Three-L-D-K-Nine-Four-Two-S-S-I-Seven-Five," Wallis reported.

There was a beat.

"Someone please tell me she's joking," Soler asked slowly.

"Sadly, no," Mwangi admitted. "It's just that practically *no one* pays any attention to the catalog numbers for trade-route stops."

To make a nova, you need detailed information on both the gravitational data of where you were and where you were going. Where you were was, of course, the easy part. With decent sensors and computer support, a pilot could calculate the current status of a destination based on light-lagged data—up to about a light-day. A light-week, potentially, for the truly specialty ships that mapped new nova routes.

To make a full six-light-year jump, a navigator needed to either be jumping into a stellar gravity well—where small variations were completely overwhelmed by the mass of the star—or have excruciatingly detailed information on every possible natural effect at the destination.

Putting together that information was what "mapping a nova point" entailed, and it could easily take weeks or months. Once the map was complete, it would be constantly updated by every ship that passed through the nova point. Part of the subscription cost for the maps of "civilized space" was providing that updated information for every stop a ship passed through.

Those maps were cheaply available to every ship—and regardless of the low price for individual ships, the coalition of corporations behind them had grown *fabulously* wealthy.

And maintained a list of stops Kira had seen estimated at over two *quintillion* individual locations. The catalog numbers got mind-boggling after a while, and people actively tried to ignore them.

"Okay, so while we all try *not* to think about Wallis using actual catalog numbers on us," Mwangi said, "what was Commander Bueller's 'hmm, that's interesting'?"

Bueller chuckled.

"So, *Springtime Chorus* is a twenty-kilocubic fast packet," he said. "A cursory scan shows that she's operating a two-kilocubic class one nova drive. So, simply enough, they used a cheap nova drive."

"Who cheaps out on their consular ships?" Wallis asked.

"Nobody who can afford better," Mwangi replied. "So, what's the answer, Konrad?"

"She's running a thirteen-X nova drive," Bueller said. "That drive can take twenty-*six* kilocubics into FTL—and the reason why is these."

An image of *Springtime Chorus* appeared in the main bridge holodisplay—mirrored to the main flag-deck display for Kira. She was a smooth disk shape roughly fifteen meters thick and forty meters across. Standard iconography flickered across the hologram, and Kira caught at least part of the issue before Bueller explained it.

"She has *way* more external airlocks than she would normally have," the engineer said. "And these ones, spaced evenly around the dorsal and ventral turrets, have concealed hatches around them."

"Docking gear," Kira concluded. "Our consular ship can carry her own escorts. I make it twelve nova fighters, Konrad?"

"I get the same," he agreed. "Of course, Samuels has the same 'big, expensive and overengineered' style of plane as Colossus, so I don't think they could actually *fit* twelve of their birds on her.

"But she's not supposed to rely on her turrets for self-defense."

"Which begs the question: where *are* her nova fighters?" Kira asked. "And if they don't normally carry them...does Samuels's diplomatic corps even realize that their consular ships are pocket carriers?"

KIRA WAS TAKEN ABACK when she first saw Doretta Macey over the holographic call. The Samuels woman had traded out the formal but stylish pant suit and tied bun for an extremely old-fashioned blue-and-white dress and loose hair.

Assuming that Macey had access to the health care Kira would expect of a wealthy Mid-Rim world, the gray in her hair and wrinkles on her face suggested that she was likely into her second century. Despite that, she mustered flowing curly locks of silver and gold hair that hung down past her shoulders with a grace that Kira, who lived in a military officer's short ponytail, could only envy.

"Mrs. Macey," Kira greeted her employer. "I figured now was as good a time to check in as any. My bridge crew and yours are keeping in touch to manage the logistics of the trip."

"Captain Hennessy is very good at their job," Macey told her. "They'll keep things well in hand."

"I'm not overly worried about the trip," Kira admitted. "Very few people get up in the morning and decide they need to pick a fight with *anybody's* heavy cruiser without real reason. Random piracy is something our mere presence tends to suppress."

"I see," the older woman murmured, shaking her head. "I suppose that is the reality of the world. One wishes it were different—I dislike appealing to even the implicit threat of violence, let alone its active use."

"I can understand that," Kira said. "Apollo is...nominally pacifist as a culture, though we're bad at it under pressure." She shrugged.

"Apollo is nominally many things that they are bad at under pressure, Admiral Demirci," Macey said acidly. "Including *democratic*."

Kira couldn't even argue. Officially, Apollo was a "democratic oligarchy." The franchise to vote in planetary elections for the Council of Principals was limited to those who paid taxes in the highest tax bracket.

Standing in those elections wasn't officially limited at all, but looking back from the outside, Kira could see the way those forty-eight seats had been passed back and forth among a hundred or so families.

Her planet's saving grace, in her opinion, was that it had a very carefully maintained rule of law, where higher-level courts answered to the lower-level courts, not the Council of Principals, and lower-level courts were managed by the municipal governments, which *did* have a universal franchise.

"I won't defend Apollo's system, Mrs. Macey," Kira replied. "I've grown to be fond of Redward's style of constitutional monarchy, but I recognize it only succeeds when provided with a certain grade of monarch."

"And it makes my skin crawl almost as much as organized church," Macey replied. "Organization has always been where the groups of Quakers split, I suppose. But we are a true democracy, in both worship and governance."

That was a sufficiently broad statement that Kira had to check her headware database. She hadn't paid that much attention to the governing structure of their employer. Macey spoke for some kind of executive branch, and she'd assumed Samuels was a relatively standard presidential republic, much like Colossus.

She was apparently wrong.

"How does that even *work*?" she asked as her download filled her in on a government structure where the lower house of the legislature was, basically, the *entire population*.

"The First Minister and the Quorum are directly selected at each election," Macey told her. "The First Minister presents a list of Ministers to the Quorum for approval, and those Ministers run the day-to-day government of our planet.

"The Quorum—who are unpaid, I must note—prepare and review potential legislation in coordination with the Ministries. Twice a local year—three times a standard year—all legislation that has passed the Quorum is presented to the populace via the system datanet, and we vote."

"Sounds complicated as all hell," Kira admitted. "And likely to result in all kinds of confusion."

"Part of the Quorum's job is to make sure that nothing goes to the wide vote without being simple enough that it can be explained in a one-hour presentation," Macey told her. "Our founders, though, were of the Interstellar Society of Friends. They believed that faith was between an individual and God—and felt that governance should be similar.

"Power derives from the will of the people, after all."

"Or the barrel of the gun that convinces the people to lie down," Kira murmured.

"That option is not one the people of Samuels will ever accept," the diplomat said. "The reality of the world is that we must have defenses and soldiers, so we do. But even our soldiers recognize that violence is the last option. No military junta will ever rule our world."

"Military juntas don't have a great success rate over the long term," Kira said. "But militaristic states... That's a different story."

Kira, at least, knew that the Equilibrium Institute existed and was happily getting involved in politics, economics and war in their area of the Rim to twist the galaxy toward their vision, where military hegemons maintained peace in carefully delineated territories.

"Hence why we came to you for help."

"True," Kira conceded. "Though that leaves me with an interesting question, Mrs. Macey."

Macey leaned back and adjusted her dress.

"We are, as you said, on the same side now," she noted. "I will endeavor to assist in any way I can."

Macey had already signed a twenty-million-pound transfer to cover Memorial Force's deployment to Samuels. That was the kind of "help" Kira mostly cared about.

"Where is *Springtime Chorus*'s nova-fighter escort?" Kira asked. "My people noted that she's designed to carry two squadrons as Apollo counts them, and I would have expected you to bring them with you, coming this far out."

Macey shook her head.

"It was a point of discussion, yes," she admitted. "I overruled our military advisors. I did not want to draw attention to ourselves on what was supposed to be an economic mission. Plus..." She paused to consider her words. "Frankly, twelve nova fighters were more likely to make a difference in securing our home than in protecting a single ship, months away from Samuels."

"I see," Kira said. "That's quite a risk you took on yourself. While consular ships are theoretically off-limits, I wouldn't want to count on that myself."

"We traveled safely to Redward," Macey told her. "And now we have you to protect us on our way home. What do I have to fear?"

"Nothing while you're with us," Kira agreed. "I was worried you'd been attacked on the way here and concealed that from us."

"No, we simply didn't bring them," Macey confirmed.

"How many ships like *Springtime* do you have?" Kira asked. "That's an edge I didn't think Samuels possessed."

The Samuels woman sighed and shook her head.

"Three," she said quietly. "All built by my late husband. *Springtime Chorus* and *Autumn Songs* were eventually bought into Ministries service, but *Summer Drums* remains the property of our corporation."

"I apologize," Kira said. "I didn't realize your husband had passed."

"A shuttle accident," Doretta Macey said. "One I now find suspicious, given that the dear man was one of the few who saw what Colossus was becoming and urged us to prepare. But..."

She spread her hands.

"I am a negotiator, a linguist and an economist," she noted. "I am not a spy or an investigator. When our law enforcement tells me there was nothing abnormal about Jacob's death, I must accept that."

"I appreciate the warning," Kira said. "It's good to know what concerns may yet await us."

It was one thing to face the enemy she knew about, but if there was rot in Samuels itself, she and her people would need to watch their backs.

9

THE DISADVANTAGE of having personal communication hardware installed in everyone's heads was that it was impossible to truly disconnect. Software locks and codes existed, but especially for someone with large responsibilities—like the Admiral of a mercenary fleet—someone always had an override to ping them regardless.

And headware implants were able to wake their human from a deep sleep if their metrics decided that the alert was important enough. Anything where Kira's subordinates were flagging the message high-enough priority to even make it through the software would rouse her.

All of that meant that she went from completely asleep, snuggled in Konrad Bueller's arms, to fully awake as an emergency ping hit her implants from the bridge.

"Demirci," she answered silently, hoping to not disturb her lover. Extracting herself from his arms without waking him would take a moment, but she'd have to find clothes before doing more than taking audio calls, anyway.

"I'm sorry to bother you, boss," Akuchi Mwangi said softly, clearly aware that it was the middle of her night. Of course, his volume was irrelevant, as the message was arriving directly to her auditory nerves...but headware, in Kira's experience, only allowed humans to be human faster and with more certainty.

Instincts evolved but never truly went away.

"What's going on?" she asked, carefully laying Konrad's arm back on the bed and pulling a blanket over the man.

"We've got a cruiser bearing for us, coming in hard," Mwangi told her. "Beacon says they're from the Denzel Security Association, and we've been summoned to provide our full course and destination."

That was more information than most people would demand of a pair of mercenary capital ships.

"The Denzel System is...what, twenty light-years from here?" Kira asked. They were inside the range where the Denzel fleet could operate, but that was still strange.

"Twenty-two," Mwangi confirmed. "I haven't responded to their demands yet, but you know where we're at in the cycle."

Kira didn't even need to manually check the time. Her two ships and their consular companion had novaed to this trade-route stop eleven hours before. It was still nine hours before they could nova away—but that wasn't the only cycle Mwangi was talking about.

Her ships were nearly at the maximum level of tachyon and electrostatic buildup they could safely carry. They needed to discharge after their next nova, which limited them to exactly two possible destinations.

"Inform them that we are en route to the Serigala System to discharge static," Kira told him. "Hopefully, that's enough. If it isn't..."

She kept her sigh off the audio channel as she looked back at the warm bed with its warm human.

"I'll be on the flag deck in three minutes," she concluded. "If the locals are still being troublesome, we'll get it sorted."

THE VIRTUAL MERGER of bridge and flag deck was online within moments of Kira entering her space, but it was sparser than usual. There was only a small bridge crew on duty, and she was truly physically alone in the flag deck this time.

While *Deception*, like most flagships, ran on a ship's day of "the Admiral is up," there was no point in waking everyone up just because Kira had been flagged for a concern.

The next step would be to bring both of her ships to full battle stations and start scrambling fighters, after all. They could wake everyone up then.

"Current range is just under one light-minute," the junior Tactical officer running the dark watch reported. "Contact is... Contact has launched nova fighters, but they appear to be falling into formation around her."

Kira took her seat and brought up the main tactical display.

"That's a response, I suppose," she told the bridge crew. "What are we looking at, people?"

"Fifty-kilocubic light cruiser, presumably local design, as she draws a blank in the databanks," Mwangi said instantly. "Looks like she's got space aboard for ten nova fighters, which is a...choice."

"Marking two of them as bombers, Captain," the Tactical officer noted.

"Eight interceptors and a pair of bombers isn't a bad sucker punch for a light cruiser," Kira replied. "What do we know about this Denzel Security Association?"

"The DSA is the nova fleet for the Republic of Denzel," Mwangi listed. "EG says they're a pretty standard presidential republic, above-average GSP per capita... Nothing to scream *troublemaker*, but they *have* a nova fleet and are listed as carrying out security patrols in the surrounding region."

"Junior over there is picking a fight with over three times his cubage of unknown warships," Kira said. "Any further communication?"

"Not yet. She's an hour away still, unless those nova fighters jump at us," Mwangi reported. "Permission to request a CSP from *Huntress*?"

"Granted," Kira replied. "Wake up Scimitar and Nightmare. They put ten fighters into space? Let's get twenty up."

"Battle stations?" Mwangi asked.

"Not yet," she told him. "Get me a link to Macey. This is her neighborhood. I hope she knows the Denzelites better than we do."

"Ronaldo."

The single name was a clear instruction, one that the assistant com officer had clearly picked up as he flashed a thumbs-up and got to work.

A moment later, Kira was connected to an audio-only link with Doretta Macey.

"Mrs. Macey, I apologize if I'm interrupting anything, but has your crew advised you of our incoming visitor?"

There was a long, silent pause.

"You woke me up, Admiral, so give me a moment," Macey said slowly. A few more seconds passed. "Captain Hennessy informs me that there is a cruiser heading our way, but so far they have only communicated directly with *Deception*."

"Have they?" Kira asked quietly. "We didn't realize that here, Mrs. Macey. They asked for our full course plan and destination, which isn't something I want to turn over without a good reason—but they've also deployed nova fighters and are continuing to close.

"Now, I'm not overly concerned about the threat of this one ship, but I don't want to fight a battle I shouldn't have to, and I'm not sure they'd be picking this fight unless they thought they had backup," Kira continued. "What do you know about what's going on?"

"Not much more than you," Macey told her. "I've led or been part of five trade missions to Denzel. They're a major trading partner of ours, if a bit more cutthroat than I really like.

"They've been pushing their economic edge for influence in the systems around them recently, so..."

"Wonderful. We've walked into someone feeling their oats," Kira concluded. "I'll loop you in on our further communications with them, Mrs. Macey. I would very much like not to have to get into a pissing match—but I'll take that over a *shooting* match."

KIRA WATCHED as the Denzelite warship continued to approach with its starfighters in formation around it. She figured she had a decent idea of what the DSA was doing there, but the cruiser Captain was being an idiot about it.

She sighed.

"Ronaldo," she addressed the com officer on duty. "Get me a wideband transmission directed at our friends. What's the time delay?"

"Hundred-and-ten-second round trip," Jacen Ronaldo replied quickly. "Plus however long they take to think and record."

"Thank you."

A green icon popped up in her headware, and she mentally clicked it to start recording.

"Denzel Security Association vessel," Kira addressed the stranger. "This is Admiral Kira Demirci of the Memorial Force mercenary squadron. My people have provided the information you have asked for, but you are continuing an aggressive approach on our position.

"We have neither business nor conflict with the Denzel System that I am aware of, and I would prefer not to get into a fight over a misunderstanding. Communicate your intentions before someone does something drastic and regrettable."

She ended the recording and shook her head. Unless the Denzelite Captain was an idiot, they knew that Kira could wipe them out. The DSA's handful of starfighters were potentially a useful augment to a light cruiser's capabilities, but against a carrier or a heavy cruiser, they were still utterly outgunned.

Kira might lose nova fighters if it came to a fight—something she did *not* want to do—but the DSA cruiser was outnumbered and outgunned.

She was considering her battle-stations alert when the DSA ship finally replied. A recorded video of a sharp-featured older man with visible cybernetics wrapped over his head glowered at her.

"This is Captain Fikri Sparacello of the Denzel Security Association," he said in a clipped and evenly paced accent. "You have entered a security restriction zone enforced by the DSA.

"As you were advised originally, we require your *full* course, destination and intentions, or your vessels will be interned and auctioned to cover the costs of your detainment."

Sparacello glared at the camera.

"This is not negotiable, Em Demirci."

The recording ended and Kira sighed. She considered for a moment, then forwarded Sparacello's message to her ship Captains and Macey before linking them in for a virtual conference.

"Mrs. Macey, any idea what's going on?" she asked the Samuels delegate.

"None," Macey admitted. "This didn't happen when we came out, but that was...weeks ago."

"It's a blockade," Mwangi said quietly. "The question is what system are they blockading and why are they being quite so irritable about it."

"They're being irritable because they don't know the standards, is my guess," Kira replied. "If Denzel has never run a real blockade before, they're being overly aggressive—not least because we just showed up with a pair of ships that can probably *breach* their blockade."

"So, what do we do?" Macey asked, the delegate looking concerned.

"First, we talk Captain Sparacello off the cliff before I have to shoot him off of it," Kira said drily. "We've got him talking, which is halfway there." She shook her head. "There's a good chance they're blockading the Serigala System, so we'll have to deal with that.

"I'm not being *paid* to breach their blockade, so we go around if that's the case," she admitted. "Plus, while our friend here isn't up to our weight, my understanding is that the DSA has a carrier group or two that could give us a real headache.

"We're probably going to have to pay a 'toll' to save their face," she continued. "That's covered under our contract, Mrs. Macey. By which I mean you have to pay for it."

The representative chuckled.

"I did read the contract, Admiral; I just didn't think there *were* any tolls or blockades on the route home," she admitted. "But you can handle this?"

Kira nodded.

"One way or another, Mrs. Macey," she told her employer. "But if I leave Captain Sparacello's ship in pieces, that's going to be a very big problem for *somebody*."

10

The first step, Kira figured, was to set the terms of the discussion. *That* meant hitting the battle-stations command at last.

Alerts rang through both of her warships, and more nova fighters began to blaze off the deck within moments of the order being issued.

"*Finally*," Nightmare told her. Mel Cartman had clearly been sitting in her fighter, waiting to launch. "My planes are up. Scimitar is on his, but we've got a full strike group in space. Shall we go kick a twit?"

"Not yet," Kira ordered. "Plot your novas, but hold position around *Springtime Chorus* for now."

It was a pointed, if silent, response to Captain Sparacello's message. Squadron after squadron of fighters launched into space, taking up positions around Kira's three starships. Thirty Wolverines and Hussar-Sevens apiece launched from *Huntress*, accompanied by twelve Wildcat-Four bombers.

Deception "only" put twelve Wolverines and eight Hussar-Sevens into space, but that still brought the total to ninety-two starfighters forming a steady protective sphere around Kira's warships.

If Kira was expecting this to come to a fight, that would have been the last thing the Denzelites would have seen before her warships and fighters vanished behind a shield of multiphasic jamming.

The *problem*, though, was that the moment she raised jammers, she committed her people. There could be no communication once the jammers were online.

She waited until the last fighters were in formation and then activated the recorder again.

"Captain Sparacello, I will be...blunt," she told him. "If you attempt to detain my ships, I will use all necessary force to protect myself, my client and my employees.

"I am, of course, prepared to respect Denzel's security restriction zone," she continued. "If you provide further information on what you are attempting to *secure*, we will comply with all reasonable requests and restrictions.

"However, I do not see how my course or intentions are of any relevance to a star system I am about to leave thirty-plus light-years behind me."

She smiled.

"We've already made this a bit messier than it ever needed to be, Captain. Let's breathe and talk this out."

Leaning back in her chair, Kira ran the mental math on how long the message would take. The Denzelite ship was still closing, but her jammers weren't up and her fighters hadn't launched assault novas yet.

With all of Kira's fighters in space, an attack by the Denzelite bombers would be suicide, even with their escorts along.

The time lag for the transmission both ways passed, and she concealed a grimace.

"He's not going to do anything stupid, is he?" Mwangi asked from the cruiser's bridge.

"I hope not," Kira said. "I don't think so. If one of those fighters disappears to play courier, *then* we need to be worried. Until then...

it's just a question of whether he's walked far enough out on the cliff that all he can do is jump."

"Incoming transmission, Admiral," Monica Smolak reported, *Deception*'s com officer having finally taken over for her junior.

"Play it," Kira ordered.

Sparacello appeared again, his face just as motionless as before as he leveled eyes glittering with metallic flecks on the camera.

"Admiral Demirci." At least he was giving her her title now. "We may have had a miscommunication here."

There was a long pause after he spoke, still staring at the camera. He didn't blink, Kira noted. That was unnerving.

"The Serigala System is currently under a security restriction by the Denzel Security Association due to a...contractual dispute between Serigala and Denzel," he said, his tone still eerily level and measured.

"Given your armament and stated destination, we have a clear and present concern about your vessels and purpose in this region. If I have reason to believe that your nova will be to the Serigala System, my orders require me to detain or destroy your vessels.

"If you are heading to the Deva System, however, I am merely required to request payment of a transit toll to recognize the DSA's efforts in securing the region. Details will be transmitted shortly."

His unblinking gaze stared into the camera.

"We will require detailed information on your planned nova to make certain that you are not violating the restriction zone," he continued. "Any attempt to nova toward Serigala will be met with all necessary force."

The transmission ended and Kira nodded silently.

"Wallis?" she addressed *Deception*'s navigator. "How much does going through Deva increase our journey time?"

"It'll add four novas, mostly because we'll need an extra discharge stop before the Samuels-Colossus Corridor," Lyssa Wallis replied immediately. "We'll have to discharge in the Mowat System, whereas if we went through Serigala, we would be able to make a six-nova course directly to Samuels or Colossus."

That added a minimum of five days to the trip, which was an annoyance Kira really didn't need. But avoiding it wasn't worth a cruiser duel and killing several hundred people.

"Mrs. Macey, we'll get the amounts for the toll from the DSA shortly," she told her employer. "We pay up and we chart a nova to Deva. I'm not going to kill anybody to save a few days."

"Thank you, Admiral," Macey told her. There was a long pause, then the Samuels delegate switched to a private channel. "A question, if I may."

"Answers are mostly free, Mrs. Macey," Kira replied. "I'm going to be on the bridge until our Denzelite friends pull their fighters back aboard at least."

"Is this...what a blockade looks like?" the Samuels woman asked. "This is what Colossus will do around my system?"

"Normally, it would be spread at least two novas out in every direction," Kira said. "That gives people more time to be diverted—only the fact that this trade-route stop is within nova distance of two systems makes this not criminally irresponsible on the DSA's part.

"But yes." She sighed. "A six-light-year nova takes a few seconds to charge up, and you can project the destination."

That meant you either novaed under jamming or made sure there was no one around to see you if you were trying to jump without being followed.

"So, the DSA will put a nova fighter—or a bomber or a warship—near any ship they see in the trade-route stop," Kira continued. "Even an interceptor will wreck a freighter if they fire into them while they nova.

"We have a bit more shielding than a freighter, but they've asked for—and we'll give—enough information to counteract that." She shook her head. "This setup is a bit amateur—they don't quite know what they're doing yet—but the basic concept is correct."

Over the course of the war between Apollo and Brisingr, Kira had both broken and taken part in multiple blockades. She knew the drill.

"So, what happens if Colossus already has a blockade in place when we arrive?" Macey asked softly.

"The difference there, Mrs. Macey, is that I'm already contracted to break a blockade of the Samuels System," Kira said quietly. "Here, I needed to avoid a fight. If Colossus is blockading Samuels...the criteria are very different."

11

WORLDS habitable by humanity were common enough that marginal ones—planets that were too cold for too much of the year, whose soil lacked nutrients for Terran-derived crops, whose atmosphere required filtration masks, and similar issues—were often left alone but equally rare enough that almost all *non*-marginal worlds in "civilized space" were colonized.

Kira's Encyclopedia Galactica listed three thousand two hundred and eighty-six inhabited worlds inside the fifteen hundred light-year sphere around Earth that contained the Core, the Heart, the Meridian, the Periphery, the Fringe and the Rim.

With that many inhabited systems, it was rare to find a spot on the trade routes where it was necessary to stop and discharge static in an uninhabited system. That happened in regions where there was a lack of systems of any kind in the next area around the trade routes—like the outer portion of the Samuels-Colossus Corridor.

After bouncing off the blockade of Serigala, Kira's ships had headed in the wrong direction, to discharge static at the Deva System. That meant that they needed an extra discharge stop before they reached Samuels—and that stop was the Mowat System, "empty" as it was.

The Mowat System was positioned to cover most routes into the Corridor that weren't served by Serigala and a handful of other systems. It lacked the inhabited worlds of the other entry points into the Corridor from the Outer Rim, but it had a super-Jovian gas giant that would make discharging static slightly faster.

Kira was in Engineering as they completed the final nova, sitting with Konrad and watching the static flash up and down the visible capacitors used to give the engineer an idea of how close the ship was to trouble.

"Short hop this time," her lover said, shrugging as he glanced at the capacitors himself. "But we don't have the capacity to make it to Samuels."

"And that's why this system exists," Kira replied. "Run by crime lords?"

"A syndicate of local corporations," Konrad said drily, then chuckled. "Given that Mowat has been set up and operating for about two centuries, it's a safe assumption the crime lords have taken over."

The isolation away from traditional sources of oversight and law enforcement made uninhabited stopover systems like Mowat incredibly attractive and valuable for organized crime. Kira hadn't been to Mowat before—her trip out to Redward had gone through Colossus—but she'd seen similar systems.

One of her handful of combat experiences prior to the Apollo-Brisingr war, in fact, had been an Apollo-led multinational effort to take control of a discharge-station network in an uninhabited system away from an organized crime group that had grown too greedy and blatant.

That had been an unmitigated disaster, since there was nothing stopping an uninhabited system from having the same asteroid fortresses as an inhabited one. The ASDF had let their allies, the fleets of the not-entirely-voluntary Friends of Apollo, take the brunt of the losses in the abortive assault, and Kira suspected a direct line could be drawn between that battle and Brisingr's numeric edge in the later war.

Everything had consequences.

"So long as the crime lords are accepting the usual tolls and not giving anyone headaches, it won't impact us today," Kira told her boyfriend. "Anything with the ships I need to worry about?"

In theory, after all, she was in Engineering to talk work, not just hang out with Konrad. She doubted she was fooling anyone, though.

"*Deception* is as solid as ever," Konrad said. "*Huntress* is shaking out even better than I expected. I know that Larry put a great deal of pressure on the shipyards to make sure nothing went wrong with *our* ship, but I think they also avoided a lot of mistakes on a light-carrier design.

"The *Bastion*-class are probably as solid a seventy-kilocubic design as I've ever seen—and they only involved me to look for mistakes." He shook his head. "They were paying attention when we put together the *Barons*."

"Redward *had* designed ships before you came along, Konrad," Kira replied. "You didn't change *everything* for them."

He chuckled and grinned at her.

"I like to take credit where I can. To go with the blame."

The smile faded and she reached over to squeeze his hand. The original emergency construction program to put the *Baron*-class cruisers into commission had been Konrad's work—and it had been a true *emergency* program.

The workers who had died had known the risks, but it had been Konrad Bueller who'd put together the program.

"I'm told *Konrad* is a popular boys' name in Redward these days," she teased him.

Before he could reply, there was a ping on the command net, and both of their focuses fully snapped to work.

"Demirci," Kira replied crisply. "What's going on?"

"This is Smolak; I need the full command team," *Deception*'s coms officer told her. "Everyone needs to hear this."

"Davidović here," *Huntress*'s Captain linked in. "Linking in my senior officers. What's going on?"

"Mwangi here," *Deception*'s Captain said a moment later, but he'd clearly caught enough to wait.

"Okay, got everyone," Smolak noted. "I need to play a recording for you all."

There was a pause, then Smolak's voice resumed—but a notation in Kira's headware told her that it was now from a recording.

"Anoteelik Central Control, this is Commander Smolak aboard Memorial Force cruiser *Deception*," the recording said. "Requesting orbital slots for discharge for three ships, en route into the Corridor."

"Understood, Memorial Force," an unknown man replied. "Do you need access to resupply or other amenities?"

"Negative, MCC," Smolak said. "We are discharging from a short hop due to the blockade at Serigala before heading into the Corridor."

"Understood," the stranger said. "Transmitting coordinates now."

The connection didn't drop the way Kira would have expected, and the MCC official's tone changed.

"Be advised, Commander Smolak, that Anoteelik has received notification from the Colossus Nova Wing that they have imposed a formal blockade of the Samuels System. We have been asked to inform all ships entering the Corridor that access to the Samuels System is currently not available.

"The CNW is instructing all ships to proceed to Colossus for discharge and warns that attempts to reach Samuels will be blocked on the trade route. Vessels attempting to breach the blockade will be detained or destroyed.

"Anoteelik Central Control cannot recommend travel to Samuels at this time, and we advise that CNW's warning meets all standard regional insurance criteria."

That meant that most ship crews would find their insurers saying

"You knew the risks" if the blockade seized or destroyed their vessel. Colossus, unlike Denzel, apparently knew the steps required to make their blockade look good on paper. The Colossus Nova Wing—the nova-capable branch of the Colossus System's military—had been around long enough to have learned the dance, even if this was their first time actually performing it.

"It seems our new friends moved faster than anyone expected," Mwangi said quietly. "Admiral?"

"It doesn't change anything for us," Kira noted. "Our contract says we break the blockade if it's in place, and that we're paid combat and risk bonuses for doing so.

"We need intel, though," she continued. "Sounds like we might need some of those amenities we just told MCC we don't want, but I'll touch base with Mrs. Macey. I can hope that Samuels has some intelligence assets in place here, right?"

"That begs an interesting question, doesn't it?" Mwangi muttered. "Does the planet run by pacifists have *great* spies...or *no* spies?"

"THERE IS a trade attaché station on the main orbital platform," Macey told Kira when they spoke a few minutes later. "Em Sandal is supposed to keep his ear to the ground and send reports home."

"I hope that entails a bit more than just listening in bars," Kira replied. "Because I'm planning on having a few of my people do that, but it can only give us so much."

"If anything else, any communication from Samuels will be sitting with Em Sandal," Macey replied, the delegate looking nervous. "We weren't expecting them to move this quickly. I don't know how much information will have made it out."

"You left almost three months ago, Mrs. Macey," Kira pointed out. "Em Sandal's reports will be only a week out of date. You've been receiving mail all along, haven't you?"

"Not the last two stops, but…I put that up to missed connections," Macey admitted. "How bad is this, Admiral?"

"Most likely, Colossus focused their efforts on getting one of the light carriers online," Kira told her employer. "But there are diminishing returns with that kind of effort. They may have a handful of ships right now, but it likely means it will be longer until they have the full flotilla in play.

"Given that I'm confident in our ability to handle the full flotilla split up to maintain a blockade, I'm *quite* certain we can handle whatever portion of it they've brought online. This may well work in our favor, Mrs. Macey.

"They've initiated the blockade, which is bad, but it makes the positions and situation clear, and it could easily have cost them a level of immediate superiority that was their only real chance." Kira shrugged.

"I need more data," she admitted. "But this looks like they've played into our hands. We'll discharge static and we'll move on to Samuels. When we find this blockade, we'll neutralize it.

"That was the contract, Mrs. Macey. I said we'd protect Samuels, and nothing in the current situation suggests to me that we won't be able to."

12

THE ORBITAL CONSTRUCTS above the super-Jovian gas giant Anoteelik were of a familiar style to Kira. The Mowat System wasn't up to the level of local industry necessary to build significantly sized space stations for themselves, so the stations came in two varieties: prefabricated facilities assembled from components that would fit in standard cargo containers and midsized nova freighters; and asteroids from the local belts and trojan clusters that had been moved into orbit and hollowed out.

Wolf Station was the largest of the facilities and was a mix of both types. Massive assemblages of prefabricated structures emerged from the surface of a kilometer-long asteroid towed into low orbit of the gas giant.

It was close enough to Anoteelik that ships orbiting near Wolf could actively discharge static into the gas giant, while high enough that its orbital velocity was manageable for ships matching course with it.

And in case anybody thought that the Mowat System was going to be a pushover, Uncle Albert was in the same orbit and just fifty thousand kilometers "ahead" of the commercial station. The Uncle was slightly smaller, only nine hundred meters long, and lacked Wolf's prefabricated surface segments.

What surface segments Uncle Albert *had*, though, were very clear in their purpose. Immense plasma-cannon turrets, quadruple arrays of guns that had four times the throughput of *Deception*'s weapons, dotted the asteroid's surface. The weapons were old enough that they were ten times the *size* of Kira's cruiser's guns to pack in that firepower, but *Deception* was less than two hundred meters long.

Uncle Albert had a *lot* more guns than the heavy cruiser, plus hangars for both nova fighters and their slower sub-fighter kin. Small compared to the forts that guarded even Redward, it was still a near-insurmountable monster compared to any nova fleet of the Rim.

From her shuttle making its way over to Wolf Station, Kira could easily see why the Mowat System's corporate government could afford the four battle stations that orbited the gas giant. She could count a dozen starships around Wolf Station alone, and at least three times that in even lower orbits as they discharged static.

There were as many nova ships discharging in orbit of Anoteelik as would be present in Redward on most days. The closer to Sol Kira came, the greater the breadth and depth of human civilization and the interstellar economy became.

Even this was in the Rim, and she intellectually knew that a similar system in the Core would have literally *thousands* of ships discharging around a gas giant. But Kira had never even entered the Fringe, the systems between seven hundred and a thousand light-years away from Sol. Apollo was twelve hundred and twenty light-years from the human home system.

Redward was fourteen hundred and eighty, nearly at the invisible line where the trade-route mapping coalition stopped being able to maintain updates.

The closest Kira had ever come to Earth was roughly eleven

hundred light-years, a long-range operation during the war. The last time she'd even been *this* close was when she'd been fleeing her home system.

And on that depressing thought, her shuttle reached Wolf Station, and she inhaled a deep breath. It was time to see what she could find out from a source she hadn't touched since leaving home: an office of the Apollon government.

WOLF STATION WAS INTENTIONALLY ECLECTIC. Kira could think of no other reason why the station was full of so many different clashing esthetics. If they'd been the kind of cheap faux replicas she'd seen elsewhere, she'd have written it off as the place just being gaudy.

But they weren't. The reconstructionist Hellenist décor of the Apollon Trade Attaché had been done extraordinarily well, with the columns carefully matched to each other and the façade behind them. The twenty-third-century Centauri-style faux-cyberpunk decoration of the high-end restaurant next door was equally well done...and clashed ridiculously with the attaché's office.

"Never seen you hesitate at anything," Milani muttered at her ear, and Kira realized she was woolgathering.

"Are you looking at the same décor I am?" Kira asked, pushing away the ground commander's quite accurate assessment of her feelings on entering an Apollon office. She wasn't *entirely* sure why Milani had decided they should accompany her instead of Jess Koch, but that was the commander's prerogative.

"Yeah. I was expecting a sheet of permafrost, to be fair," Milani told her. "I'm not sure this fits."

"Fits *what*, exactly?" she asked.

Milani laughed, the dragon on their armor joining in their amusement and visibly giggling at Kira.

"The books?" they asked. "Everything in this system is named for an Old Earth activist author, but the *station* is named for *Never Cry Wolf*. Which was" —they waved around—"about wolves in the Arctic, so not exactly this!"

Kira snorted.

"We prefer not to have ice on a space station," she pointed out. Liquid water was denser and easier to store than its solid form. "And yes, I'm hesitating to walk into an Apollon government office and lean on my retirement rank for information. It's been five years since I turned in my papers."

And her government had let Brisingr send assassins after her *on Apollo*. She was wearing her blaster-proof armored leather jacket over her uniform shipsuit, *and* an armored vest under the jacket, but she was still nervous.

Even the Mowat System was far enough from both Apollo and Brisingr that she was well beyond any active attack at this point, but she was finally back in the diplomatic radius of her homeworld.

A strange feeling.

"The Samuels woman will probably get as much intel as we will," Milani pointed out. "We can skip your countryfolk if you want."

"Enabling my fears is not your job, Milani," Kira replied. "And Macey *does* have a name."

Milani sniffed.

"And when I'm talking to her, I'll use it," they said. "The rest of the time, I'm going to remember that the Samuels woman thinks everyone should marry off and pop out babies."

"Culture clash happens, Milani," Kira pointed out. "At least she wasn't asking what was in your armor."

Even *Kira* didn't know if Milani had the equipment to actually "pop out babies," and, given the mercenary's complete lack of a romantic life that she knew about, Kira suspected only *Deception*'s doctor *did*.

The armored mercenary growled.

"Was tempted to tell her I'd had all of that crap burned off or out or whatever," Milani finally said. "But...as you say, culture clash. Surprised *you* haven't got an earful on that."

"I'm surprised she spent enough time with you *to* give you an earful," Kira admitted. "And I suppose I'm at least paired off, even if we aren't married by whatever rules she's using."

She paused thoughtfully, studying the Apollon office and considering what she knew of the Quakers like Samuels.

"Actually, it's possible I *am* married by whatever rules she's using," she realized aloud. "*Culture clash.*"

That epithet covered a *lot* of problems, in Kira's opinion. It was, at least, not a problem she was going to have in an Apollon government office.

"Let's go," she told her bodyguard. "Suddenly, talking to a fellow shepherd's kid is sounding much more comfortable."

THE INTERIOR of the attaché office was built in the same style as the exterior, the extravagant neo-Hellenist style favored by Apollo for public works. It was a surprise to find something in that style there, at the very edge of Apollo's reach, but from the quality of the disparate elements of Wolf Station's interior, Kira suspected it had been partially paid for by the station's owners.

"Good afternoon," the artificial stupid hologram receptionist told her. "Welcome to the Mowat System Trade Attaché for the Republic of Apollo, Em Demirci. We have confirmed your citizenship and look forward to assisting you.

"What do you need today?"

Kira had updated her personal headware beacon to run the Apollo standard information before they'd come in, allowing the artificial stupids running initial contact to know who she was.

In another country's offices, she probably would have been greeted by her former military rank as a courtesy—or potentially even by her current mercenary rank, depending on how well informed they were—but Apollo, as always, engaged in the appearance of pacifism.

"I need to speak with the attaché or one of their senior analysts," Kira told the hologram. "I'm leaving in under a day, so I don't have time to make an appointment."

"Of course," the digital image of the decorative young man replied. "Em Argyris is a busy individual, of course. We will see if—"

"I can make time for Major Demirci," a voice cut through the AS's patter. Kira looked up to see a massive man with graying hair and thickly muscled upper arms standing in the door to the inner office.

The AS shut up instantly as the Apollon man bowed his head slightly to Kira.

"I am Angelos Argyris," he introduced himself. "Trade attaché to the Mowat System. I'm also my own senior analyst—my staff is quite limited and, frankly, this posting is boring as sheep shit.

"Can I get you a retsina?"

Kira blinked. She hadn't even *thought* about the fact that she was close enough to Apollo to get her homeworld's traditional resin-infused wine.

"I would be delighted, Em Argyris," she told him. "May my body-guard accompany us?"

Argyris eyed Milani up and down and shrugged his massive shoulders.

"I'm guessing you don't want retsina, Em..."

"Milani," the merc introduced themselves. "And no. I don't drink on duty."

"Of course. Come in, both of you."

Argyris led the way through the door into a gorgeously decorated but tiny rear office. They walked through a small kitchen and dining area into a conference room, but Kira only counted five office doors.

The attaché wasn't lying about having limited staff. She wasn't sure if he was going to have what she needed—but, on the other hand, she hadn't had retsina since she'd put her last bottle up as a prize in a training exercise for her pilots several years earlier.

And the big man might surprise her.

KIRA DIDN'T RECOGNIZE the brand of the bottle Argyris produced to fill two wine glasses with, but the smell was unquestionable. She'd found one tiny winery on Redward that made a kind of retsina, but something in even Terran pines adapted to the Syntactic Cluster world made the resin taste wrong.

She suspected that part of what made Apollon retsina work so well was that exact effect, in truth. Something in how the imported pines had adapted to her homeworld had changed their resin in a way that impacted how it interacted with alcohol.

The first sip confirmed that it was definitely the right stuff, and she just took a second to delight in the taste of home.

"What is it, Demirci?" Argyris asked as she closed her eyes in warmth. "Four years since you left home? Five?"

"Almost five," she told him. "I'm surprised even that much information is on your mind."

He laughed.

"The most famous mercenary Admiral of the Outer Rim is an Apollon native," he pointed out. "Believe me, Admiral Demirci, most of the outward diplomats and attachés know who you are. Plus, I had a cousin who survived one of the last battles of the war because the Three Oh Three showed up at the right moment."

"Credit for that probably belongs as much to *Victorious* and Commodore Heller as anything else," Kira said. "The Hellions pulled a lot of people's irons out of the fire at the end."

And Heller had died for it—or so Kira suspected, anyway, given the fate of so much of the 303 Nova Combat Group. Officially, it had been an aircar accident.

"Perhaps, but it was Three Oh Three interceptors that took out the bomber strike heading at *Sun Arrow*," Argyris reminded her.

"Ah. *That* battle," Kira murmured. *Sun Arrow* had been the ASDF's most modern and powerful battlecruiser. Ambushed by two Brisingr fleet carrier groups in the final days of the war—*after* the Agreement on Nova Lane Security that had ended the war had been signed, in fact—she'd lost the carrier she'd been escorting and most of her escorts before Task Group *Victorious* had arrived.

They'd crushed two BKN fleet carrier groups but lost the entirety of Task Group *Salutations* except for *Sun Arrow*. A tactical victory but a strategic draw at best—and Apollo had already basically surrendered.

"I figured you'd remember it," Argyris told her. "Now, I'm not one to claim debts that don't really exist, but I'll confess to warm, fuzzy feelings over the fact that I still have a cousin.

"I'm guessing that you're looking for information on the Samuels-Colossus mess?"

"Got it in one," Kira conceded. "Samuels hired Memorial Force to provide security after Brisingr provided a fleet to Colossus. From the messages Anoteelik Control is passing out, Colossus already made their move?"

"Yeah," Argyris confirmed. "I got the update from Intelligence about Brisingr selling them the demilitarized ships around the same time we got the notice of the blockade. Somebody dropped the ball on putting that information in my hands.

"A lot of Apollon merchants got squeezed by that," he continued. "I'm *supposed* to be able to warn our people in advance of crap like this, but without knowing that Colossus suddenly had an actual nova fleet..."

He growled, a low rumble deep in his chest.

"I'm a damn good analyst, Admiral Demirci, but I need the data to do the analysis," he told her. "We have assets in both Colossus and Samuels, but I get their reports the long way around: via Apollo.

"So, if someone drops a ball back home, I don't get the info to help our merchants. The only reason I'm even *out here* is to help our merchants."

"Is the detour from Samuels to Colossus that big a deal?" Kira asked. "My understanding, even from my employers in Samuels, is that Colossus is the faster trip through the Corridor."

"So Samuels is cheaper," Argyris told her. "And Colossus has been ratcheting their toll up of late as well. Now we know why.

"Samuels is, in general, simply the better stopover," he continued. "Their toll was down to *half* of Colossus's as of the last numbers I saw. The fuel they provide is cleaner and cheaper as well—their gas giants are better proportioned, so the hydrogen and helium they extract requires less refining.

"They have better amenities, down to the level of having better food, cleaner hotels and, I'm told, prettier boys and girls." He finished with a chuckle at the last. "So, unless the cargo was time-critical, over the last ten years, the balance of shipping has been swinging further and further toward Samuels."

"And Colossus just kept raising rates and preparing for war," Kira concluded.

"Exactly." Argyris shook his head. "I'll be honest. This blockade is an inconvenience to our people, not a deal-breaker, but a few smaller shippers got hurt pretty badly who could have dodged it if I'd been able to give them a few weeks' heads-up."

"But Apollo isn't going to complain if I kick Colossus's Brisingr-provided fleet back to the dust heap of history," she said.

Both Argyris and Milani chuckled at the description, and the attaché saluted her with his retsina glass.

"I can't put up any money to help cover your costs," he warned her. "But yes, we would be quite pleased to see Colossus brought back down to the level. The competition between the two systems keeps the Corridor open, and the Corridor is damn handy for Apollo."

"What *can* you give me?" she asked.

"Data," Argyris said instantly. "Officially, my Intelligence reports are classified top secret—but I checked. You haven't done anything sufficiently egregious since retiring to have your clearances revoked.

"Technically, I shouldn't hand over reports to you without you, say, having a contract with Apollo...but you're still cleared."

Kira's headware chimed with an incoming report.

"I imagine Samuels got you as much information on the makeup of their flotilla as I have," he admitted.

"They gave me a pretty detailed list," she agreed. "Though I wasn't expecting any of it to be in action just yet."

"Ah. *That* is a question I can answer—and it's in the report, as well," Argyris told her. "*N45-K* was listed as part of the Secondary Service Reserve until six months ago. She was leased as private security to the Syndulla System."

Kira nodded grimly. That confirmed at least one of her suspicions —*Deception*, as *K79-L*, had been "leased" to an exploratory corporation out of the Syndulla System that had actually been an Equilibrium Institute front.

If *N45-K* had been in the Syndulla System, she was almost certainly also an Equilibrium asset.

"I'm guessing she was never fully demilitarized?" Kira asked.

"The timeline that I have between the arrival of the flotilla of 'decommissioned' ships and the deployment of enough vessels to begin the blockade aligns with a basic refit and test flight," Argyris noted. "That would suggest that *N45-K* arrived in Colossus fully functional, if outdated by Brisingr standards.

"They gave her a quick dusting and ran her through some trials before loading their fighters aboard and sending her out to blockade Samuels," he concluded. "*N45-H*, however, was definitely fully demilitarized and basically sold as a scrap hull. Assuming they began a refit the moment she entered their hands, I'd guess she's at least two months from deployable."

"That does help," Kira agreed. "We'll review the intelligence you provide, Em Argyris. It's appreciated."

"Like I said, it's in Apollo's interest to keep Samuels and Colossus in competition with each other," the diplomat told her. "But that means not having one of them blockaded!

"So, while I cannot afford any official approval or support, I can certainly provide some information under the table."

He raised his glass in salute.

"Good luck, Admiral."

13

Back aboard *Deception*, Kira linked into a virtual conference with her senior officers and Macey. She hadn't even had time to steal a kiss from Konrad, but the timer before they got underway was ticking down.

"Apollo Intelligence was late on the ball for this," she told them all. "The trade attaché figured our mission is in Apollo's interest, so he gave me their report.

"Numbers and types of ships match up with Samuels's intel, but at least one carrier was in the Secondary Service Reserve in the Syndulla System." She glanced at Macey and didn't elaborate further. From their expressions, her officers understood completely.

Konrad Bueller especially looked...frustrated. She was going to have to pin her boyfriend down for more than personal reasons after the meeting.

"The Apollo staff here figures that Colossus did a quick refit on an SSR ship that hadn't been demilitarized at *all*, then loaded her up with their fighters and sent her out," she concluded. "Mrs. Macey, what did you dig up?"

"I don't have any useful background," the Samuels delegate said quietly. "So, you know more about where these ships came from than I do. I did have a conversation with our people here who've been trying to sort out a way around the blockade."

Macey paused and looked down, making an unnecessary attempt to straighten her dress.

"The Mowat System is perhaps not the best place for my people to look for help," she conceded, "but there has been a surprising lack of support or even empathy for our situation. Even shipping lines that have used Samuels exclusively for decades appear to simply be shrugging and replotting their courses to go through Colossus."

"It's not a freighter captain's or a shipping line's business to breach a blockade," Kira reminded her. "They have to do business, one way or another, and so long as there is *a* way through the Corridor, they can do that.

"They may personally regret what's happening with Samuels, but very few people get involved in other star systems' politics. And of those who do, it's rarely a *good* thing for the star systems in question."

"Perhaps," Macey said. "I feel we're lacking even any *personal* regret. The people our staff here have dealt with don't seem to care at all, barring some minor complaints about the change in cost. We know some of what is out there now, but that's mostly thanks to our own ships that have turned back after being forced to discharge at Colossus."

"I'm surprised Colossus is letting your ships go," Mwangi said. "A blockade implies a state of war. No one is going to blink if they started interning all of your ships that had to discharge there."

"They may well be now," Davidović pointed out. "Any ship that Mrs. Macey's people have made contact with left Colossus at least six days ago."

"What *do* we know?" Kira asked Macey gently. "The more information we have, the easier it will be for us to break the blockade."

"You will break it, then?" Macey asked.

"That was our contract, Mrs. Macey," Kira reminded the other woman. Again. Sometimes, it was very obvious that the Samuels diplomat had never played this game before. "There are specifics in the contract for what Memorial Force gets *paid* for doing so. I wouldn't have added those if I hadn't planned on breaking whatever blockade Colossus put in place."

She shrugged.

"In truth, I figured the likelihood that Colossus was moving sooner than you expected was at least fifty-fifty," she told Macey. "It wasn't in their interests for you to have months of warning. We were prepared for this."

"I hate to accept that this must come to violence," Macey said. "But...thank you."

She made another pointless attempt to arrange her dress, then straightened.

"The information we have on the blockading force is limited," she told them. "But we have confirmed the presence of at least one carrier, multiple squadrons of Liberator MFNCs, and at least two active destroyers. Our analyst here said... Delta-Nine-Charlies?"

"D-Nine-C heavy destroyers," Kira filled in. "They were on the list, and I'm familiar with them."

A handful of Brisingr-built D9C heavy destroyers had played a role in one attempt by the Equilibrium Institute to reshape the Syntactic Cluster.

"We don't have a lot of extra maneuvering room as far as nova jump on the starships goes," she continued. "But we'll be arriving through one of the most heavily trafficked stops coming in from the Outer Rim. If they haven't secured that stop, they haven't blockaded Samuels."

A mental command linked a map to the rest of the conference.

"Here and here," she told them, highlighting two trade-route stops. "We take one extra jump before we head to Samuels, and we should clear two major entry points to the system. Once we've discharged static at Samuels, we sweep back out and hit the other parts of the blockade."

Four more trade-route stops flashed on the screen.

"We don't know how many ships are in play yet," she reminded everyone. "We can *guess* that it's only one N-Forty-Five and the four D-Nine-Cs. A carrier and four destroyers are sufficient for an effectively unopposed blockade of a star system if they're bold enough."

She glanced at Macey's image and smiled at the concerned expression the older woman was trying to conceal. Macey was *good*, but Kira hadn't expected the pacifist to be comfortable with going into the middle of a fight.

"*Springtime Chorus* will *not* accompany us into the battlespace," she said drily. "Once we reach the blockade zone, *Chorus* will wait twelve hours before following us into nova. She will then nova directly to Samuels before we move on to the second trade-route stop.

"Your people and your ship can't contribute to the fight, Mrs. Macey, and you're paying us to protect you. I see no reason to risk a consular ship in the middle of a firefight."

"I...appreciate that, Admiral," Macey said calmly. "Of course, once *Huntress* and *Deception* have engaged the Colossus Nova Wing, I will authorize payment of the combat portions of your contract."

She paused.

"Is there any chance of resolving this without violence, Admiral?" she asked softly. "I understand the advantage of surprise in this situation, but if we can avoid unnecessary bloodshed..."

"There's a protocol," Mwangi pointed out. *Deception*'s Captain had served aboard *Conviction* under John Estanza before Kira had ever joined them. He'd been a mercenary for longer than any of the other senior officers with them.

"They'll challenge us to honor the blockade; we'll inform them of our contract and give them a chance to lift the blockade of their own accord," he continued. "It's...effectively a declaration of war on the part of Memorial Force, as opposed to Samuels."

"Were Samuels engaging in active operations on their own and we were supporting, the rules would be different," Kira told Macey.

Inasmuch as any of the "protocols" Mwangi mentioned *were* rules. More like...a recommended voluntary code of conduct.

"But we will give them a chance to back down before we bring up jammers," she continued. "After that... Well, it's damn hard to talk when every wavelength used for communication has been turned into hashed garbage."

"I have faith that you will do the best you can," Macey finally said. "I understand the realities of the situation, Admiral Demirci, Captains, Commanders. I just...do not like them."

That was fair. Kira was *very* good at her job—but that didn't mean she liked killing people.

At all.

"SO?" Kira asked from the bed as Konrad came out of the bathroom, teeth freshly brushed.

"So?" he echoed back.

"You had a *look* when we were talking about where the active N-Forty-Five came from," she told him. "She's *N45-K*, if that helps with the feeling like you just ate a lemon."

Her lover sighed and shrugged, which did fascinating things to his broad-shouldered physique when he was shirtless.

"It confirms the lemon, at least," he told her. He leaned against the bulkhead and eyed her. "I don't know if it's relevant citrus, though. It's old."

"And we've officially killed that metaphor," Kira told him. She was still wearing her shipsuit, but she was still enjoying the way Konrad's gaze clung to her body. That said...

"But you do think it's relevant, don't you?" she murmured.

"*N45-K* was in Syndulla when we were," Konrad admitted. "That was back when *Deception* was *K79-L* and in the SSR herself. Working for Ghost Explorations... Equilibrium."

It wasn't something either of them talked about much, but

Konrad Bueller had been a knowing Equilibrium agent before they'd met. He'd actively defected after a sickening synergy between the Equilibrium standard of "no witnesses" and the Brisingr standard of "test before battle" resulted in the massacre of thousands of innocents.

"They were with Ghost?" Kira asked. If *N45-K* was actively an Equilibrium asset, this whole contract was closer to home than she'd feared.

"No, *N45-K* was being leased to the Syndulla government," he told her. "I didn't think of it earlier because they were also leasing a newer N-Sixty-class carrier and a destroyer flotilla, and frankly, I assumed the N-Forty-Five had been scrapped by now."

"But if they're using the SSR ships from Syndulla, that explains a lot," Kira murmured. "And gives us more data, if they're using ships of the same vintage."

"I'm not sure any of that is *useful*, though," he admitted. "They had eight D-Nine-Cs on the same lease, two I-Fifties, and another K-Seventy like *Deception*. Plus their own home-built nova ships."

Kira whistled silently, and not at Konrad's physique.

"I thought Brisingr's tributaries were limited to half a million cubic meters of nova ships?" she asked. That was what Brisingr had imposed on the former Friends of Apollo as part of the surrender agreement.

"SSR leases don't count," he said. "The BKN and the Kaiser keep a tight leash on those ships. We both know that those leases entail them acting as deniable assets for Brisingr or Equilibrium as often as assets for their supposed operating navies."

Like *K79-L*. The ship that was now *Deception* had been brought out to the Syntactic Cluster with a mixed BKN/Equilibrium crew. Not a soul aboard had actually been in the service of the Syndulla System, though most had been employees of the Ghost Exploration front on paper.

"So, most likely, all four of Colossus's new D-Nine-Cs came from Syndulla," Kira concluded. "Or, at least, we won't be underestimating them if we assume that. And they might have grabbed the I-Fifty as well, though no one was reporting her at Samuels."

"They'll have split their forces pretty evenly if they sent all of that forward to lay the initial blockade," Konrad said. "I'm not the tactics guy, so you'll know better than I if that's the right call."

"It depends on your threat environment," Kira replied. "Most likely, they have sent the I-Fifty and she's just on the other side—I'd split my heavies between Inner and Outer Rim routes in their place."

"And we change the threat environment, do we?" he asked.

"We do," she confirmed, grinning at him.

"I'm sorry, Kira," he said softly. "I really didn't think it was relevant until you mentioned Syndulla...and even then, I still think the data is badly out of date."

"It is and it might still be useful," she told him. "It's all good, my love. Even tells me something entirely new."

"And what's that?" he asked.

"That Syndulla is entirely in Equilibrium's pocket, even more than we thought," Kira murmured. "But also that Syndulla is the *only* real asset they have to play with out here, with resources flowing through Brisingr.

"After almost half a decade of feeling like they've got their fingers in every pot and pie around here, it's reassuring to see them going back to the same well—even if they're doing so to mess with someone else."

"Hadn't thought of it that way," Konrad admitted.

"That's because you're not the tactics guy," she echoed back to him. "You're the engineer and the reason we even have a home base."

Still grinning at him, she ran her finger down the seam of her shipsuit and let it fall open to the waist.

"We nova shortly, but I believe we still have *quite* some time before we actually get into trouble, don't you?" she purred.

14

"All squadrons have reported in and are ready for combat operations," Colombera reported. "Any problems on the ship side, Captain Davidović?"

"None," *Huntress*'s CO said brightly. "I want Queen Sonia to loom threateningly over *all* of my construction crews in future. This ship is still purring like a kitten."

Kira grinned at that image. While Sonia cultivated the image of a gorgeous socialite, one focused on networks, economics and getting the right people in the right rooms, there was very much another side to her. One that could use every scrap of the woman's near two meters of height to *loom* very effectively indeed.

"I suspect she's leaning over our next carrier's build team in much the same manner," she noted. "Mwangi, Nightmare? Status on *Deception*?"

"Guns are charged and clear, deck is clear, all systems are green," Mwangi said instantly. "Bueller would *hurt* me if this ship wasn't perfect."

"Scimitar has all of the planes," Cartman complained. "Why are we even worrying about *my* little wing?"

"Because twenty nova fighters of ninety-two is actually pretty damn relevant," Kira told her old friend. "And we all know that if *you* shout jump, Abdullah will be three feet in the air before asking 'Which way?'"

"I take offense to that," Colombera said. "I am a *much* better jumper than you give me credit for. I'd be *least* five feet in the air."

"Be that as it may, Nova Group *Deception* is fully operational and ready for combat operations," Cartman said with admirable equanimity, though it sounded like she'd barely swallowed her laughter to manage it.

"*Springtime Chorus*, you have our course?" Kira asked Captain Hennessy.

The blond-haired and blue-eyed enby commander of Macey's consular packet arched a perfectly groomed eyebrow at Kira.

"We have your course," they murmured. "We will follow in twelve hours, barring an emergency alert from one of your fighters."

"Everything looks safe here," Kira told them.

That wasn't entirely a good thing. The trade-route stop they currently occupied was safe because it was *empty*. And that meant that there was no traffic heading toward Samuels. Their next stop was the last place where a ship could safely divert to Colossus from a Samuels-bound course—but anyone who, say, adjusted their course after receiving the warning in Mowat would take a different route entirely.

"Good luck, Admiral Demirci," Hennessy told her. "My principal can't bring herself to wish you the same, unfortunately, but she hopes for the best conclusion possible.

"I understand where Mrs. Macey is coming from, Captain. Her best wishes and yours are appreciated—but if things go according to plan, *luck* won't be a factor today."

They gave her a crisp nod and dropped the connection.

Kira turned her attention back to her four senior officers.

"Last chance, people. Anything going to explode that isn't supposed to?" she asked.

Silent headshakes answered her, and she smiled.

It still felt awkward to be going into battle from a flag deck instead of a nova-fighter cockpit, but that was her life now.

"Memorial Force...nova."

"CONTACTS IDENTIFIED," Soler snapped moments after they arrived. "I have five freighters on the scopes, clustered together *here*."

The navigational slash tactical display was shared between the two bridges and Kira's flag deck. Soler's marker lit up around a location two light-minutes away. Five freighters together like that suggested the Colossus Nova Wing was corralling captured ships there for easy management.

"Unclear what's in place to defend them," the Tactical officer continued. "I would expect to see nova fighters or gunships, but I have nothing showing up around the freighter cluster.

"I *do* have nova-fighter squadrons—*here* and *here*. Initial data suggests eight to twelve fighters each. Probably Liberators, but our resolution isn't that solid yet."

Two new markers appeared. One was just as far away as the freighters but on a different vector. One was in the opposite direction but only a single light-minute away.

"I have one destroyer at three light-minutes, past the freighter corral, and another at ninety light-seconds past the closer fighter squadron. No further active contacts."

Kira processed silently as the data appeared on the screen. They still had almost forty seconds before the first fighter squadron even realized that Memorial Force was there. Her *warships* couldn't nova for twenty hours—but that was why she'd brought the nova fighters that were spilling out of both ships in a tide of green dots on the display.

"Form by squadrons," she heard Colombera bark on the fighter tactical network.

The Colossus forces had spread out to provide coverage against freighters breaking through the blockade—while keeping enough of a concentration to deal with any nova-fighter strikes out of Samuels.

Lacking real carriers, Samuels's military couldn't do what Kira could. The CNW was divided and vulnerable, and her instincts said to take advantage of it. The lightspeed delay would let her fighters swarm half the destroyers and fighters before anyone even knew her people were there.

"Plot your jumps, Nightmare, Scimitar," she ordered. "But stand by. They're badly outgunned, and we promised we'd try to end this without violence."

A silent message to Smolak brought up Kira's recording software, and she focused on the pickup with a sad chilly smile.

"Colossus forces, I am Admiral Kira Demirci of the Memorial Force mercenary fleet. We have been contracted to break the blockade of the Samuels System. You have one chance to withdraw. If you do not nova homeward within five minutes of the receipt of this message—eight minutes from transmission for the farthest of you—I will take that as a sign of determined hostilities with my employer and act to reduce your forces.

"Demirci, out."

She sent the message and leaned back in her chair, a timer automatically starting in the corner of her vision.

"When do we jump, boss?" Cartman asked.

"Mwangi, Davidović, set course for the freighter corral," Kira ordered, half in response to her old friend. "I expect them to converge on the depot ship holding those ships prisoner."

"Depot ship, sir?" Mwangi asked, then nodded as he caught up.

"There's no carrier here," Kira explained to the others. "So, one of those freighters is both armed and has docking ports to resupply fighters. She's not even a junk carrier, but she can extend the operating time of a fighter wing indefinitely.

"They'll converge on her, because the freighters are the most valuable thing in the area, and then decide if they're going to make a fight for it as a group."

She shook her head.

"Which they will," she warned her people. "Scimitar, Nightmare —I want a plan for punching both those destroyers out with a single bomber pass. I don't want to lose anyone today, not when we have this much of an edge!"

"On it," the two Commanders, Nova Group, replied in sync.

That was the worst part of being one of the galaxy's *ethical* mercenaries. There wasn't truly a standard code of conduct, but there was enough of one, and it aligned well enough with Kira's own morals to set a standard for Memorial Force.

She turned down jobs she didn't think were moral, she didn't open fire without warning unless she was involved in a clear and active war, and she followed the regular rules of war to the letter *and* the spirit.

And sometimes that meant she gave up one hell of a tactical advantage, she reflected as she took in the light of the closest nova-fighter squadron reacting to her arrival. They blipped out instantly, following the age-old adage of nova-fighter pilots:

If you're in trouble...be somewhere else.

"Nova-fighter wings and the closer destroyer have converged on the freighter corral," Soler reported. "As expected. Sixty seconds before we'll see the second destroyer arrive, if that's her call."

"I hope your fingers are on the jammer buttons, people," Kira said. "These guys haven't said anything yet, but they didn't come out here to back down."

"Incoming transmission," Smolak reported.

"Play it for everyone," Kira ordered.

A shaven-headed woman of about Kira's own age appeared on the screen. Tattooed whorls of silver Celtic knots wrapped up around the sides of her face and over where her hair should be, and her irises were a matching silver.

"I am Senior Captain Nadia Hopson of the Colossus Nova

Wing," the silver-eyed woman declared. "I must inform you that the Samuels System and surrounding trade-route stops are under a formal blockade due to a contract dispute between Samuels and Colossus. Any attempt to breach the blockade will be met with all necessary force.

"I will give you this one opportunity to accept that your contract is pointless and stand aside, Admiral Demirci. Our conflict with Samuels is longstanding and deep-rooted, and an outsider such as yourself has no idea of the crimes that have been committed.

"If you do not withdraw your nova fighters aboard your vessels, I will assume you are hostile and treat you as active combatants of the Samuels System. Choose carefully before you involve yourself in a war you know nothing about."

The recording ended and Kira chuckled.

"Presumptive of her to think we haven't done our research, isn't it?" she said aloud. "But it's the only card she has to play."

There was still almost three minutes left on her timer.

"Second destroyer has arrived at the corral," Soler reported. "As of a minute ago, the nova fighters were forming up. Likely preparing for a nova strike. Their jammers are still... Never mind. Multiphasic jammers are live; we have lost our sensor lock."

A two-light-second-wide sphere of chaos suddenly appeared on Kira's display. While it was reasonably certain that the CNW ships were at the center of the sphere, it wasn't *that* perfect a radius from the transmitter. Hitting the Colossus ships at any range was now impossible.

"Understood," Kira said. "Scimitar, Nightmare?"

"Admiral."

"Jammers up. Nova and attack."

15

DECEPTION's and *Huntress*'s multiphasic jammers went up the same moment that the nova fighters' did. The two capital ships were at least moving sufficiently in sync to remain in contact with each other via direct laser link, though. They lost some bandwidth but coms remained stable.

The nova fighters maneuvered too quickly and too randomly even at sublight for that to work for them for long—and they vanished into nova seconds after the jammers went live, anyway.

Which left Kira waiting for news of what was going on a full light-minute away as her two starships hurtled toward a battle that would, hopefully, be over before they could join it.

"Anti-fighter systems are online," Soler reported, her voice soft. "Link with the CSP is...intermittent but active."

While it had never been *explicitly* mentioned in the orders Kira had given, everyone had known they weren't sending the entire nova-fighter fleet at the enemy. Two squadrons of Wolverines and two squadrons of Hussar-Sevens—all from *Huntress*—had remained behind to form a twenty-four-fighter combat space patrol.

Those fighters were moving around the two capital ships rapidly and randomly, taking full advantage of their superior maneuverability to throw off any sight lines anyone would get. It would also make them harder to hit if—

"Contact!" Soler snapped. "Multiple contacts. We're having difficulty resolving them, but they're inbound from the edge of the jamming bubble and coming in *fast*."

"Time from nova?" Kira demanded.

"At least fifteen seconds," the Tactical officer replied. "Forty-five seconds to exit nova... They must have barely missed *our* people."

"Confirm identity," Mwangi snapped.

"Approach vector and maneuvers are all wrong to be our people," Soler told him. "Acceleration is wrong, mass is wrong, direction is wrong. CIC makes it ninety percent likely Liberators."

"*Huntress* CIC agrees," Davidović confirmed.

"CSP is released," Kira ordered. "Huntress squadrons, Ranger squadrons—break and attack!"

Huntress carried three fighter groups: Huntress Group with her Wolverine interceptors, Ranger Group with her Hussar-Seven fighter-bombers, and Avalanche Group with her Wildcat-Four bombers.

The Liberators were multirole fighters, similar in intent to Kira's Hussar-Sevens, which meant they carried torpedoes. Both *Deception* and *Huntress* could take *some* torpedo hits...but not many. The single-shot plasma cannon were at least as powerful as *Deception*'s main guns, after all.

"Contacts at sixty thousand klicks and closing," Soler said grimly. "Estimate thirty seconds to exit nova. We believe twenty targets."

"They're good," Kira murmured. "We're better."

She felt *Deception* vibrate underneath her as the heavy cruiser opened up on her incoming enemies. The cruiser could hit nova fighters, but the odds weren't great. Any of them she did hit, even with her secondary lighter guns, were blown to pieces, though.

To reliably hit a nova fighter in a multiphasic jamming field required rapid-firing guns from less than ten thousand kilometers' range. Given that a plasma torpedo had a roughly *fifteen*-thousand-kilometer effective range, no capital ship wanted to get that close to a torpedo-armed nova fighter.

The best counter to a nova-fighter strike was another fighter, even the much-maligned sublight sub-fighters.

And unfortunately for the Colossus Nova Wing, Kira had more fighters in her defensive patrol than the CNW had in the entire area. The Liberators were fast for their size, but they were also *big* nova fighters, almost as large as Memorial Force's Crest-designed bombers.

Her fingers curled out of view of the cameras, the instincts of a fighter pilot trying to wrap around a set of joysticks she didn't have. There were few orders she could give at this point, and part of her still wanted to be out there, flying a Wolverine alongside her people.

There was even an extra Wolverine tucked away on *Deception*'s flight deck for just that purpose. But even Kira had to admit that Memorial Force would suffer for losing her—and nova-fighter combat was risky.

"Fighters are breaking off," Soler snapped. "Exit nova in ten seconds. No contacts remain on approach."

"Hold turret fire," Kira ordered. "Let them go."

She couldn't order the fighters to make the same allowance, but she didn't need to. The Liberators were solid fighters, but their *pilots* had been utterly outmatched. They'd been decently trained—but *Kira*'s pilots were a mix of veterans and pilots *trained* by said veterans.

With the numbers on her side, the Colossus fighters had never stood a chance. Four lived long enough to nova away to safety.

"Lock down those locations," Kira ordered. "We need to do a Jianhong radiation review once the jammers are down."

They'd be able to establish where the nova fighters had gone. If they'd only jumped a light-minute, they might be back in sixty seconds—that was the minimum cooldown of a class two nova drive.

If they'd jumped six light-years, however, they *definitely* weren't coming back. With the thirty-six hours' cooldown on a class two drive for a long nova, that was a getaway jump and *only* a getaway jump.

"New contacts," Soler reported swiftly. "Multiple contacts, at least forty... Acceleration, mass and vector are correct for our people."

"Flash the running lights, Captain Mwangi," Kira ordered. "Let's see how they did."

It took a few seconds to establish a laser link, even with the fighters flying in easy, straight lines—though the very fact that nova fighters *were* flying in easy, straight lines told Kira everything she needed to know.

"Mission accomplished," Colombera told her. "Cartman stayed behind with three squadrons to keep an eye on the freighters. They still have Colossus Army troops aboard, but they and the depot ship surrendered after we blew both destroyers to pieces in the first pass."

"The bill?" Kira asked.

"Zilch," her old comrade replied. "Couple of the bombers got dinged up, but nothing we can't buff out. Clean sweep, boss."

Kira released a layer of muscle tension she hadn't realized she'd been holding.

"Well done, Commander," she told Colombera. "Mwangi, Davidović. Let's drop the jamming and link up with the fighters. Once we're closer, Milani will send teams over to secure the depot ship and clear the freighters."

One trade-route stop down. They could hit one more before they had to discharge at Samuels—and Kira's map suggested that Colossus would be blockading four.

Today's results said that wouldn't be for much longer.

16

"Everything is secure," Milani reported as *Deception* decelerated into the freighter corral. "Depot ship isn't much use to anybody at the moment, though. They locked her systems down hard.

"We've got...housekeeping control, nothing more," the mercenary continued. "Airlocks and life support. Couple of my smarter electronic warfare grunts that Bueller trained are trying to crack the computer core, but it's not looking promising."

They shook their head.

"I'm moving the prisoners over from the other freighters and locking them down here. Your orders with the rescues?"

"Make sure the Colossus ships didn't leave any surprises in the systems," Kira ordered. "Otherwise, we wave them on. So long as they aren't prisoners of the CNW, they're not our headache.

"What's the breakdown?"

"Three ships from Samuels, one from the Bodega System," Milani told her.

Their tone suggested that Kira shouldn't know where the Bodega System was...which was good, because Kira didn't.

"EG says the Bodega System is...almost ten degrees around the Rim," Kira murmured as she checked the entry on the system. "I don't know anything about them."

"Me either," her ground commander confirmed. "Which I figure is why the Colossus detained them. *Wanderer* is a long way from home, so it would be about half 'That's suspicious' and half 'No one's coming for you.'"

"Well, someone came for them," Kira replied. "Anything else?"

Milani paused, the dragon flickering across their faceplate on the video feed, then the armored suit seemed to sink in on itself slightly.

"We lost a commando taking the depot ship," they admitted. "One of those damn stupid things. Idiot mook got into the armory, got her hands on an armor-piercing grenade launcher. Came around the corner, found herself face-to-face with Crush.

"Put an AP grenade into his armor at point-blank range. Neither of them lived."

Crush was a name Kira knew. He'd been part of her original welcoming party when she'd first come aboard *Conviction*, a combat trooper visibly addicted to combat drugs. Somehow, he'd managed to ride a functional addiction for long enough to die from something else.

"Pígaine me theó," Kira half-whispered. *Go with God.* She didn't know if Crush had been religious, and *she* certainly wasn't, but Apollo had traditions.

"One of those damn stupid things," Milani repeated. "No one had a chance to stop it, no one saw the idiot coming, and the idiot didn't even survive herself. Just...fucking bad luck."

"Keep reminding yourself of that, Milani," Kira ordered. Crush had been part of Milani's squad, one of the dozen or so mercs her ground-force commander had commanded the longest. That loss had to hurt as much as the Three-Oh-Third pilots she'd lost since reaching Redward.

"I will," they promised. "Like I said, things are secure. We'll load everybody onto the depot ship for now. Then, I guess we're waiting for Samuels to send someone for them?"

"We may move them to one of the other freighters for transport, but that's for Macey to negotiate," Kira told them. "Well done, Milani."

The dragon saluted for the mercenary, then the video channel closed and Kira leaned back in her chair on the flag deck.

One fatal casualty to take down a quarter of a blockade and eighty kilocubics of enemy starships was an exchange rate most commanders would sell their soul for. But in some ways, Crush's loss hurt worse for being the only one.

And for being so random. As Milani had said, it was "one of those damn stupid things."

"Admiral?" Smolak pinged her headware. "We have an incoming transmission from *Wanderer*. They want to speak to you."

"I can do that," Kira agreed.

"Check your headware trans software," the coms officer told her. "Doesn't seem like the gentleman speaks English. Just French."

"Send me a pack," Kira replied. "I don't think I have that one."

Her headware contained datapacks for over two hundred languages, but she'd never needed French before. An icon popped up on her vision and rotated for a few moments as the pack downloaded from *Deception*'s computers.

"Should be good to go; linking him through," Smolak said.

A new hologram appeared in front of Kira's desk. The image was of a tall and heavily fleshed man in a long and high-collared black coat. His salt-and-pepper beard was thick and long graying curls framed his face as he smiled widely at her.

"Admiral, thank you for speaking with me," he greeted her. His words blurred in her hearing for a moment before the translator software caught up.

"I had some time," Kira allowed. "How may I assist you, Captain..."

"Reverend, Admiral," he corrected gently. "I am Reverend Pierre Benowitz. My wife is the Captain of *Wanderer*, but she took injuries when those thugs boarded our ship, and they limited our access to things like the ship's medical facilities.

"Her younger sister, our doctor, is seeing to her injuries now, but she isn't available to speak to you herself," Benowitz continued. "I must pass on my family's gratitude for your timely rescue. Having no concept of what exactly Colossus believed we were doing, we did not know if there was any chance they would release us."

"The other detained ships were all from Samuels," Kira noted. "I'm not sure just why the CNW seized your ship, Reverend. Any ideas?"

"None, I must admit," he told her. "Though governments are known for being paranoid and we are a long way from home. Which leaves me even more grateful for your rescue. If there is any way that I or the rest of my family aboard *Wanderer* can assist you, please let us know. We will be heading on to Samuels with the other ships, I suspect, once you release us."

"We have no reason to hold anyone," Kira said. "Though..."

Some instinct told her that there was more to the family-owned freighter several hundred light-years from home than Benowitz was saying. His calm reaction to both his ship being seized by a local military—and, apparently, his wife being *injured* by said military—was out of line with his presentation.

"The depot ship—*Indigo Iris*—that Colossus was using to maintain their fighters has her systems locked down," she told him. "You were in position to have some records on her operations. Any assistance you could give my people in accessing her files and systems would be greatly appreciated."

"I'm sure we have some scan data or something that may be of use to you," Benowitz said cheerfully. "And my sons and I have toyed around with various tools over the years that might be helpful.

"If you can connect us with your people aboard her, we will attempt to assist."

"Thank you, Rabbi."

"Consider it the least aid I can offer for your assistance," he told her. "You have done my family a great service. Any service we can provide in return, we are delight to offer."

17

Kira watched as the four liberated merchant ships vanished into nova in silence.

"Well?" she finally asked Milani.

This time, a full-size hologram of the armored mercenary had joined her on the flag deck. Her link to the cruiser's bridge was active, and another hologram of Captain Davidović stood across from the ground commander.

"I do not know what our Bodegan friends are," Milani said slowly. "That is outside the scope of a mere and lowly grunt to guess."

"But they're not a merchant crew," Kira guessed.

"We shut down the external firewalls and gave them access to *Indigo Iris*'s systems," her ground commander continued, their voice still slow and measured. "It took them eleven minutes to undo the encryption and lockdown that had baffled my best electronic warfare troops for *six hours*, Admiral.

"*Eleven minutes*."

"So, *Wanderer* is a spy ship," Bueller concluded. "Whose, I wonder?"

"Bodega's, I suspect," Kira told her people. "I can see many Rim systems wanting more intelligence than they can easily acquire on the greater galaxy. How far does Redward's knowledge truly extend, for example?"

"Not even to here," Davidović—who had been a Redward Royal Fleet officer until the last year—replied. "We know little of the Samuels-Colossus Corridor, let alone of Apollo or Brisingr, except at the highest levels. We know more of the Royal Crest—we knew more of the Crest before you worked for them, even—but that is because the Bank of the Royal Crest has made itself the currency of choice in much of this sector of the Rim."

And the royal family of the Royal Crest owned their bank. It was one of their key sources of power—and the money that came from it had funded the coup that Kira had helped birth.

A strange galaxy they lived in, where the Crown Zharang of a constitutional monarchy helped launch a coup to make said monarchy *more* democratic. But, of course, the Royal Crest's lack of democracy had favored their dominant political party, not their monarchs.

"Maps, the Encyclopedia Galactica and rumors," Kira concluded aloud. "That's all the people of most systems know once they're more than *maybe* a hundred light-years from home. Ninety percent of humanity never leaves the planet they were born on. Another eight percent never leaves their star system.

"An intelligence network that can give reliable, even if dated, information about the galaxy can be worth its weight in gold."

Not that any government she'd ever worked for had spent the time and money to achieve that. The only one that she knew of that *had* was the Solar Federation, the loose coalition of most solar systems in the Core around Terra.

SolFed Intelligence had operatives even this far out. She'd met one in the middle of their op against Crest, even engaged in a trade of favors to help complete the *Fortitude* mission.

"So what have we learned?" Mwangi asked.

"I'm just finishing up going through the data Milani sent me now," Soler reported, the Tactical officer looking up at the meeting going on around her. "It's not our worst-case scenario, but it's more than Samuels told us to expect."

"Lay it out," Kira ordered.

"It looks like Commander Bueller's guess of them pulling the older ships from Syndulla was correct," Soler said. "*N45-K*, *I53-R*, *D5D-12*, *D5D-09*, *D5D-A2*, and *D5D-B1* were all Brisingr SSR, leased to the Syndulla government, and they were all transferred to Colossus.

"The files on *Indigo Iris* suggest that she and her sister ship, *Violent Variance*, were undergoing conversion to act as junk carriers for Colossus before they acquired their stack of BKN ships. There was a quick and dirty completion job to use them as depot ships instead, while the yards did a refit sweep on the six immediately useful ships.

"From *Iris*'s files, all of those ships are here, spread across the three trade-route stops the CNW flagged as the most efficient for blockading the system—the fourth we'd IDed they figure is covered by the other three. Two of the destroyers are with *N45-K* at the far side, where we can't reach without discharging static."

"And *Violet Variance* is with *I53-R* at the third nova stop?" Kira asked.

"Exactly, boss," Soler replied. "Twenty Liberators and a light cruiser."

Kira nodded as the regional display updated with the marks of the three trade-route stops and their known blockading forces. Samuels and Colossus were on either side of the rough triangle of mapped nova locations. Theoretically, someone could hit each of the three spots the CNW had blockaded and not stop at either system.

Of course, each of the three spots was four or five novas from the next nearest stopover *except* Samuels or Colossus. One stop was where they were currently, the closest if coming in from the Outer Rim toward Samuels. One was on the opposing side, the closest stop if coming from the Inner Rim toward Samuels. The last was "north," based on the poles and ecliptic plane of the Sol System per ancient tradition, for those coming in from "above."

If anyone had built a nova drive that didn't need a couple of planets' worth of mass to discharge static and tachyon buildup every thirty-odd light-years, Kira didn't know about it. That meant that anyone coming to Samuels had to stop at one of those three trade-route stops—unless they had a secret addition to the standard galactic map.

"Anyone think we'll have a problem taking *I53-R*?" Kira finally asked. "We can nova into Samuels to discharge static and resupply first if needed."

"*Deception* alone could probably take her and her escorting fighter wing down," Mwangi told her.

"Probably, but we need to realize that four Liberators jumped from here," Davidović reminded them all. "It's only two novas from this stop to Colossus, so they might have gone home...but there's a good chance they jumped to the I-Fifty. Forewarned is forearmed, and they almost certainly know we're coming."

"Agreed," Kira said. "But we'll go by the plan, people. We send *Springtime Chorus* and Macey's people back home, then we jump after the cruiser. Even if they bring *N45-K* and the destroyers into the mix, we still have the edge in fighters and firepower."

"And that's assuming that *N45-K* is fully loaded," Bueller added. "If she's split her fighter group to provide the blockade wings rather than just ferrying squadrons from Colossus..."

"The two depot ships can theoretically carry their own fighters," Kira pointed out. "They can't launch them quickly enough to act as carriers, but you can stuff any freighter full of planes. I don't want to assume that *N45-K* is under-armed."

Fully loaded, that would give the Colossus Nova Wing eighty

fighters, a cruiser, a carrier, and two destroyers to go up against Kira's carrier, ninety-two fighters, and heavy cruiser.

She figured the odds were still in her favor, though she'd far rather take on the cruiser separately.

"If *N45-K* is there, we'll need to be a lot more careful," Kira noted. "But I don't think Colossus even *has* the hulls to make a real fight of this just yet."

18

Springtime Chorus's countdown to nova was running in one corner of Kira's vision as she settled back down in her flag deck. The last thirty-six hours had been surprisingly calm, once the battle itself was over, but her people were about to go back into action.

"Captain Hennessy, any concerns on your end?" she asked the Samuels ship's CO.

"None," they replied. "We'll get everyone home safe and sound and have the party ready for when you arrive."

"I'm not sure many people in Samuels are down for celebrating a military victory," Kira pointed out.

"They won't celebrate the deaths, no," Hennessy agreed. "But liberation from the blockade and security for our future? They'll celebrate that. Your people will get a heroes' welcome."

"Save the heroes' welcome for when the work is done," she said. "We've only cleared a third of the blockade, and we have no idea how close the rest of the CNW is to being ready."

"You know that," Hennessy said. "I'd put that together as well. But most of my people? We just need to know that traffic will flow again. Good luck."

"Thank you, Captain," Kira said as her timer clicked to zero. "Fly safe."

Hennessy threw her a salute, and then their image vanished from her displays—and so did their ship.

"We ready to nova, Captains?" Kira asked Mwangi and Davidović.

"Yes, sir," Davidović confirmed.

"We were ready twelve hours ago, boss," Mwangi replied.

It was sometimes very easy to tell which of the two Captains had been in a traditional military more recently.

"All right."

Kira leaned back in her chair and took a glance down at the readiness reports for her two ships and their fighters, then exhaled a sharp sigh.

"Nova on schedule," she ordered.

UNLIKE THEIR JUMP to the first nova point, this time they had a damn good idea of what the enemy strength was and where they were positioned. Almost as importantly, Kira had gone through the steps required by her code of conduct and her morals to attempt to prevent unnecessary deaths.

She wasn't playing that game this time. There would be no warnings, no attempts to communicate.

Unfortunately, it turned out that their data wasn't *quite* as up to date as they'd hoped.

"Contact, contact, contact!" Soler snapped. "Major contact at two hundred thousand kilometers!"

"Jammers up," Mwangi, Davidović and Kira all snapped at the same time.

"Full deck launch, maximum scramble," Kira followed up. All of their nova fighters were crewed, but "maximum scramble" cut the intervals between launching the fighters tight. *Too* tight, in Kira's informed opinion, given the safety radius of Harrington coils at full power.

But it would shave the time to launch her fighters from seventy seconds to forty-two. And sometimes that was absolutely necessary.

"Set assault course," Mwangi barked. "Guns up. ID the target!"

"Jammers are live," Soler confirmed. "Target appears to be an I-Fifty-class light cruiser. She is... She is aware of our presence and maneuvering. I read no fighters in the jamming zone."

"That won't last," *Deception*'s Captain replied. "Target the cruiser. All guns!"

Kira almost bit her tongue. There was a point where the task of the fleet commander was to *shut up* and let her subordinates work.

Plus, in all honesty, she had no business meddling in a capital-ship action. She could apply a lot of her training in general tactics to running a *battle* at the capital-ship scale, but she had very little applicable knowledge in the minutiae of actually running a heavy cruiser.

Twelve heavy guns fired as one, flinging plasma across the void as the starfighters got *very* clear of the big cruiser's guns.

A quick glance at the imagery showed Kira why it was *only* twelve guns: *Deception*'s angle of approach was wrong and two of her turrets couldn't bear. They'd expected the Colossus force to be almost three million kilometers from where the cruiser actually was.

But Mwangi and his people were on it, and the cruiser finished turning in time to watch *I53-R*'s first salvo fly wide. *Deception*'s own initial fire was no closer, Kira suspected, and the two warships were now hurtling toward each other at the best acceleration their Harrington coils could throw out.

"And now you see why we went to single turrets on this generation," Bueller murmured in her ear. "The turret-cubage-to-gun went up about twenty percent, but watch."

Kira wasn't sure what her engineer partner was saying for the next few seconds...and then realized as Soler plotted the firing pattern on the displays. *I53-R* had three triple turrets. While she had more guns per cubic meter than *Deception* did, they fired in sets of three. So while they were trying to track a target through multiphasic jamming, they were only hitting three *vectors* at once.

Deception was cutting through *fourteen* individual vectors, allowing Soler to narrow down the space that didn't hold her enemy far more quickly than the smaller ship.

"New contacts!" Bueller snapped from CIC, acting as XO more than engineer at the moment. "Liberators are on the board. Marking twenty-plus contacts—some of our friends from the last go-around are definitely here!"

Kira had no link with her fighter wings by this point, but Cartman and Colombera had learned their trade from her. The interceptors and fighter-bombers had stuck in close this time, recognizing that either there was no *need* for bombers once the cruisers had started shooting at each other—or the bombers' contribution would be too late anyway.

Now most of the Wolverines and Hussars boiled away in a chaotic mess that even Kira had trouble distinguishing in the chaos—and *Huntress* swung around behind them, positioning the carrier between the incoming fighters and the cruiser.

Deception was better able to take a hit than the carrier was, but *Huntress* carried no heavy guns.

Instead, she had almost as many *light* guns as the bigger cruiser did, and they joined her fighters in laying a hail of plasma across the space the Liberators were charging into.

"Got a hit, recalibrating," Soler announced, her voice technical and calm as a spark of light that cut through even multiphasic jamming allowed her to nail down her target. "Tightening the salvos. We have them."

The range was down to eighty thousand kilometers, marking the one clear advantage of capital-ship turrets over the one-shot torpedoes that duplicated their firepower at close range. Capital-ship guns fired plasma packets with magnetic fields to keep them together over as much as a hundred thousand kilometers.

A nova fighter's torpedo was more on the order of a shaped-charge explosive, a space shotgun versus a heavy cannon's rifle round.

Of course, at this range, they couldn't really *see* the enemy ship, and even *Deception*'s guns weren't doing a lot of damage to *I53-R* when they hit. Still, as Soler tightened her vectors, more and more hits hammered into the light cruiser.

"Fighters are down," Bueller reported. "None of them even got close."

"Nova!" Soler snapped. "Target has novaed. Wait...no..."

There was a sick tone to the Tactical officer's reassessment.

"Soler?" Kira asked gently.

"Target has *attempted* to nova, Admiral," Isidora Soler said in a small voice. "I have visual on a debris field. We must have hit her nova field while it was forming. Would have caused a...critical stability failure.

"She didn't make it."

Kira nodded slowly. A class two drive cycled too quickly for that to happen outside the absolute *worst* of luck, but it could happen. The threat of it was what made a blockade feasible in the first place.

"Understood," she told her people. "Bring down the jammers; locate the freighter corral and the depot ship."

If *Violet Variance*'s crew were smart, they were taking advantage of that moment to be somewhere very far away—probably even under *N45-K*'s metaphorical skirts.

The question Kira wasn't sure of was whether the CNW depot ship's crew were callous enough to abandon whatever soldiers they'd put on their captured freighters.

19

After two chunks of not merely void but *hostile* void, the Samuels System was a relief to see. Following Macey's instructions, they'd novaed in close enough that their scans immediately picked out the six asteroid fortresses guarding the inhabited planet.

"It's a nice star system," Kira observed wryly to Konrad. They were alone in her office, though she was expecting to be linked with the locals shortly.

"Especially the planet," her boyfriend replied, looking at the virtual window covering one wall of her office. "I've seen a few by now, but few quite that pretty."

Bennet was a green and blue marble, with shades slightly different from Apollo or Redward that somehow still felt *exactly* right. With a minimal axial tilt and an equatorial set of continents, the data feeding into Kira's headware said it was comfortably warm across most of the landmasses despite being in the latter stages of an ice age according to the geologists.

Inward from Bennet were Fox and Hound, two balls of rock and toxic gas that would be useless to almost anyone. The wealth of the

Samuels System was outward from Bennet, first in the Pennsylvania Belt and then in the gas giants Haven and Sanctuary.

The outer wrap of the system was the Washington Belt, an ice asteroid belt to match the Pennsylvania Belt's rocky asteroids. Five worlds and two asteroid belts to provide everything a wealthy colony needed.

And yet the true wealth of the Samuels System, Kira knew, was its galactic position. Without the impact of the Samuels-Colossus Corridor, the system would have been self-sufficient and better off than many—but *with* the Corridor, Samuels's wealth was nearly in the league of Apollo or Brisingr.

The Ministries were careful with their people's wealth and kept a low profile on the interstellar scene. The people of Samuels controlled their government quite directly—and the people of Samuels, from what Kira could tell, wanted no trouble with anyone.

Unfortunately, that meant they had no fleet whatsoever. Just asteroid forts and a dozen squadrons of nova fighters.

"It's a pretty world, but that's uglier," Kira told her boyfriend, highlighting a familiar-looking set of structures near one of the asteroid forts. "Thrown-together military shipyards."

"Why are you assuming military?" Konrad asked, eyeing them.

"Because the civilian yards are at the Samuels-Bennet Lagrange point over here," she said, tagging the point of gravitational stability "ahead" of Bennet in its orbit. "But those aren't protected enough for warship construction, so the locals are putting together new slips under the guns of the fortresses to build a fleet."

"You're not wrong," he agreed, studying both sets of yards with a practiced eye. "Slips aren't done yet, though. It's going to be another month or two before they even lay keels for nova warships, unless they've got some under construction at the civilian yards."

"I'd do both in their place," Kira told him. "They can afford it. *If* the populace voted for it."

"Universal e-democracy," he said with a sigh. "I like it. I just hope they don't shoot themselves in the foot *too* badly."

"Macey seems to have her head on pretty straight, pacifism and all," she noted. "I suspect they know what Colossus is throwing their way."

She shook her head.

"I hope you have a clean dress uniform tucked away somewhere," she said. "We might be sending the ships to discharge at Haven, but some of us have to go make nice with the Ministries—and if I have to play politics, I am bringing my arm candy."

"Oh, I think I can manage that," he promised with a chuckle.

"ADMIRAL DEMIRCI, please allow me to extend the First Minister's warm welcome to the Samuels System," Doretta Macey's familiar image told Kira. "From Captain Hennessy's discussions with you, we understand the blockade is...not entirely broken?"

She sounded a bit confused by the concept, which was fair in Kira's opinion. Macey was a negotiator, not a soldier.

"There are three mapped trade-route stops that need to be blockaded to seal Samuels in an efficient manner," Kira told her. "There are six a ship can actually nova to Samuels from, but those three cut off any approach far enough out that they can still detour to Colossus."

The third was actually two novas away from Samuels, past the fourth point Kira would have blockaded but the CNW had chosen to ignore. There was still no way Kira's ships could have reached it without discharging. Speaking of...

"My vessels will need to discharge static and tachyons at Haven before proceeding," she continued. "But we believe we know roughly what awaits us at the final blockade point, and I am confident in our ability to handle it."

"That was what our military officers told us to expect," Macey agreed. "As promised in the contract, all tolls and fees for fueling and discharging in the Samuels System are waived for your vessels.

"The First Minister has also asked me to invite you, and any of your officers you choose, to join them for dinner this evening. That would be in about two and a half hours," the Samuels native explained with a smile.

"Of course," Kira said. "Commander Bueller and I would be delighted to attend, though most of my officers will need to deal with the damage from our engagements so far."

"Is there any assistance our yards and personnel can provide with that?" Macey asked instantly.

"Not needed at this point," Kira told her. "We were lucky and didn't take significant damage in either engagement. *Deception* is a little banged up around the edges, but we have replacement armor plates and dispersal netting in storage."

She smiled.

"Such costs are what the additional combat fees are intended to cover," she reminded Macey.

"And those fees will be paid shortly," the local confirmed. "Shall I inform First Minister Buxton of your attendance this evening?"

"Please," Kira said. "I will be bringing a shuttle down from *Deception*. If you can pre-arrange our flight path, that will smooth the way."

"It will be taken care of," Macey promised. "I look forward to seeing you again, Admiral."

The channel closed, and Kira linked to Mwangi and Davidović.

"Akuchi, Marija," she greeted them. "As expected, I need to politick on the surface. I'm taking Bueller, but both of you know what you need to do?"

"I'm pretty sure we can both manage a static discharge into a gas giant in our sleep, boss," Mwangi said drily. "And the repairs we need are minor enough that, yes, it *is* okay that you're stealing my chief engineer to be your arm candy."

"Rank hath its privileges," Kira reminded her flag captain. "And if I have to go make nice, I'm at least bringing my boyfriend to back me up!"

"Better you in the politics than me, sir," Davidović noted. "I know how the game works on Redward, and I know the players. A strange new world with strange new rules? I'd be lost."

"Half of my career for Apollo was working with our allies," Kira told them. "And *then* I had to survive in Redward." She grinned.

"I think I can handle the snake pit of politics that is a planet founded by pacifists."

20

THERE HAD BEEN a time when Kira could be convinced to let other people fly the shuttle carrying her. That had been *before* she'd been forced to almost entirely give up flying her nova fighter, and now she clung to every chance to actually fly a spacecraft she could get.

With only Cartman acting as copilot and Milani and Bueller as passengers, the shuttle was effectively empty as she whisked over the low-slung and widespread districts of Quaker City.

Even from above, Samuels' capital city was impressive. While the locals had chosen a more horizontal style than many diaspora cities, and Quaker lacked the sweeping skyscrapers Kira was used to, the carefully plotted concentric circles of a high-speed transit network were clearly visible from the air.

The transit network was laid out with sufficient density that she saw far fewer personal vehicles than she would have expected for such a sprawling city—but what was truly impressive in some ways was that the *network* extended farther out than the *city*. It had been built for the Quaker City of the future, and at least two full concentric rings of magnetic tracks and transport stations existed past where the current city ended.

And even amidst the city, there were greenery and parks—and her course took her to one of the largest parks, a hundred-hectare, seemingly wild forest surrounded by transit lines on all sides. The landing pad was just past the transit line on the north side, where a still-green collection of red stone buildings filled almost as much space as the park itself...and her threat detectors pinged as she began her final approach.

"Missile launchers on the grounds of the Ministries Compound," Cartman muttered. "And, unless these sensors suck in a way I know they don't, those are the *only* defensive weapons in a city of seven million people."

"Different cultures, Nightmare," Kira replied as the Compound fully spilled out beneath them. Unlike the park to its south, where the transit network had been rerouted around it, Quaker City's transit network interpenetrated the complex of buildings that held much of the Samuels System's government.

The Quorum and direct democracy might write the planet's laws, but its day-to-day governance was handled from there. This was the home of the Ministries' bureaucracy—and in an oddly familiar-looking red stone building with two wings and a central hub, the home of the First Minister themselves.

"Link established with ground control," Kira said aloud as a silent communication finished and she removed her hands from the flight stick. "Everybody dressed up and ready to party?"

"Did anyone warn them we're bringing a suit of armor?" Cartman asked, glancing back over her shoulder at Milani.

The dragon flickered across Milani's armor to offer a rude hand gesture in response, and Kira chuckled.

"Don't worry, Mel; they have a doctor's note."

KIRA and two of her companions wore black and dark-teal dress uniforms, long jackets over full-body shipsuits. Milani, of course, was the fourth, clad in digital-camouflage battle armor currently rendered as light gray with a flickering pattern of a content red dragon.

Doretta Macey was their only greeting party, adding to her sense of a surprising lack of security at the capital of a star system. The negotiator had returned to the neatly tailored pantsuit of the meetings on Redward, though here she had a dark blue kerchief tied over the top of her head.

"Welcome to Bennet and Quaker City, Admiral," Macey greeted them. "Mix Buxton got tied up in a late committee meeting but *should* make it to the dining room in time for the meal itself."

Kira nodded with a small smile, remembering Queen Sonia giving her the same reason for why King Larry had missed *Huntress*'s commissioning ceremony. Some aspects of leading a world never changed, it seemed.

"If you'll follow me, please?" Macey asked.

"Is security always this light?" Kira said as she and her companions fell in with the Samuels woman.

"Why would we need security?" Macey replied. "We are a universal e-democracy, Admiral, with a highly religious population dominated by traditions of pacifism. We are not unobserved, if that is your concern, but we have generally low levels of crime and have no recorded cases of political violence in our entire history."

The native shrugged.

"We take certain precautions because we recognize the realities of the universe, but they have never been needed. There was a time, in the past, when we were recruiting many of our top police and security officers from Colossus."

Macey looked sad at that and sighed.

"We have not done so for a long time, obviously," she noted. "But for a while, most of the officers of the First Minister's detail were veteran bodyguards and security officers recruited from Colossus, often on the personal recommendation of their President or other senior officials."

That was...new and an odd bit of information. It was a sign, Kira realized, of just *how* friendly the "friendly competition" between Colossus and Samuels had been until the last twenty years or so.

No wonder it had taken Samuels's leadership so long to adapt to the possibility that Colossus might actually wage war on them.

"Welcome to the Rouge House, Admiral, Commanders," Macey told them as they approached the red stone building at the center of the Ministries Compound.

BUXTON ENTERED the dining room from the other side as Kira's party, though only a few seconds after the mercenaries. A pair of suited bodyguards scattered to the corners of the room—the first sign of security she'd seen since the threat detectors on the shuttle had pinged.

The First Minister of Samuels was nothing like what Kira had expected. She'd known from pronouns and honorifics that she was dealing with a nonbinary individual, but even that had only led her off the track.

They towered well over two meters in height, easily rivaling the largest humans she'd ever known. Their shoulders were immense, clearly rippling with muscle under the perfectly tailored burgundy skirt suit they wore—and if the skirt hadn't been cut to free up Buxton's range of motion, Kira would eat her own uniform.

Expertly delicate makeup accentuated the curves of the First Minister's face and drew attention to their dark brown eyes, with the kind of gaze that even Kira would call soulful and intense.

"Admiral Demirci," they greeted Kira, striding across the room to offer her their hand. After a brief-but-firm handshake, they pressed a swift kiss to Macey's cheek and then gestured everyone to the table.

"Please, I am running late—but the food is not," they noted. "Mrs. Alarie informs that the turkey has been carved and the plates are being finished as I speak. Sit, sit!"

Kira obeyed with a smile, squeezing Bueller's hand under the table as her engineer sat at her right. Cartman and Milani settled in on either side of them, pilot and trooper alike seeming bemused by the First Minister.

"We were advised of Commander Milani's requirements by Mrs. Macey," Buxton continued. "Mrs. Alarie has prepared a nutrition shake that you should be able to both easily scan and intake through your armor's emergency induction port."

Milani bowed their armored head.

"I appreciate that, First Minister," they said carefully. "To use that port, I may require a straw."

"Mrs. Alarie believes she has included everything. We shall see, of course, but she rarely disappoints," Buxton replied.

A pair of middle-aged men in tuxes emerged from the kitchen as the Minister spoke, each carrying a platter loaded with plates—and one large, surprisingly decorative, sealed jug with a flexible metal straw emerging from the top.

The jug was placed in front of Milani, who ran an armored gauntlet up and down it in a clear scanning gesture.

The irony to that, Kira knew, was that Milani had no need to make any kind of gesture. They would have scanned the plates presented to the other Memorial Force officers from across the room. They were only making a show of scanning the shake because the locals were trying to be accommodating.

Though, to be fair, Kira had *never* seen Milani touch food anyone else had prepared and was a bit shocked when they pulled the flexible straw up and connected it to a covered port on the side of their helmet.

"Please, eat," Buxton instructed. "There is business for us to discuss, but a full stomach always clears the air!"

The food was unsurprisingly excellent. Kira wasn't entirely sure the bird was what *she* would have called a turkey on Apollo, but the subtly different flavor could have been entirely preparation as well.

Once they had all eaten, the servers reappeared at a silent

command from the First Minister and cleared the plates, leaving cups of steaming hot coffee in their place.

Kira sniffed the coffee carefully. It met her minimum standard—of being hot, black and caffeinated—but it didn't smell nearly as smooth or rich as she was used to. On the other hand, she knew she'd been spoiled by living on a planet that *exported* coffee.

"You said there was business to discuss," she reminded Buxton after the first sip confirmed her initial impression.

"There is," the First Minister agreed. "You understand that Mrs. Macey arguably exceeded her authority by only hiring the two ships you had available, yes?"

"Mrs. Macey's documentation was sufficient to sign on your government's behalf by any common-law statute our lawyers are aware of," Kira said calmly. "While she may have been given different *instructions*, her legal *authority* to sign the contract was not in question."

"No, of course not," Buxton conceded, laying Kira's worst fears to rest. "But, as you are aware, the contract was written to allow the Ministries to decide on the activation of several ancillary clauses."

"Extensions and reinforcements," Kira confirmed. "The base six-month contract and stipulated bonuses and fees for engaging blockade forces are not subject to additional approvals."

"My Minister for Legal Affairs argues differently on the bonuses and additional fees," the First Minister told her. "Several other Ministers in my government believe that combat bonuses mis-incentivize your operations toward an armed conflict that we wished to avoid."

"That would be an annoying discussion to have in court," Kira murmured, leaning back in her chair and studying Buxton. They didn't seem nearly enough on edge to be trying to screw Memorial Force over in the way their words implied, but they were also a politician.

They could easily lie as well as she flew.

"And, of course, while such a discussion was tied up in court, there would be an open question over whether my forces were actually obligated to engage the remaining blockade forces," she continued. "I dislike even raising that point, First Minister, but I must act to protect the interests of my organization and personnel."

"I understand that, Admiral," Buxton told her. "Frankly, I believe that engaging in that level of legalese wrangling with regards to people who have already fought on our behalf would be churlish of us.

"Plus, unlike my colleagues in that meeting, *I* have had time to engage with initial reactions from our voting populace. It is very clear to me that if we were to attempt to deny your people the compensation due for acting in our service, our voters would be quite displeased.

"Pacifist leanings of the majority of our populace or no, we recognize that we are under threat and that you have already acted decisively to protect us."

"Do you," Kira murmured.

"Regardless of the technical reading of the contract, I feel that we are bound by its intent, and I wish to formally confirm that we will be honoring the bonus and additional fees for combat operations," Buxton told her. "I feel that a government that is obliged to be able to explain everything we do to our populace, usually in short video lectures, should be more careful in our uses of intentionally obfuscatory language."

"Your world is fascinating, First Minister," she said drily. "A trade-route stop remains under the control of the Colossus blockade. My ships are discharging static as we speak, but we will deploy to clear that last piece of the blockade when we are done.

"I appreciate knowing that I'm not going to have to fight two wars: one against your enemies to protect you, and one against you for my money.

"Even if the latter would be fought in a courtroom and not the battlespace."

"You must understand, Admiral Demirci, even having recognized the slowly growing hostility of Colossus's governments over the last twenty years, we never expected it to come to this," Macey told her. "And what the *Ministries* didn't realize, our voting populace certainly did not. To build a nova fleet required legislation passed by the body politic."

"The Ministries did not recognize the threat until too late," Buxton agreed. "We are not, by nature, a warlike world. Finding personnel for our defenses and fighters has always been a struggle."

"If it weren't for the Gurkhas, I'm not sure we'd succeed at all," Macey admitted. "They're Nepali-extract Hindus. Old, *old* martial traditions. While most of our Hindu population is on similar pacifistic paths as our Quaker and Buddhist citizens...the Gurkhas—the Gorkhali—are quite different."

"I suspect that some of our Gorkhali founders came here with the explicit intent of protecting their more peaceful coreligionists," Buxton noted. "They are approximately three percent of our population and provide roughly seventy percent of our military personnel.

"Without them, I am not certain we would have been able to do anything except surrender to Colossus," the First Minister admitted. "We are barely prepared to defend our own star system, Admiral Demirci. In many ways, we are at your mercy."

"I told Mrs. Macey when we completed the contract that the negotiations were the last time we would be on opposite sides," Kira told Buxton. She felt Bueller squeeze *her* hand under the table and drew strength from it as she smiled.

"We are mercenaries—I make no attempt to conceal that—but I have always attempted to find contracts where I believed we were on the right side," she noted. "There are enemies out here that few people know of, that play games with worlds and lives. I take their presence on the other side of the battlespace as a hint that I'm in the right place.

"And yes, I have reason to believe they are involved in the scheme to arm Colossus," she told them. If Samuels's government wasn't aware of the Equilibrium Institute, well, she'd have to educate them.

"Which brings me to our greatest fear, Admiral," Buxton replied. "These warships that make up the Colossus Nova Wing—Colossus didn't build them. They are well in advance of us in the construction of nova warships, but they have yet to commission anything of their own."

"You haven't even laid keels," Bueller said. "Do you have design work? Schematics? Plans?"

"Some," Buxton said. "Not, perhaps, as much as we would like, but we have acquired partial designs of last-generation Apollo, Crest and Santerran warship designs. Putting the three together, we believe we have assembled designs for practical and effective cruisers and destroyers."

"Commander Bueller was heavily involved in the updating of the Redward Royal Fleet to a by-Rim-standards modern nova fleet," Kira noted. "He was also both a combat-duty engineer during the war and a post-war design engineer for the Brisingr Kaiserreich Navy.

"For a small fee, I'm sure he could take a look through your designs and have some suggestions."

"There are easy mistakes to make that can cost you weeks or months to fix if you catch them later," her boyfriend told the Samuels politicians. "I can identify them relatively quickly."

Buxton and Macey shared a long look.

"I will talk to my husband," Buxton finally said. "Batsal has been central to the organization of the construction and design work. He retired from our defense force as commander of one of the orbital forts... He will be far more qualified to assess if Commander Bueller can be of use to us than I am."

"The first priority remains fully clearing the blockade," Kira told them all. "If there's nothing else, we'll return to our ships in short order and prepare for that strike. Once we have secured the trade routes around Samuels, we can discuss patrol plans and patterns while you send couriers to the key entry points to the Corridor.

"Colossus has passed the word that Samuels is blockaded," she warned the locals. "Once my job is done for the moment, *you* must make sure that the word of the blockade's failure is passed as well."

"We have the ships and the contacts," Buxton confirmed. "We will wait until you confirm the blockade is completely lifted, but the couriers are already standing by."

"Give me forty-eight hours to finish discharging static and investigate the last trade-route stop," Kira requested. "That should be plenty."

"You are that confident in your ability to defeat the Colossus Nova Wing?" the First Minister asked.

"With all due respect, First Minister, the CNW are amateurs with old ships," Cartman pointed out. "We expect their second wave, the refitted units, to be more dangerous—but they still lack real experience at this.

"It's not like we're facing the Kaiserreich Navy."

Kira figured there were likely BKN *advisors* supporting the CNW, but it wasn't the same—especially not with the balance of forces until the rest of the ships came online.

"And yet," Buxton said softly, "that is where these ships came from. We know Apollo and Brisingr of old, Admiral, Commanders, but we know neither well. The Kaiser has armed our enemies. I will not—I cannot—set my system on course for *more* war.

"Yet I must fear the man behind the war we already face," the leader of the Samuels System told them. "Between the four of you, there are two Apollons and a Brisingr. Is the Kaiser truly likely to have simply sold the ships and care nothing for what happens next?

"Or is this simply the first stage in a plan to seize the Corridor for himself?"

Kira shared a long glance with Bueller, then sighed.

"The Kaiser does not simply sell old warships on a whim," she conceded. "And I see the hand of a different enemy behind this all—the Equilibrium Institute."

"That is a name I have heard," Doretta Macey noted. "But not an entity I know of beyond rumor. A conspiracy theory, a shadow."

"And all too real for that," Kira warned. "Three times they launched schemes against the Syntactic Cluster, before we finally convinced them their return on investment wasn't going to be there." She shook her head. "They are ideologues driven by flawed Seldonian psychohistorical calculations.

"They believe there is only one way that humanity can be stable and at peace—and they are prepared to destabilize regions and start wars to get to that status. The irony, it seems, eludes them."

"The Corridor was stable until one side of Colossus's political divide decided to use us as an outside enemy," Buxton noted. "And now this Institute, what, arms Colossus in pursuit of a goal of peace?"

"Suffice to say, I don't find the Equilibrium Institute's logic or methods overly convincing," Kira replied drily.

"They can make a very convincing pitch, though," Bueller warned.

Kira squeezed his hand under the table again. He didn't need to say more than that, at least. No one there who didn't already know needed to know he was an Institute defector.

"We have encountered Brisingr ships being supplied or even operated by Equilibrium fronts before," she told the Samuels politicians. "We have reason to believe that the Institute has its claws deeply into Brisingr's power structures, potentially even into Kaiser Reinhardt himself.

"This has allowed them to draw on ships from the BKN's Secondary Service Reserve in the past," she continued. "We have traced several of the ships Colossus now possesses not only back to the SSR but back to a particular SSR deployment that we *know* the Institute has drawn on before."

She smiled coldly.

"We know that, I should point out, because it's where *Deception* originally came from," she told them.

"All of this is...useful context," Buxton told her. "But it does not allay my fear. If we are victorious today, will we see the full force of the Kaiserreich Navy blockading my system in six months?"

"The full force? No," Bueller said quietly. "The BKN has set itself too many tasks since the end of the war. If they cannot secure the trade routes they claimed from Apollo, they cannot enforce the other, less...positive aspects of the treaty.

"But...if Reinhardt sees this as a project of his, you may well see further forces committed. Either more modern ships, still through the shield of the SSR—or potentially, depending on the importance the Diet and the Kaiser's government place on this operation, a full carrier group of the BKN under their own banner."

"If it's an Equilibrium project as opposed to a Brisingr one, we're more likely to see SSR ships or mercenaries from other Rim powers," Kira noted. "We ran them dry of mercenary assets a few years back when we took out Cobra Squadron, but the Rim is wide and the Institute has a vast amount of money by our standards."

Until recently, there would have been a decent chance that the Institute would have been able to access forces from the Royal Crest, too. Thanks to Crown Zharang Jade Panosyan, with some help from Kira and Memorial Force, their control of that power was no more.

"So, you agree, then, that we have not seen the last of this with just the forces Colossus now possesses," Buxton said. "I know more than I did at the start of this dinner, and for that I thank you all.

"It does not, however, change the decision that I discussed with my cabinet earlier today. I am grateful that Mrs. Macey was wise enough to include the possibility in the contract—and I must state clearly that I am grateful for your presence here and the work you have already done.

"But looking to the future, I see a growing threat to the people I am sworn to serve. A threat that we will not be able to defend ourselves from...and a threat that will require far more than a single cruiser and carrier to stand off."

They shook their head.

"Admiral Demirci, we are activating the reinforcements clause in your contract," they told her. "While I understand that you have other commitments for your forces in the Outer Rim and I will not ask you to breach those commitments, we wish to contract for the arrival of *Fortitude* and her escorting ships as quickly as possible.

"When Memorial Force's full strength guards the routes to my people, then, perhaps, I will be able to breathe while we build our own fleet. Until then, I must fear the dark and hate every minute of the time that has come to me."

"No one ever wants to live through a war, First Minister Buxton," Kira told them. "Fate and experience have made me *good* at war, but even I would rather never raise arms again.

"If you are prepared to pay the fees written into the contract, I will send the messages to Obsidian," she continued. "With the communication time, the contract in place with Obsidian and the travel time for Commodore Zoric to bring the rest of the fleet to Samuels, we are looking at four months or more before *Fortitude* can arrive."

"And that, Admiral, is why we are activating that clause now and not when the CNW shows up with a Brisingr carrier group in support," Buxton said drily. "I wish for peace, Admiral. I will pray every night that I have made a mistake and the money we pay for this is wasted funds.

"But the day I became First Minister of Samuels, I accepted that there were certain ideals and beliefs that I would have to sacrifice on the altar of my sworn duty," they told the mercenaries. "Were a threat merely to me, I would stand aside.

"But the threat is to Samuels...and I swore an oath."

"I understand completely, First Minister," Kira said. "One of my pilots, Evridiki Bardacki, chose to retire rather than face war again after fleeing Apollo. I was tempted to join him—but then I learned of the Institute and all that they sought to do to the people of the Syntactic Cluster...and the rest of the Rim.

"I took up arms to defend my homeworld once. I may take up

arms for money now, but I also stand for a cause. And that cause, First Minister, will be well served by protecting Samuels."

She would be well paid for that task, but she had a fleet to maintain out of those funds. Kira herself, after all, was already wealthy beyond many people's dreams of avarice.

Even if *she* tended to forget that part.

21

It was a telling part of the limitations of Kira's current main operating base that they didn't have enough class two nova drives to spare for shuttles. While *Fortitude* had carried a handful of nova-capable pinnaces when they'd stolen her, the vast majority of their fighter-sized nova drives came from Redward.

And Redward, until recently, had only had the one manufacturing plant, stolen from an Equilibrium patsy. Class two nova drives had *very* specific manufacturing requirements, down to a precise level of natural gravity. Even Kira's Wolverine was based on the nova drive core of her old Hoplite-IV starfighter, as Memorial Force recycled every class two drive they possibly could to keep their fighter strength up.

That meant it took ten hours for Kira to make it back to *Huntress* and *Deception* on the shuttle they'd taken to Bennet, which was almost half the time the two capital ships needed to discharge their static buildup.

"*Deception*, this is Memorial Actual on approach," she told the control center. "Any news on the home front?"

She presumed anything *major* would have been communicated

to her by radio. Worst-case scenario, Colombera might even have sent a nova fighter to act as courier.

"Quiet and calm out here, boss," Dilshad Tamboli told her. The cruiser's flight deck boss shouldn't have been the person answering the coms for flight control. That they were suggested that things were *very* calm indeed.

"Locals have a damn good idea of how to run a discharge station," Tamboli continued. "If we'd been willing to let them, they'd have docked a sub-boat with its restaurants and casinos aboard to our airlocks."

Kira chuckled.

"Can't be *that* many people who'd let them do that," she replied.

"They've got four of them out here that I've seen, so at least *some* people aren't paranoid about the idea," the deck chief replied. "We've taken deliveries of food and let some people take leave, but it's quiet out here, boss."

"Good." Kira checked her implants. "I have the bouncing ball, Tamboli," she told them, confirming the computer link between *Deception* and the shuttle. "Turning over control."

"We have the link," Tamboli confirmed. "Welcome home."

Kira glanced back at her passengers and smiled. It might be weird to a lot of people for a warship to be home, but to all four of the people aboard her shuttle that day, *Deception* was definitely home.

A NIGHT'S SLEEP, a shower and an impressive breakfast later, Kira settled into a virtual conference with her senior commanders.

"All right, people," she greeted them. "My math says we should finish discharging everything in about half an hour. What's our status across the board?"

Her attention focused on Davidović first, and the carrier CO smiled calmly.

"*Huntress* went through her first two combat actions with flying colors, sir," Davidović noted. "A few of the fighters took glancing blows, though that's Scimitar's area to speak to. *Huntress* herself didn't take any fire and didn't take any self-inflicted issues, either.

"We are good to go as soon as the static levels are cleared."

She gestured to Colombera in turn and the dark-skinned CNG coughed.

"As Captain Davidović said, three of our planes took hits in the second engagement," Scimitar told them all. "Mostly zigged when they should have zagged. It wasn't anything that the deck team couldn't patch up, and none of the pilots or copilots were injured."

Both the Hussar-Seven fighter-bombers and the Wildcat-Four bombers had a copilot aboard, managing the heavier defensive electronic warfare suite and the torpedoes. The Wolverines traded that copilot space and life support for more powerful Harrington coils.

"All three of my flight groups are fully back up to speed and itching to get back out there," Colombera concluded. "Couple of my fresher pilots made ace in the kerfuffle, and the couple dozen who *haven't* want the chance to even up the numbers."

Even on Apollo, the "three kills make a pilot an ace" rule had been sacrosanct tradition. Kira had never hesitated to allow it, even encourage it, among her mercenary recruits.

"And *Deception*?" she asked, turning to Mwangi. "I know I stole your CNG and your chief engineer, but my impression is that everything is in hand?"

"We took a few more hits than the starfighters did," *Deception*'s gaunt Captain confirmed. "But given that we went toe-to-toe with another cruiser, however much smaller, I'm content with how we handled ourselves.

"We did take half a dozen real hits from the I-Fifty's guns but nothing that breached the armor," he continued. "We've replaced two thousand four hundred and sixteen square meters of external armor and refitted the energy-dispersal networks behind roughly thirty percent of the exterior hull.

"Bueller can speak to the tests as well as I can"—he gestured to the engineer—"but they all show as green from my end. Our armor did exactly what it was supposed to: sacrifice itself to protect the function and personnel of the ship.

"We *do* have wounded, but Dr. Devin assures me none require off-ship treatment, and the worst should be out of sickbay in a few days," Mwangi concluded. "I don't see any reason to hold off from deploying as soon as we're finished discharging."

Kira glanced at the three who'd accompanied her to Bennet.

"Mel, Milani, Konrad. I know it's not fair for me to ask you to know more than I do," she noted. "But still. Anything in your areas I should be worrying about?"

"*Deception*'s fighters didn't take any hits," Cartman replied. "We've got a lot fewer newbies than *Huntress*, though."

Despite the expansion of the nova-fighter wings of Redward and King Larry's allies, there were still very few nova-fighter pilots in the Syntactic Cluster—and the vast majority of the ones who existed were still in their tour of duty with the system militaries that had trained them.

Memorial Force had to recruit volunteers and train them from scratch, a process that left them far more inexperienced than most mercenary fleets would prefer. Kira's people were sufficiently veteran in both combat and training that they came out better than they might have, but almost half of *Huntress*'s pilots had flown their first combat op against the Colossus blockade.

Not that that was something any of them would admit to outsiders.

"Mwangi covered my part," Bueller said. "*Deception* is clear for combat."

"I'd like time to hold a funeral for Crush," Milani said. "That can wait a few days, at least. Ground forces are clear to deploy and carry out boarding actions, but I want to make sure that's on the schedule."

"This one is a strike-and-return," Kira told her people. "We'll be back in Samuels in four or five days, most likely. Shit can always happen, but we'll make sure there's time for us to remember our lost."

She looked around at the collection of faces and smiled slightly, drawing strength from the sheer competence and camaraderie around her.

"We will *always* make time for our dead," she promised them. "Our intel suggests it will be another month or so before Colossus can roll out their second wave of ships.

"That gives us a few weeks, once we clear the blockade, to set up patrol and work with the locals on a strategy for long-term security," she continued. "They have activated the reinforcements clause in the contract and put a courier ship at our disposal.

"That ship is already on her way."

The courier vessel was the standard ten-kilocubic "small hull" that any system with access to the standard colonial database could build. Coming out of Samuels, her one-thousand-cubic-meter Ten-X class one nova drive was dirt cheap and strapped to an abundance of Harrington coils.

She didn't carry much in terms of crew or cargo, but the little ship would make it out to Kavitha Zoric and *Fortitude* as fast as anything human-built reasonably could.

"That puts our objectives into four phases, basically," Kira told her people. "The first phase is to clear the blockade, which will be done shortly. The second will be to establish patrols through the zones we expect Colossus to cause trouble in and keep an eye on their activities.

"The third phase will be when they finish refitting the rest of their Brisingr hand-me-downs," she continued. "That will probably be the riskiest, because they'll know what we've got and will likely attempt to concentrate their forces."

"They can't concentrate their forces against us *and* blockade the Samuels System," Cartman pointed out. "That's the whole concept of a fleet in being, after all."

"Exactly," Kira agreed. "Depending on what the Nova Wing does with their ships, we may attempt to defeat them in detail, or potentially, depending on how many ships they bring up at once, we may even accept the fleet battle they are near-certain to court."

She didn't think that was going to be a *good* idea, but it would be even numbers on cruisers and carriers, and hers were bigger. The destroyers and other escorts would tip the balance, though, and she'd prefer a fleet battle to come after reducing the escorts one way or another.

"The final phase is when *Fortitude* and our destroyers arrive," Kira concluded. "At that point, we will use our local superiority to engage in counter-force operations against Colossus, reducing the CNW until their government is prepared to negotiate with Samuels.

"The Samuels government is concerned that there is an additional third party behind the delivery of even obsolete warships to Colossus," she told her people. "Given our own history, my concerns are directed at different targets than theirs...but the fundamental long-term risk is the same."

"Whether it's Equilibrium or Brisingr themselves behind this, we're still most likely to see Brisingr ships deployed to finish the job," Konrad Bueller warned. "If it's an actual *Brisingr* operation, I suspect the Kaiser will order more ships in than he would to help Equilibrium.

"We don't know, after all, just what hold the Institute has on my home system."

"Money," Mwangi said bluntly. "Any nation at war needs it, and Equilibrium has it. I wouldn't be surprised if the Kaiser still regards Brisingr as being at war as they try to secure an entire sector of the Rim."

"Either way, the fourth phase of our operations here is primarily to play security blanket until the Samuels System has enough of a home-built nova force to secure their own trade routes," Kira told her people. "They have the industry, the technology and the wealth to do so. Unfortunately, so does Colossus.

"The long-term astro-political ramifications of an arms race between these two systems are ugly, but they're also outside our control," she admitted. "Our job, in all of the phases I've gone through, is to maintain open passage to and from the Samuels System for the carrying trade that supports their economy.

"We will maintain those trade routes until Samuels is either capable of doing so themselves or otherwise decides our contract is no longer necessary. This is not a retainer contract, people, and active patrols and other activities will be required—but I do hope that by being a fleet in being for Samuels, we can bring Colossus to the negotiating table sooner rather than later.

"Right now, however, we know one of the three access points to the Samuels System is blockaded by the Nova Wing. Conveniently, it would also help my plans for the third phase of this mess if the N-Forty-Five carrier doing said blockading ceased to be a problem."

No one had raised any concerns yet, and the clock was ticking down until they were ready to nova.

"I believe, my friends, that it's time to go hunting."

22

"Nova."

The world flickered around Kira as she double-checked her links. She was beginning to understand some of the problems with not having a flag-deck crew—not least that it felt weirdly lonely in the empty space, even with the holographic link to the bridge.

There were half a dozen stations around the big holotank at the center of the flag deck, but all of them were empty. Several were completely covered by the illusory merge with the bridge. If Kira had had people at them, those people would have been available to answer her questions without being focused on the minute-to-minute combat operations of the heavy cruiser.

Of course, if she was being honest, *Fortitude*'s flag deck was almost four times the size of *Deception*'s. The K70-class cruiser's flag facilities were very much an afterthought, where the Crest-built *Fortitude* had been designed from the keel out to be one of the flagships of the Navy of the Royal Crest.

She *should* be commanding Memorial Force from the flag deck of the supercarrier. Instead, she was on *Deception* for personal reasons—well, those and the fact that she'd lost the coin toss with Zoric.

Right now, Kavitha Zoric had the supercarrier and the bigger contract. Kira got to spend time with her boyfriend. It had seemed a fair enough deal, though the contract with Samuels was expanding on them.

"Scopes are clear of hostiles," Soler's hologram reported crisply. "I have a cluster of transports at sixty-five by ninety-three, eighty-two light-seconds. No other contacts. No warships or fighters."

"Well, that's not what we were expecting, was it?" Kira murmured. "No sign of *N45-K*?"

"Nothing," the Tactical officer confirmed.

"They may have recognized the blockade was broken and abandoned the whole affair until they had reinforcements," Mwangi suggested. "They lost their only active cruiser and half their destroyers. *N45-K*'s CO could have chosen to withdraw while they still *had* a carrier and two destroyers."

"It would probably even be the right call," Bueller said. "I'm not sure I've met many officers I'd trust to *make* that call, but from everything we know of the situation..."

"From *my* perspective, it's a pain," Kira told them. "But Bueller is right. Given that we expected to roll over her and her escorts in a single fight, the carrier-group CO had every chance to recognize the same balance of forces.

"Those three ships will be worth more to Colossus in two months when they have the rest of the fleet than they would be right now in a battle all of us can fight in our heads."

She shook her head.

"That said, *I'd* have laid a trap," she admitted wryly. "So, let's get the fighters into space and send a squadron of Wolverines to check on those freighters. If everything is as it appears, we just waste some fuel that Samuels has already agreed to pay for."

"And if they're playing silly buggers, we can lure them out and kick their asses rather than getting hit by surprise," Mwangi agreed. "Cartman?"

"I'll take the recon squad out myself," Nightmare said instantly.

"Puts a senior, maybe even wiser, head on the scene rather than waiting three minutes for an answer."

"Agreed," Kira said after a moment's thought. "Be prepared for surprises. I don't *think* the Nova Wing is good enough to pull the wool over our eyes, but I've *been* underestimated too many times to want to get into the habit!"

KIRA WATCHED Nightmare's *Deception*-Alpha squadron bear down on the cluster of merchant ships with an edge of nervousness. She'd seen this kind of post-blockade cleanup operation go very, *very* badly in the past—and their only fatality so far on this particular contract had been in *exactly* this situation.

The six Wolverine interceptors were over eighty light-seconds away, which meant that everything Kira was seeing was almost a minute and a half out of date. Given the sixty-second cooldown on the nova drives after this short a jump, in theory she should have already seen them retreat if things had gone obviously wrong.

Or, of course, all of her people could already be dead. Lightspeed delays did not help Kira's nerves.

"All contacts are showing dead in the water," Cartman's voice reported. The transmission was just as old as the light they were receiving. "I'm reading zero Jianhong radiation across all contacts. Their nova drives are either off-line or missing.

"Power, heat and gravity signatures are...weak but live," she continued after a moment. "I'd say primary power is off-line on all eleven ships. No Harringtons, no fusion plants—but I think I've got active grav plants and secondary power sources.

"No active sensors or coms. We are continuing our approach and watching for new contacts."

There was nothing to stop Nightmare from simply vaporizing the eleven freighters the CNW had left behind. There was, equally, no *point* to the pilots doing any such thing. No hostile contacts, no charged weapons. Only the silence of half-dead ships.

"Freighters are a mix, about what I'd expect for this section of the Rim," Soler reported. "Two eighty-kilocubic haulers, five in the forty-to-sixty range, one twenty-kilocubic fast packet and three ten-kilocubic tramps."

The basic ten-kilocubic nova-capable hull only really had one virtue, in Kira's opinion: it was cheap and any society with the standard colonial database could build it. The ancient term "tramp freighter" had been quickly resurrected for the vast numbers of cheap freighters hauling whatever small cargo they could find that underlay the interstellar economy.

"We have no coms with anyone," Cartman continued. "I don't think I've seen this before, but I'm not sure there's any threat here."

"Commander Bueller?" Kira queried her boyfriend, her attempt at professionalism probably undermined by the fact that everyone *knew* he was her boyfriend—but necessary for the task regardless.

"It looks like they activated the hardware lockouts on the fusion cores before they left," Bueller replied thoughtfully. "They're designed as a safety measure for when ships are being built and refitted.

"Even with all of the access codes and authorizations, it can take as much as twelve hours to reactivate a locked-out fusion plant," he told her. "Assuming the CNW reset all of those codes...even the best engineering teams are looking at twenty-four hours, easy, to get the power plant back online.

"That's part of why the secondary power generators *can't* be locked down like that," he continued. "To make sure there's life support and such if someone pulls *exactly* this kind of shit."

"So, what are we looking at?" Kira asked. "Can we speed that up?"

"Maybe," Bueller replied. "But most likely we're looking at three days or so before any of them can nova."

"And no sign of the Nova Wing," she noted. "All right. Davidović, Mwangi—get us moving toward the freighters.

"Keep the guns online and the fighters up for now. We'll stand down to a lower security level once we've made contacts with the crews, but for now we'll stand watch. I can't help feeling that these bastards have another arrow in their quiver."

IF THERE WAS another shoe to drop, it was still hanging when the two capital ships settled in near the cluster of impounded freighters and Milani's shuttles started moving people around.

After that, the details began to fall into place with speed.

"They up and left about a day before you arrived," the Captain of one of the large haulers told Kira. Yoshi Sakata was an elderly man of Japanese extraction, with thinning white hair crowning fiercely sharp eyes.

"A handful of nova fighters appeared, and they started to become agitated," Captain Sakata continued. "We all had a few soldiers aboard, but up to that point, things were..."

He pursed his lips as he sought a word.

"Polite-ish?" he concluded. "We were under their guns and we were definitely prisoners, but they'd interned *everybody* heading to Samuels from the Apollo-Brisingr Sector. There are rules for handling neutrals when you do that, I suppose."

"Expectations, at least," Kira told him. She was appearing to the merchant captain as a hologram projected by Milani's suit, allowing them to have a conversation despite her never leaving *Deception*.

"Indeed. Once those fighters arrived, though, there was about a day where they were quite agitated. Then a Commodore Vanessa Rivers got on the radio with everyone and told us she was releasing us all on the condition that we not nova to Samuels for at least seventy-two hours...and that she was going to *guarantee* that we kept that condition."

"Her people locked out your power plants," Kira concluded, based on Konrad's guess.

"Exactly." Sakata shrugged. "She had a pocket carrier group. I have an eighty-kilocubic freighter with a pair of light guns to discourage pirates. Whatever her techs wanted to do on my ship, we couldn't stop them."

"And everyone else was in the same boat," Kira said. "Did you get a good look at what this 'pocket carrier group' consisted of?"

Sakata smiled.

"I may have, I may have," he observed. "But that seems like it would have some worth to everyone, wouldn't it? I have to fly the Corridor, Admiral, no matter what happens in this little tiff.

"If I'm going to irritate a star system government that I have to work with, it should probably be worth my while, don't you think?"

Kira sighed. The Admiral of a mercenary fleet had no legs to stand on when complaining about *other* people being mercenary.

"Fine," she told him. "Name your price."

Sakata had clearly been expecting at least a bit more pushback and had to think for a moment. Kira, on the other hand, knew that *Samuels* was on the hook for anything she had to pay him.

"One hundred thousand Samuels pounds," he finally said.

"Done." Kira glanced over at the holographic link to *Deception*'s bridge. "Smolak, make the transfer."

The coms officer flashed her a thumbs-up, marking it as done.

"A pleasure to do business with someone reasonable," Sakata told her. "*Shinohara*'s sensors are nothing special, I must admit, Admiral, but I will forward you our full scan information on everything we saw of the carrier group.

"We saw a carrier and two destroyers here, though there was also a cruiser present when we arrived," he noted. "She jumped away after we were interned.

"We were *instructed* to shut down our sensors, but, frankly, *Shinohara* doesn't have any active sensors except close-range collision radar," Sakata said. "Running our passive receivers is undetectable and, I hoped, might be of use to someone.

"While Commodore Rivers was perfectly polite and operated her force entirely within the letter and the spirit of those 'expectations' you mentioned, some of her people were significantly ruder...and the whole affair leaves a sour taste in one's mouth, yes?"

"So it does," Kira murmured. "Send us the data, Captain Sakata. What we do with it after that isn't your problem or your responsibility, is it?"

He bowed over his hands.

"May fortune favor you, Admiral."

23

Both capital ships hung somewhat protectively over the interned warships as technicians worked to undo the damage that Commodore Rivers had done to the civilian ships.

All thirteen ships, and the defensive shell of five squadrons of nova fighters, gleamed on the holodisplay in *Deception*'s main conference room as Kira considered the situation.

"Konrad, how long until we can take these people with us to Samuels?" she asked.

"All of them had been working on the lockouts," he replied. "But we have both hardware and software most civilians would not. We'll complete nova cooldown in about twelve hours, and we'll have most of their power cores online by then.

"It'll be a few more hours after that before anyone is ready to nova. If we want to wait until everyone is ready...thirty-six hours is my outside estimate."

"There's no need for us to rush," Kira told him, glancing around at the CNGs and Captains in the meeting. "It seems pretty clear that this Commodore Rivers isn't likely to return. We still want to be prepared for some kind of trap, but it seems she decided to play it safe."

"Not many officers would have the moral courage to order a blockade collapsed on their own authority," Davidović said quietly. "Even in RRF service, a withdrawal like this would draw a lot of attention.

"It's the right call, I agree with you, but we're her enemies. Her superiors may think differently."

"They might," Mwangi agreed. "And the Nova Wing will be poorer for it, from the sounds of it. Speaking as someone who expects to *fight* the Colossus Nova Wing in the future, I rather hope they *do* relieve her."

Kira snorted.

"We wish our enemies the worst of the superiors we've had ourselves," she said aloud. A mental command moved the current map of the area to the side, and a hologram of a squat, pale woman with oddly bulging eyes appeared above the table.

"Our intelligence files from Samuels include a surprising amount of information on Commodore Vanessa Rivers," Kira noted. "She's sixty-three standard years old and has served in the Colossus Defense Forces since her eighteenth birthday. She was a nova-fighter pilot for twenty-two years, then moved to command first one sublight monitor, then a division of three monitors.

"She then vanished from the records that our employers have access to," Kira continued. "My guess is that she was slated to command one or both of the converted carriers that became their depot ships.

"My read of the Samuels file on her is that she is probably Colossus's premier nova-fighter tactician. They cared enough to send their best—and their best was smart enough not to pick a fight she didn't think she could win."

"She'll be back," Mwangi said, grimly studying the woman's image. "Somehow, I doubt their first carrier-group commander lacks the political connections to survive whatever fallout will come from her quite rational decision to retreat."

"I agree," Davidović said. "They've got another carrier, a cruiser, four more destroyers and half a dozen corvettes coming online? We barely dented their true strength, though I doubt *they're* feeling that way."

"They're almost certainly feeling quite bruised at the moment," Cartman agreed. "But if most of their nova-qualified officers are former fighter pilots...finding even *one* willing to retreat is a small miracle."

"Are you implying something about former fighter pilots?" Kira asked sunnily.

"We both met the type in ASDF service," her friend pointed out. "And you're not as out of the target as you'd like to pretend, either. Who was it who tagged along on a destroyer patrol because she was bored?"

"That was me, yes," Kira conceded. "And I've heard the lecture a dozen times." She shook her head and glanced at the rest of the officers.

"I think we all know what kind of officer Cartman is talking about," she agreed. "And, yes, I'm of the type myself, though I like to think I'm not *senselessly* aggressive.

"We need to factor that into our planning. Their ship COs are either ex–fighter squadron COs or ex–monitor COs, after all. Or, like Commodore Rivers...both."

"That's a hell of a split personality they'll have at an organizational level," Mwangi said. "Monitor commanders who've run ship with large crews before but never had access to a nova drive at all, mixed with nova-fighter commanders who've only run a formation of maybe two dozen people before and have almost no experience handling enlisted or noncommissioned personnel in the numbers a starship commander has to."

"Every new nova fleet in the history of mankind has gone through at least one of those," Kira said. "And all of them survived. I'd worry about the same problem in Samuels, except that Samuels doesn't *have* monitors."

Monitors were heavily armed sublight ships, often assembled from asteroids in a way that lent itself poorly to vessels on a nova-drive scale. The more mobile part of the defenses that made inhabited star systems generally impregnable, they were still far too large to ever nova.

Colossus's defenses included over a hundred of them, providing a ready reservoir of experienced officers and crews that lacked only nova experience. Samuels, however, had predicated their entire system defense around large, mostly immobile asteroid fortresses.

Kira had never actually seen a star system's defenses tested, so she had no idea which method made more sense. Certainly, Samuels's defenses were more limited in the areas they covered—but, on the other hand, no sublight force could move around a system fast enough to provide mobile defense against a nova-drive attacker.

Asteroid fortresses could render sections of the system untouchable, but the general assessment was that you needed nova ships of your own to prevent a so-called "close blockade," where your enemies started nabbing ships *in* your star system.

Colossus hadn't had quite that much nerve yet, probably discouraged by the fact that Samuels did field several hundred nova fighters.

"Samuels will deal with building their fleet on their own," Kira continued. "Bueller has agreed to help them on a contract basis." She grinned. "He's got to be getting used to that!"

"Not what I expected when I defected to a mercenary company, I have to admit," he replied. "You do remember that I ended up on *K79-L* because I wanted to get *away* from a desk job as a design engineer, yes?"

"I have faith in your patience," she told him. "Building the fleet isn't really our problem. Protecting Samuels until that fleet is online is.

"We need to make sure that we're ready and able to deflect any attempt to reimpose the blockade," she continued. "That also requires intelligence and recon—including of Colossus itself.

"We need a plan for maintaining a defensive perimeter around Samuels and for getting eyes into Colossus, on at least an occasional basis."

Kira looked around her people.

"I have a few thoughts on both points," she said. "Standard Apollon tactics, in both cases, call for corvettes for those missions. Since we don't *have* any of those, I'm going to open the floor for suggestions."

24

Kanchenjunga Fortress was the centerpiece of Samuels's defenses, an eleven-kilometer-wide asteroid fortress bristling with over a thousand heavy-cannon turrets. Against its bulk, *Deception* and *Huntress* were toys.

Like many asteroid fortresses, Kanchenjunga acted as a counterweight to an orbital elevator. A civilian station hung at geostationary orbit, underneath the battle station's protective umbrella.

Anchored on the elevator cable between the civilian station and the fortress, Samuels's new nova-warship yards were taking shape. The yards added another layer of traffic to an already-busy portion of Bennet's orbital space.

From *Deception*'s flag deck, Kira could track every individual shuttle, in-system transport and work pod. Hundreds of pale green tracks flickered across the background of her mental view.

"Your call is incoming, boss," Smolak told her. "An Em Batsal Tapadia?"

"Mr. Tapadia, as Samuels classes things," Kira observed, but it wasn't even a correction. Even she was a bit confused by having different honorifics for different people. Only unmarried people used

Em there, where Kira was used to that being the standard for everyone without a formal title.

"Right," the coms officer confirmed. "Director of Space Operations, Samuels-Tata Technologies. I'm guessing the man behind our shipyards over there?"

"I hope so," Kira said drily. "Or the wrong person is calling. Put him through."

The holoprojectors on the flag deck flickered and formed an image of an unfamiliar man. Like his spouse, Batsal Tapadia clearly spent a good chunk of his spare time in a gym. Unlike Buxton, Tapadia didn't have towering height to go with his broad shoulders and barrel-like muscled torso, resulting in a more pug-ish impression.

The dark-skinned businessman's smile was wide and felt genuine as he bowed to Kira.

"Em Demirci, I appreciate you taking my call," he told her.

"The request did come from the First Minister's office," she said drily. "My current employer, until the contract runs out."

"I know, but I suspect you will shortly find yourself besieged with calls," Tapadia warned. "If you aren't already. There are parties being thrown in your honor, and people will want you to attend them *all*."

"I will have to attend some of them," Kira admitted. "That's the nature of the game. But I also need to prioritize the actual *job*, Mr. Tapadia, which means talking to the shipbuilders and soldiers.

"And, strangely, no one has actually put me in touch with Samuels Defense Command."

Tapadia chuckled sadly.

"That is on us," he conceded. "And mostly due to an unrelated tragedy: General Rajesh Nibhanupudi was in hospital when you were visiting the First Minister and, unfortunately, passed away shortly before your ships novaed out to clear the blockade.

"Which of the SDC's handful of junior flag officers will replace him is currently being discussed—but who their senior civilian contractor is, on the other hand, won't change." Tapadia shrugged.

"So, they asked me to talk to you to open up at least some channels of conversation."

"My condolences. What happened to the General?" Kira asked. Given some of the players in her affairs, she was always worried by unusual deaths. Her old Apollon CO had died of a "brain aneurysm" that had been anything but.

"Heart attack," Tapadia said. "My understanding is that his wife called an ambulance and they got to him in time to save him from the first one...and then he had another one in hospital, and the doctors couldn't keep him going long enough for a replacement to be implanted."

"Despite all of our knowledge, the human body is still a fragile thing," Kira said. Almost anything could be cured, given time, medicine or even cybernetic replacements—Kira herself, for example, had a rare and deadly blood disorder managed by an implant on her spleen—but *time* was key.

"Agreed. And the human political structure even more so," the businessman said drily. "In a perfect world, General Nibhanupudi's successor would have been known before he died. We do not live in a perfect world, and we have sixteen junior flag officers in the SDC."

He shrugged.

"Four of the Commodores and two of the Brigadiers are in the running to replace him," he continued. "Buxton could just pick one, but tradition says the flag officers agree on a candidate and present them to the First Minister unanimously."

"Sounds like a peacetime promotion mechanism," Kira pointed out. She could see the value—but it also called for a degree of negotiating and discussion that was going to take time. Time in which the SDC wasn't going to have anyone who could actually work with her.

"I need someone to communicate with, Mr. Tapadia," she told him. "*Today*. Not in six weeks. Not in three months, when Colossus reestablishes their blockade and you *still* don't have nova ships of your own.

"SDC has nova fighters, at the very least," she continued. "I need to know the full extent of their resources. I need to be able to *coordinate* with those resources."

She shook her head.

"It is not my place to tell my employer what to do," she said. "But I would strongly recommend that the First Minister does just 'pick one,' as you put it. While we have bought Samuels breathing room, you remain at war."

"I know," Tapadia murmured. "But we are not..." He shook his head. "You understand, Admiral, that our military is drawn almost entirely from a handful of regional subcultures, yes?"

"Macey and Buxton explained that to me, yes," Kira said. "I'm not sure I see your point. You are...Gorkhali, wasn't it?...yourself, correct?"

"I am," Tapadia confirmed. "Culturally, at least. My family joined the Interstellar Society of Friends several generations ago, and I am, personally, a pacifist like most Quakers." He smiled.

"I am also, like many historical members of assorted iterations of the Society, a pragmatist and a businessman. The construction of a defensive fleet is absolutely critical to the survival of Samuels in our current form, so I have taken on that task for my employer and the government of my system."

"And the fact that it's a massive contract offered by your spouse..." Kira let that hang.

"Both Buxton and I completely recused ourselves from both the decision-making and the negotiations around this contract," Tapadia said calmly. "But I was the best candidate to lead the construction project itself."

"Fair enough," Kira replied. "My apologies."

"Unnecessary. It was a legitimate concern." He made a dismissive gesture. "But as to my point, Admiral, the fact that the SDC is the primary...cultural touchpoint, let's say, for a number of cultures and regions that are otherwise sufficiently minor to be considered unorthodox creates certain pressures on the Ministries to be more hands-off than is perhaps wise.

"The First Minister and the civilian government are unquestionably *in charge* of the SDC, but it is often allowed to choose a lot of its own leadership and protocols. For the Minister to pick a leader for the Defense Command without the consent of the rest of the flag officers would be seen as an imposition by the majority populace on what is, bluntly, effectively a military caste."

She sighed.

"I'm not responsible for your internal politics, demographics or crises," she warned. "I *am* responsible for defending your system against the Colossus Nova Wing, a task for which I *need* the SDC's assistance."

"And that is why I am in contact with you," Tapadia told her. "While it would be inappropriate for, say, the commanding officer of the SDC's Nova Fighter Division to have a one-on-one meeting with you while she is merely one candidate for the command of the SDC... there is nothing inappropriate about me inviting you to a private dinner at my quarters aboard Kanchenjunga Fortress."

"To which said commanding officer may be invited?" Kira asked acerbically.

"Among others," the local said calmly. "Frankly, Commodore Mahinder Bachchan *is* the most likely candidate to succeed Nibhanupudi. Commodore Devdas D'Cruze and Commodore Apurva Rao will also both join us."

Kira raised an eyebrow.

"Commodore D'Cruze commands Kanchenjunga Fortress itself. Commodore Rao commands Everest Fortress, the second-largest defensive citadel. Commodore Maus, the CO of Fortress Division Haven, is the fourth candidate for command of the SDC from the spaceborne forces—but is, of course, currently at Haven and approximately eighteen hours' flight away."

Tapadia shrugged.

"I advised Eugene of the meeting and he laughed at the invite," the businessman noted. "While I cannot officially promise that any discussions around the capabilities of the SDC's Nova Fighter Division will take place... Well, I suspect if I put that many soldiers in a room, some shop talk will happen inevitably."

Kira sighed. It was a good thing she'd made sure to have a spare dress uniform tunic with her aboard *Deception*. It sounded like she was going to be spending even *more* time at parties than she thought, if there wouldn't be an official link with the SDC for a few weeks.

"Should I bring a date?" she asked.

"Please, the Commodores are bringing their partners," Tapadia confirmed. "Sadly, I will not—Buxton is a bit too busy to nip into space for dinner—but I would suggest you bring your partner and perhaps one of your ship Captains?"

"I'll discuss it with my people," Kira told him. "And then I will see you for dinner, Mr. Tapadia."

"Thank you, Admiral. I know this is a pain, but tradition and the balance of power between our cultures is critical to Samuels." He smiled. "Your patience is appreciated."

"My patience, Mr. Tapadia, is *expensive*," she replied. "But you are already paying for it, I suppose."

25

Kira had spent a lot of time on asteroid fortresses of various vintages and designers. They all shared certain features—they all started by taking a natural nickel-iron asteroid and hitting it with carefully calibrated heat in the form of plasma blasts and lasers while spinning them.

The result tended toward rough ovoid shapes with a massive cavern in the center. Redward's fortresses, for example, had basically stopped there. Holes had been cut into the asteroids to allow access to the central core and mount turrets, but most of the actual "station" was concealed behind a kilometer or so of natural armor.

Samuels Defense Command, on the other hand, had taken that rough ovoid shape and applied further heat and carving lasers, smoothing the surface down to clearly artificial featureless plains. They'd later used those exterior plains as the medium for immense murals of the Earth mountains the stations were named for, large enough to be seen some distance away by approaching ships.

The same boring lasers had opened up large landing bays—covered by twenty-meter-thick armor of their own—as well as hundreds of channels now filled with power cables, plasma conduits and personnel tramways.

Apollon fortresses went for a similar "built from an asteroid" rather than "guns mounted on an asteroid" esthetic, so the SDC forts looked vaguely *right* to Kira in a way few of the stations she'd seen in the last few years had.

Her home system, though, shared one tendency with Redward: they built structures on the surface of the asteroid fortresses. Academies, residences, observation domes—while the designers accepted that anything on the surface except the heavy-cannon turrets was inherently expendable in the event of an actual conflict, they were disinclined to let that surface area go to waste.

The SDC, with the sole exception of the large hangars like the one she was landing her shuttle in, had not. The surface of Kanchenjunga Fortress was an expanse of laser-carved steel marked only by the identifying mural.

Even the heavily armored turrets that provided the fort's armament were smoothed into the armored and painted plains. On an Apollon fortress, those plains would provide the base for a city of skyscrapers.

Here, only the open hatch of her immediate destination was visible. Beneath it, a hangar bay that wouldn't have looked out of place in a planetary surface starport spread out, with atmosphere shields holding the air in place as Kira brought the shuttle in for a careful landing.

"Huh. They actually have security here," Bueller commented from the copilot's seat. Between her two starship Captains and the engineer, her boyfriend was the most qualified to back Kira up in that role.

He wasn't actually *qualified* to be a copilot. Simply more so than Mwangi or Akuchi, neither of whom had ever helmed anything less than a hundred meters long.

"Light defensive turrets just outside the hatch, and looks like a pair inside," Kira agreed approvingly. "Of course, the hatch itself is the main security. Not much is getting through that without causing trouble."

"I was mostly thinking about the fact that there's actually soldiers out there," Bueller pointed out, indicating the roughly two dozen armored troopers scattered around the landing bay. "Not enough, I don't think, but I didn't see *anybody* armed on the surface."

"This is Samuels's shield," Kira told him. "Culturally and professionally different from her bureaucratic heart. I'd hope there'd be *somebody* armed around."

"Because Milani didn't have a fit at being left behind," her boyfriend muttered.

"Even they recognize that we need to trust *some* people," she said. "Plus, I can't think of anywhere safer in the area than aboard the largest battle fortress between here and Colossus."

"Oh, I know," he agreed. He unstrapped the safety harness. "Shall we collect the Captains and get to work?"

"Remember that you are supposed to be working directly with Tapadia going forward," Kira told him. "He's responsible for their shipbuilding, even if I doubt he's hands-on enough to be buried in the designs."

"At least I know who I have to work with. As I understand it, we're only meeting *some* of the potential new commander in chiefs?"

"The commander in chief is Buxton," Kira noted. "But yes. One of about seven people gets the big hat when the dust settles, but we're only meeting with three of them." She sighed and shook her head. "But one of those two commands their nova forces, which means they're the most relevant person to *us* no matter what happens."

AN EAGER GUIDE in a sharp-creased white uniform led the four mercenaries through a series of elevators and trams that eventually delivered them to an open lobby that looked like it belonged in a luxury hotel, not a heavily armored fortress.

Soft carpet and gorgeous abstract murals covered the floors and walls, with a dropped ceiling concealing the necessary fixtures of life aboard a space station. Soft hues of natural greens and browns brought a sense of walking into a forest or field.

Kira had only a moment to appreciate it before Commodore Mahinder Bachchan approached them. Bachchan was a towering woman that Kira could only describe as statuesque, with tanned skin and waist-length hair twisted into a tight braid.

She wore the same sharp-creased dress uniform as the young officer who had delivered them, with three gold circles on the left side of the uniform's high collar—and, unless Kira missed her guess, was wearing a military-grade shipsuit under the uniform.

Many of the people she'd seen on the station had been wearing dress or undress uniforms *without* the safety gear underneath, something Kira would never have tolerated aboard any vessel or fortress under *her* authority.

The SDC was not the ASDF or Memorial Force, though. The war with Brisingr had been large enough and culture-shaping enough for Apollo that she doubted anyone would even assume the home front was safe for a while yet.

Samuels, on the other hand, had never even had to *consider* the possibility of actually being attacked or facing a military threat until very recently. It wasn't Kira's place to speak to their defenses or their military culture—for their home-system defenses, at least.

"Admiral Demirci," Bachchan greeted her. "It is a pleasure to finally make your acquaintance. Our dinner is this way."

She gestured toward a set of double doors leading off from the lobby. A pair of armored SDC military police flanked the doors, looming at anyone who came near them.

"What is this place?" Kira asked. "It looks like a hotel."

"Because it is," Bachchan replied. "The Kanchenjunga Pahilō Hōṭala. We have enough civilians and dignitaries come through that it's necessary to have a place that lives up to their expectations."

She shrugged.

"The Pahilō Hōṭala is based out of the Nepali-majority regions of the surface and was delighted to lease space on our key platforms to provide a service that was outside the scope of the SDC's resources. And when people like Mr. Tapadia visit, it's always in our interests to keep them...content."

Kira didn't see any safe response to that as she followed the Samuels officer into the dining room. The space was just as luxuriously decorated as the hotel lobby, though practicality had intruded into a space that could clearly just as easily serve as an addition to the hotel restaurant.

There was a large central table, but several taller ones had been set up around the edges to allow mingling. Half a dozen people, all tall and with the dark-skinned features Kira was starting to associate with Samuels's Gorkhali minority, were standing and talking quietly.

Between her own companions and the average height of SDC's senior officers, she was feeling particularly small. Knowing her own bad habits, that meant she had to watch herself and make sure she didn't get *too* aggressive.

Bachchan walked over to one of the women, who was wearing a body-hugging red sheath dress that showed off her legs. Embracing her, she gave the woman a kiss and then gestured toward Kira.

"Admiral Demirci, this is my wife, Mrs. Chimini Bachchan," she introduced her partner. "You know Mr. Tapadia, of course." She gestured toward the businessman as he joined them.

"Please, Admiral, allow me to introduce you to my other guests," Tapadia said. He bowed to the Bachchans. "Thank you for finding them, Commodore."

He smiled.

"Remember, we aren't here to work tonight."

"Bullshit," Commodore Bachchan said flatly to an amused giggle from her wife. "We're here to sort out what the Admiral needs to defend our star system in a way that's politically acceptable while us flag officers hash out who gets to be in charge.

"Rao and D'Cruze both know that." She chuckled. "I'd be stunned if there's a flag officer in the star system who doesn't know what this dinner is about, Mr. Tapadia. But you've done what you needed to cover the tracks.

"The SDC will behave. We promise."

26

KIRA DIDN'T KNOW MUCH about Samuels or Gorkhali cuisine, but if the food served at dinner was any example, she suspected that *Samuels*'s Gorkhali population spent a great deal of time with sheep. Much like her own branch of Apollon cultural cuisine, it was focused on turning mutton into something more edible.

And the chefs at the high-quality hotel the SDC had installed in their command fortress were experts at their trade. The food was amazing, and the Commodores and their spouses proved to be excellent company.

Still, everyone was clearly waiting for the end of the meal. When the dessert plates were cleared away and the hotel staff brought out carafes of a harshly brewed black tea Kira was unfamiliar with, it was clear that the real work was about to begin.

"Admiral," Bachchan addressed her, the Samuels Commodore leaning back in her chair. "I assume everyone has explained to you the politics that resulted in tonight's particular arrangements?"

"Mr. Tapadia gave me the rundown," Kira agreed. "Only about half of the people who might end up as the commander of the SDC are in this room, and even you don't know which of you is going to get the job. Do I have it roughly summarized?"

The three Commodores shared glances, but Bachchan simply nodded.

"For reference, there are eight Commodores and eight Brigadiers in the Samuels Defense Command," she noted. "While Commodores D'Cruze and Rao are first and foremost the commanding officers of their battle stations, each is also responsible for a division of three other orbital fortresses above Bennet.

"There are three junior commodores who each command a division of two smaller fortresses making up the rest of the Samuels defensive fortifications," Bachchan continued.

"Two more Commodores, Maus and Horáček, each command a larger division above one of our gas giants. The SDC also hold responsibility for what limited army forces we have, a standing emergency security and support force of eight brigades and approximately sixty thousand uniformed personnel."

Bachchan spread her hands.

"While there are nova-fighter wings positioned on each orbital fortress, I hold overall authority on our nova-fighter force," she noted. "General Nibhanupudi and I had an...*ongoing* discussion over where the nova warships would fall in our existing structures."

She looked at the other officers and Tapadia.

"Anyone have anything to add to that summary?" she asked.

"Not truly," D'Cruze replied. "At the end of the day, Admiral Demirci, we are here to answer *your* questions. Our training, organizational structure, even our resources and equipment, are based around a defense of Samuels that we mostly regarded as theoretical.

"Even with the beginning of a nova fleet, the SDC represents barely one percent of the system domestic product. While the officers of the SDC are hardly pacifists, we serve a culture that holds pacifism as one part of true enlightenment.

"That impacts us," he conceded. "And more importantly, it impacts the political objectives of the government we serve. The

SDC exists to protect Samuels itself from a direct attack. We never expected and were never equipped to secure trade routes that had never come under attack!"

"Hence my people being here," Kira told them. She considered the people at the table and glanced over at her starship Captains.

"For the mission we face, officers, the only vessels and resources that are relevant are those that are capable of reaching the trade routes," she noted. "If it can't nova, it's not part of the equation. Colossus will never have the strength to challenge Samuels's defenses."

Rao and D'Cruze—both tall, dark men who could have passed for cousins, if not brothers—exchanged a long, long look. Then D'Cruze gestured to Bachchan.

"You were right," he told her. "I was starting to figure that, anyway, but hearing Admiral Demirci put it that way does put it in perspective, doesn't it?"

He turned back to Kira.

"We need to maintain our defenses to keep that true, but when was the last time you know of that a star system was actually attacked?" he asked.

"The *only* situation I'm aware of was the mess in Ypres in the Syntactic Cluster," Kira told them. "And that situation was complicated by the fact that Ypres was internally divided and had significant sublight fleets. A handful of more-modern nova ships were enough to destabilize the balance of power, but the real weight of the battle was expected to be carried by the monitor squadrons."

In the end, that battle hadn't happened the way anyone had expected—not least because one of those "more-modern nova ships" had been captured by one Kira Demirci and transformed into *Deception*.

"In general, strategic and operational doctrine for every nation I am aware of takes the logic that even a small number of asteroid forts of comparable technology level renders a star system impregnable to nova attack," she said. "While a nova fleet could be in the Samuels

System outside the range of the SDC's fortresses, it would take dozens or even hundreds of nova capital ships to match the firepower of a *single* fort.

"I have never heard of a star system being attacked and taken," she concluded. "Maintaining a solid level of home defense when faced with a threat like Colossus is necessary, as you said. But...this conflict, like most I know of, is being fought over trade routes and discharge spots.

"Which means it will be fought by nova ships far beyond the reach of your fortresses."

"Which means you need to know what nova ships we have," Rao said. "And that it is more important that you work with our nova-force officers than our fortress commands and ground forces."

Kira knew that question carried more weight than the immediately obvious and that she was being asked, however indirectly, to comment on the political shenanigans that would decide the next head of the SDC.

But the question wasn't one she could avoid.

"That is correct, yes," she confirmed.

Bachchan didn't say anything, but she looked...vindicated.

"We'll talk to people tomorrow, Bachchan," D'Cruze said calmly. "But that does clarify many things and may make this process shorter. For the moment, though...what do you need to know, Admiral Demirci?"

Kira was reasonably sure she'd followed the undertone. It sounded to her like D'Cruze and Rao were going to drop their own campaigns for the leadership of the SDC and throw their influence behind Bachchan, since the Nova Fighter Division CO was the best-qualified officer they had for the task at hand.

It was what *Kira* would prefer, she suspected, but she did *not* need to get involved in her employer's politics.

"I need to know more about what your nova fighters' capabilities are and how many of them you have," she told them. "And then I need to know what other nova ships you have and if you have any, say, carrier conversions under discussion."

"We have at least a twelve-plane squadron of nova fighters on every fortress," Bachchan said instantly. "Several of the larger fortresses have extra squadrons aboard, and we have several more squadrons located at a base on Bennet's moon.

"All told, the NFD musters thirty twelve-plane squadrons. Three hundred and sixty nova fighters, all of our own Guardian design."

Tapadia concealed a cough.

"The Guardian design may...not be *quite* as home-built as Samuels-Tata Technologies likes to claim," he murmured. "The current Guardian-Three design is almost entirely unique to us, but the original Guardian was based on an *acquired* copy of the Apollo Phalanx-Three heavy fighter."

"Send me the current schematics," Kira asked. "I am hardly concerned about a thirty-year-old counterintelligence failure on the part of my former government."

"That is fair," Tapadia conceded. A gesture tossed her a pair of schematics.

Kira passed them on to her companions and examined them in a virtual space in front of herself. The Guardian-Two and Guardian-Three designs were decent heavy fighters, she concluded. She could see the Phalanx heritage in their design in several places, but they also had a good bit of the Colossus's Liberator in their DNA.

Big, heavy, expensive planes with dual torpedoes and heavy guns. Designed to be able to perform all roles instead of specializing in one, with the newer fighter generally superior in all ways.

"What's the split between the -Twos and the -Threes?" she asked. "I'm presuming you have both still in commission?"

Otherwise, she figured they wouldn't be giving her information on the Guardian-Two at all.

"Two to one," Bachchan said instantly. "Currently, each squadron has two flight groups of Guardian-Twos and a flight group of Guardian-Threes, usually led by the squadron commander. One hundred twenty Guardian-Threes, two hundred forty Guardian-Twos.

"We have no carrier-style spacecraft," she continued. "I'm trying to get authorization from the Ministries to make you an offer for the two depot ships you seized from Colossus, but they're understandably hesitant to buy mediocre ships when we should have real carriers...eventually."

"You also have the consular packets, which can carry nova fighters, correct?" Kira asked.

"Ah, yes, the Macey Industries ships," Tapadia confirmed. "None of those are actually in SDC service. *Springtime Chorus* and *Autumn Songs* serve as consular ships, as you said. We have used their ability to carry nova fighters in the past to provide escort for diplomatic missions, but they are not regularly available to the SDC."

"Might be worth having a conversation with the Ministries on that, though," Kira pointed out. "Each of those three ships can carry the entirety of one of your squadrons of nova fighters."

"I'm not sure I see the need," Bachchan replied. "My fighters can make it to the trade routes easily enough. Takes us longer if we're going farther, but the key blockade points are only a single nova way."

Kira sighed and resisted the urge to bury her face in her hands.

Systems that were second-tier in their own regions—as opposed to on any kind of interstellar scale, by which standard even Apollo and Brisingr were roughly seventh-tier powers—seemed to fall into two categories of mistakes in her growing experience.

The first group never managed, either through lack of tech or lack of will, to acquire the ability to build class two nova drives. They ran their interstellar security with full-size nova ships and a handful of purchased nova fighters, which left them at a distinct disadvantage when running up against people with proper combined-arms forces.

Samuels, it seemed, fell into the second group. They had nova fighters and were only interested in local security, so they saw no need for carriers.

"The problem with that, Commodore Bachchan, is what happens

when your nova fighters make that one jump and engage a Colossus force," Kira said quietly. "Your people's drives will still be cooling down for thirty-six hours, whereas the CNW's fighter will be able to nova every few minutes and fly circles around you.

"You sacrifice your nova fighters' greatest tactical advantage by using their nova drives for operational mobility. It's something that shouldn't be neglected, but the cost of nova fighters jumping long distances on their own is high. Hence, carriers."

There was a long silence in the room. *Her* officers fully understood that problem at the kind of bone-deep level that only years of living it could instill.

Very clearly, a military that had *never fought a war* hadn't quite absorbed that reality.

"I think I may have to repeat that, word for word, when I next argue for the depot ships," Bachchan noted. "I was thinking they would be useful—but I now think they may be *critical*."

"They will be," Kira agreed. "Especially if you have no other nova combatants at all."

"We have a single twelve-ship squadron of gunships that we use for anti-piracy patrols," D'Cruze noted. "They are...not new."

"We also bought them *from* Colossus, so we are currently going over them with a fine-toothed comb," Bachchan pointed out. "They're fifty years old, so they're probably fine, but given the circumstances, I want to be absolutely certain they're clean before we deploy them against Colossus."

She sighed.

"Plus, I doubt they're even worth the fuel to send them out against what the Nova Wing has now," she admitted.

Gunships were the basic "minimum viable combatant" constructable by anyone with access to the standard colonial database. They were basically a minimum-sized, one-kilocubic Ten-X class one nova drive attached to Harrington coils, antigrav coils and a set of light plasma cannon. Ten thousand cubic meters didn't go very far and often resulted in a nova "warship" that would lose a one-on-one duel with nova fighters a thirtieth of their size.

"Potentially not," Kira conceded. "And Mr. Tapadia has promised a new fleet, but from what I have seen, you're still building yards?"

"Exactly," Tapadia confirmed. "I believe the First Minister discussed engaging some of your technicians to review our designs before we laid keels? We'll be commencing some test builds in the civilian yards within the next ten days, but we still have time."

"I can only really flag the easy problems," Bueller warned. "There are a number of easy-to-make mistakes I can help you avoid, but bigger issues...are harder to both find and fix."

"Anything we can do now to save the lives of our people in the future is absolutely critical," Tapadia told him. "If your skills are available, we will hire them. I will have my people make arrangements."

"That's roughly where we're all at, I think," Kira said. A hovering pattern of starfighters flickered across her vision as she considered the numbers and capabilities of the SDC.

"Commodore Bachchan and I, plus whoever ends up in charge of the SDC, will need to review a combined patrol-and-scouting schedule," she continued. "*That* meeting will need to be more formal than this.

"I know what resources you have now, and that impacts my plans." They were both better and worse than she'd feared, in many ways. It would be handy if the SDC bought the two captured depot ships into commission, though turning them into even crappy carriers would take time Kira didn't think they had.

"The next step will be to make the arrangements to lay out that schedule," she continued. "I'm pleased that we were all able to sit down and get a feel for each other. The next few months appear to promise a chance to fine-tune processes and patterns before the Nova Wing is ready for round two—but also remember that the Nova Wing retains a carrier and two destroyers that are fully functional combatants."

She shook her head.

"I don't expect Colossus to come to the negotiating table," she admitted, "but that is something your government should attempt anyway. Regardless of discussions, though, my next critical piece of intelligence is going to be hard to find.

"Somehow, Commodores, Mr. Tapadia...we need to find out how long it's going to take for the Nova Wing to get the rest of the Brisingr ships refitted and crewed."

Because if the Colossus Nova Wing put two carriers, a cruiser and a dozen escorts into the field before the rest of Memorial Force arrived...Kira was going to have to get *very* clever to fulfill her contract.

27

Batsal Tapadia's party turned out to be the smallest and lowest-key of the events that Kira was dragged to over the next week. It seemed like every major business leader in the Samuels System wanted to show their support for the woman of the hour and the mercenaries who'd saved them all.

Kira knew the drill, though, and she played along. While keeping the Quorum and the general electorate happy wasn't part of her *contract*, she knew perfectly well it was part of her *job*. In any democratic society, the government had to have faith that *enough* of the population supported the deployment of mercenaries to keep the contracts intact.

It was still a relief to receive an invite from a name she knew: Doretta Macey.

"Any details on her invite?" she asked Smolak.

She'd coopted the coms officer as her planetside secretary and aide—and given that the assignment came with a suite on the penthouse level of the Quaker City Pahilō Hōṭala, if one shared with Jess Koch, Smolak wasn't complaining too loudly.

"Cocktails and live music in the garden of the Quaker City house of a Mr...Broderick," the lanky green-eyed coms officer told her. "Emilio Broderick, significant minority shareholder and board member for Macey Industries. Widower, three teenage daughters by his late wife."

Smolak's gaze was fixed in the mid-distance, ignoring the luxurious furnishings of the penthouse around them as she scanned Bennet's news feeds.

"Business news has him as Mrs. Macey's usual proxy on the Macey board," she continued. "Political and personal allies, though the chairperson is *Roy* Macey, her eldest son." Smolak paused. "It does not look like the younger Mr. Macey will be at the party, but about half of the board is on the list I have access to.

"So are several key members of Samuels-Tata," she noted.

"Security?" Kira asked. After a week of parties on Bennet, she could guess the answer.

"Exists," Smolak said drily. "Mrs. Macey having spent time with us, she had her staff actually include the details with the invite. Mr. Broderick has a relatively standard executive home-security system. Perimeter sensors and exterior cameras linked to a third-party response agency.

"He has also contracted with said third-party agency to provide a discreet perimeter patrol unit for this event, four officers."

"Four," Kira echoed. "Which is, I believe, three more than the next-best security I've seen at one of these events."

Smolak chuckled.

"I'll pass all of that on to Milani and Jess," she promised. "I do have to note, boss, that *Deception* is supposed to leave on patrol six hours before the party. If you're attending, Captain Mwangi will be deploying without you."

"Captain Mwangi and Commander Cartman are capable of handling a three-waypoint patrol without me," Kira said. "I'm keeping his chief engineer and XO anyway, since Commander Bueller is buried in datawork at Samuels-Tata's head office."

She'd seen her boyfriend awake for roughly two hours in the last seven days. While his dedication to the tasks set in front of him was always hugely valuable, it was also occasionally frustrating in more ways than one.

"I should probably be reporting back aboard myself, though," Smolak pointed out. "I can swap out with Ronaldo. I'll fill him in and he can play aide as well as I can. So can Jess, for that matter."

"Fair," Kira allowed. She'd probably done her bodyguard slash steward a disfavor by using anyone else as a secretary at all. "That's your call, Commander. For myself... Well, let's inform Mrs. Macey's people that I'll be there. And then Milani and Jess can sort out how they're going to back up those four hapless security guards."

"I UNDERSTAND, in theory, where these people are coming from," the armored mercenary told Kira with a sigh. The digital dragon on Milani's armor was currently sitting on its tail, glaring at the Admiral with crossed arms.

"At the same time, they have a bad habit of drastically understating their own domestic crime rate," they continued. "Their *violent* crime rate is unusually low, but their property-crime rate is actually slightly above average for the Rim."

"Which is why someone like Broderick has sensors and alarms but not armed guards," she replied. "They know their own environment, whatever line they like to talk for public consumption."

"And they have *zero* consideration for the possibility that Colossus has infiltrated covert teams of any kind onto the planet," her senior ground commander grumbled. "My math says that something like twenty percent of the board members of the top five space industrial companies on the planet is going to be at this party.

"That's a *hell* of a strategic soft spot."

"And that's why I'm telling you twenty-four hours in advance," Kira noted. "You have permission to move armored troopers around so long as we don't spook people or abuse the privilege.

"We want to watch our own backs, but I'm not going to mind if we help protect the senior leadership of the companies building Samuels's new nova fleet at the same time!"

"Of course, of course." The red dragon uncrossed its arms and did a triple back-flip while shaking its frilled head at Kira.

"I'm just...professionally offended," Milani admitted. "I look around Bennet and I see *so many* points of vulnerability that the locals don't seem to recognize. It's a blind spot that Colossus is going to ram a fucking *nuke* through if this war goes on for long."

"Planet full of pacifists," Kira reminded them. "Not every last one of them, no, but it's a strong value of multiple cultures that make up major sections of the population. It's hard to see military vulnerabilities when you don't *think* in terms like that."

"Yeah, well, their *enemies* do," the merc said. "They are, thankfully, keeping an eye on the most recent imports from Colossus, but there were a lot of people going both ways for a long time."

"That's part of why their leadership never really considered a war as likely."

Kira shrugged.

"Plus, downside of direct democracy. The Ministries needed to convince a majority of the planetary population the threat existed. Easy *now*, but...harder before Colossus moved."

"Well, *my* job is mostly to make sure *you* survive the party," Milani told her. "So, you wear the *armored* dress uniform, you understand?"

"Yes, Milani," she said meekly. "This one feels more dangerous because of the other attendees, right? Too much potential value for an attack."

"Exactly," they confirmed. "If *you* are the target, any party you're at becomes a vector. But if Colossus is trying for the most bang for their buck, knocking out a chunk of the leadership of the companies building warships..."

"I mean, are the companies *really* going to suffer for losing their boards?" Kira asked. "They aren't the people holding wrenches and torches. They aren't even the ones leading building teams or coordinating logistics."

"It depends on who replaces them," Milani said. "I don't know what the split on Samuels-Tata's board was on whether they should get involved in building warships...but I doubt it was unanimous.

"This isn't a place where people are going to be overly willing to get blood on their hands for money."

Kira sighed her agreement.

"Fair. I'll keep my eyes open and my ears wide," she promised. "I'm in the middle of this war, 'getting blood on my hands for money,' but I don't plan on dying for it."

"Good. Because I *won't* let you," Milani stated firmly.

28

EMILIO BRODERICK's house was a sprawling villa of ancient design, a style that Kira's headware labeled as "North American Colonial." While the government structures had similar heritage, they'd been built of the local reddish stone.

The industrial magnate's house, on the other hand, had either been built of stone carefully sourced for its color, or someone had applied a small fortune worth of dyes and chemical transmutations to turn it all white.

It made for an impressive backdrop for the full acre of carefully manicured grounds resting between the two extended wings of the horseshoe-shaped structure. The plants, at least, were local, though they'd been carefully shaped to conform to the overall esthetic.

Kira found the whole affair distinctly artificial, but she couldn't argue with the impact or the effect. It was pretty. Just not to her taste.

"How are you finding Quaker City, Admiral?" Doretta Macey asked, separating herself from a cluster of older women to intercept Kira at the drink table.

"Fascinating," Kira murmured. She watched Koch refill her glass, eyeing the heavily sweetened local iced tea with scant favor. Whatever Samuels people grew for tea—and it was quite probably the standard Terran-stock *camellia sinensis* tea plant—combined with the local soil to taste distinctly *off* to Kira.

In the same way as Redward's unique biochemistry produced some of the best coffee she'd ever tasted, *Bennet's* unique biochemistry produced some of the *worst* tea she'd ever been given—and she wasn't sure exactly what fruit cordial had been mixed with it at Broderick's party, but it managed to make it even worse.

She took it from her bodyguard and sipped it anyway as Macey poured her own drink.

"That sounds like mixed feelings, I have to admit," the older woman noted. She eyed Koch for a moment, but the Redward woman's beatific smile made it clear this wasn't going to be a private conversation.

"It's an interesting experience to watch a bunch of people have an internal war over the fact that they need me to keep them safe and the fact that they despise everything I am and stand for," Kira murmured.

Macey sighed and took a sip.

"Fair enough, Admiral. We *do* need you, though. I've been having conversations all night, and I now know the answer to a question my son kept changing the subject on."

Kira arched an eyebrow.

"Your son? The CEO of Macey Industries?"

"I do have two others, but yes," Macey confirmed. "Roy was being cagey about the orbital yards to me. We're one of the key partners in the Lagrange-point shipyard, so I figured we were involved in the new military yard."

"And?"

"We are, but he's trying to keep the board from realizing," Macey said grimly. "Neither he nor Broderick nor I think we have a majority on the board to support the project. We've got the votes to save Roy's job when it comes out that he did an end run *around* the board—

especially given that a one-third share in the warship yards stands to make us a *lot* of money."

"Ouch." Kira grimaced. "The support for building your own warships is that thin?"

"Fifty-six percent," the local told her. "That's what we're projecting when the bill for long-term funding goes to general vote next week. Everything up to this point has been funded out of standing SDC allotments, but we can't maintain a significant nova fleet out of those."

Macey shook her head.

"For that matter, *I'm* not sure I really want to fund a permanent warship fleet," she admitted. "I just know we need it now. It goes against the grain, and I worry that once we have a standing fleet, we'll find reasons to use it."

"Everything I can see, Mrs. Macey, suggests that Colossus is *also* going to have a standing fleet, which means that keeping an eye on *them* is going to keep your ships busy," Kira pointed out. "It's not my place to tell you how to protect your world, but Memorial Force won't be able to stay here forever."

"You were at Redward for a long time," Macey said.

"And we'll be going back to Redward. We home-base there, for a few reasons," Kira replied.

Not least that she *really* wanted the carrier they were building her. That she owned a penthouse apartment there was quite a bit lower on her priority list.

"That is fair. We will build our own ships," Macey said. "It just feels wrong, after two centuries of living by the values of our various faiths, to find ourselves funding a major military now."

"Your nova fleet will likely never even *begin* to rival the costs and personnel requirements of your defensive forts," Kira observed. "Without a major change in strategic priorities, it will never even need to."

"Fair." Macey turned to survey the garden. "A year."

"A year?" Kira echoed. "Before you have any nova ships, that is?"

Macey nodded.

"That was the other answer I got out of the fact that Samuels-Tata and Macey's boards and senior executives are both well represented here," she noted. "The military yards are still weeks away from being ready, and the plan is to lay down cruisers at the civilian yards. They'll take a year to build, and our first destroyers will come out of the military yards around the same time."

"Once the keels are laid, it's harder to stop the process," Kira murmured. "Not impossible...but harder. There's a momentum at that point."

"And Colossus has laid their own keels. We don't know how long until their ships commission."

"We have a good idea how long before their Brisingr acquisitions are online," Kira said. "Memorial Force is still only contracted for six months right now."

"That will be extended soon enough," Macey promised. "The First Minister can't say that officially yet, but the decision's been made."

"Useful to know," Kira said.

She looked around the garden with its swarm of VIPs.

"Do me a favor, Mrs. Macey," she told the other woman.

"What's that?"

"Find some damn bodyguards," Kira instructed. "Look at this. Samuels-Tata and Macey are both well represented here, you said. Who else, industry-wise?"

"Oats Orbital. Shindig Manufacturing. A few others, but Oats and Shindig are the other—"

"Partners in the military yards?" Kira finished.

Macey sighed.

"Yes," she conceded. "There are five companies that run the Lagrange-point yards. Several of the yards are solo operators, others are joint ventures, but it's basically five corporations that manage ninety percent or so of the civilian yards.

"Four of us are directly or indirectly involved in the military yards, though Samuels-Tata leads the work."

"And all four of those firms have major executives and board members *here*, in a basically undefended garden with four glorified *mall cops* running exterior patrol," Kira said flatly. "Tonight, there are another dozen armored mercenaries discreetly running backup. But if I wasn't here, the rest of you would be, and those mercs wouldn't be."

Macey was even safer than Kira was implying, given that she was within the "operational radius," so to speak, of Kira's covertly soldier-boosted bodyguard.

"A single shooter could throw the entire balance of power in the boards of the companies building Samuels's new fleet into disarray." She shook her head. She knew she was repeating Milani's point...but it was a good one.

"Colossus may not be thinking in terms of sabotage and assassins just yet, Mrs. Macey...but if they are working with Brisingr, the suggestion is going to get made," she told the other woman. "You want to make sure you have security precautions in play *before* someone decides to start causing trouble."

"This is Quaker City," Macey pointed out. "There are no killers for hire here. There aren't even many *blasters* in the city. We are safe here."

"You are safe from *your people*, most likely," Kira countered, glad that Macey *probably* couldn't read Koch's body language with the Redward agent behind her. "But your entire economy hinges on the flow of people and goods through Samuels. Most of that is passing through, stopping at Haven and Sanctuary, but people stop here on Bennet, too.

"The trade routes are open, and people will be coming back quickly enough. Infiltrating covert operators will not be hard. You. Are. Vulnerable."

Macey stared off into the distance for a few long moments, her gaze seeming to traverse over the gathered crowd of Very Important People.

She sighed.

"I'll talk to Roy and Batsal," she murmured. "Because both of them should *also* get security—and because Batsal Tapadia is probably the best person I know to find that kind of resource. I'm...*guessing* there are some Gorkhali SDC veterans running something of the sort, if nothing else."

"Buxton has security," Kira pointed out. "They're hired from somewhere."

"Mostly off-world, if we're being honest," Macey admitted. "Not from Colossus anymore, and not generally from Apollo or Brisingr for obvious reasons, but...from elsewhere."

"Might be time to change that. And that's speaking as a mercenary you hired from elsewhere," Kira said. "You are at war, Doretta Macey. You cannot continue to rely on the good faith and general peaceful nature of your people for the security of your leaders. Not if you want to *stay* peaceful."

"I get it, Demirci," Macey said sharply. "And I will make arrangements for myself and my son, and encourage others to do the same. You're right."

She shook her head.

"I just hate it," she whispered.

DESPITE ALL OF her and Milani's fears, the party went as smoothly as planned. Kira mingled and made nice with the industrialists building the fleet that would eventually replace her people. She said the right things, smiled at the right people.

She'd been...*okay* at that part of the job when she'd arrived in Redward. No one made it to squadron commander in *any* military without having some ability to play the game, but she'd been under her old CO's wing for much of her time in the ASDF.

Queen Sonia of Redward, however, had made something of a project out of Kira, and she could handle the game well now. She was confident that, over the course of the last week, she'd helped nudge the balance in the boardrooms and investor community of Samuels in favor of the military buildup.

Kira knew perfectly well the value of her work. She'd probably done as much to secure her employer's safe future with a week of parties and dinners as Konrad Bueller had done spending the same week reviewing and improving their warship schematics.

Unfortunately, because she knew it was important, she put just as much work into it as she put into actual combat, and after a week, she was *exhausted.*

"Aircar is standing by," Milani said in her implants. "J has taken Bravo team and fallen back on the hotel to pre-sweep before our arrival. Charlie team is in a second aircar for overwatch. We're ready to move, boss."

"And where are you?" Kira asked drily.

"Aircar with Alpha team," they replied instantly. "Watching threat detectors and leaning on a black box that I swear is entirely decorative."

"I do not believe the locals okayed us bringing heavy weapons to the surface," Kira observed as she located the aircar and started crossing the front lawn. There was enough space for two dozen vehicles in front of Broderick's house, and her vehicle wasn't even the only aircar present.

"Like I said, the box is *entirely decorative*," Milani replied. "Emotional support armor and a decorative box. What's the problem?"

The *problem* was that Kira knew perfectly well that the box contained either a heavy assault cannon or a hyper-velocity missile launcher. Both unquestionably qualified as heavy weapons, designed to take down combat aircraft and tanks.

If there were twenty of either of those things on Bennet, Kira would be surprised.

"Someday, Milani, you are going to get me in a lot of trouble," she told them. "On my way to the aircar. Threat detectors showing anything?"

"Negative. Got you on my headware, tracking. Everything is looking surprisingly calm."

Kira half-expected the world to reach out and explode after Milani taking things that much in vain, but she made it to the aircar without incident. Her armored troop commander gave her a calm nod and slid the big black box—shaped more like an HVM launcher than an assault cannon, Kira judged—into the aircar's storage bay.

"Charlie team is the air," Milani noted. "Linked with Quaker City Air Control. We are clear back to the hotel, where Jess has commenced the security sweep."

"I wish I could regard all of this as unnecessary theater, you know," Kira said. But she stepped into the aircar and nodded to the pair of armored troopers already inside.

"The thing is, boss, that the hope *is* for it to be unnecessary," Milani replied. "The point, in fact, is for us to do more than is necessary to convince any potential attacker that it's just not worth it."

The aircar door closed behind Milani and they took their seat across from Kira as the vehicle took off. Antigravity coils made liftoff supremely smooth, to the point where Kira knew a lot of people might have even missed the moment.

She linked her headware into the car's sensors, checking the area around them as they moved over Quaker City.

"I do wish we could borrow an antigrav fighter or two," Milani admitted. "Charlie team has blaster rifles, but that's it. They're covering us, but even a single fighter would be better protection."

"I don't think the SDC has enough AG fighters to lend anyone," Kira replied. "Including *themselves*."

"I could love this planet if they weren't at war," the enby merc told her. "If I didn't think that their enemies were lurking, waiting for the right moment, a place like this could be rela—"

"Charlie is down!" the pilot suddenly snapped—in the same instant as an explosion lit up across the sensors Kira was watching.

There'd been no threat ping, no warning—the second aircar with three of Kira's people aboard it had just *exploded.*

"Get us on the ground!" Milani snapped. "AA lasers in play!"

The pilot did *something* and the aircar dropped like a stone. Even knowing what was coming, Kira barely picked out the coronal effect of the laser beam that clipped their vehicle. If the pilot hadn't moved as fast as she had, they'd have died right there.

"Starboard AG coils are out," the pilot said grimly. "Down, down, down. I have control, but they have a fucking laser. Only one option."

Kira could *fly* an atmospheric aircraft, but she had only theoretical knowledge about air *combat.* Even she could guess what the one option was: a rapid miss-generation maneuver.

In layman's terms: crashing the aircraft before it could be shot down, and hoping everyone walked away.

"*Brace for impact!*"

29

There was what Kira *hoped* was a brief flash of darkness, and her head started ringing as the aircar settled around her. She shook her ahead against a brief spike of dizziness and a warning message popped up in her vision.

Minor concussion detected. Refrain from aggressive motion. Repairs initiated.

A moment later, though, Milani's voice echoed through the aircar cabin.

"Move!" they bellowed. "Everybody out of the car; we almost certainly have incoming."

Kira obeyed, despite another warning message flashing across her eyes. An override order to her headware released an emergency stimulant, and she exhaled as her vision and ears settled around her.

She followed the armored mercenaries out of the aircar and looked around to situate herself. The pilot—Juliet Whittaker, her headware absently informed her—had somehow managed to put the aircar down in the only open space in a neighborhood of four-story walk-up apartment buildings.

There were small parks in front of each of the buildings, but the three that Kira could see in the darkening twilight actively had kids and parents in them. The one Whittaker had landed in was currently sealed off by a cordon of yellow light and a sign warning about new grass seeding.

Given the apparent choices, Kira was *glad* to ruin an apartment building's carefully managed grounds—and damned impressed with her pilot.

"Milani, what's our status?" she demanded.

The armored Commander was removing crumpled plating to get at the storage compartment and their "decorative" black box.

"Try to raise *Huntress* and you'll see," they replied. "We're jammed. *Hard.* It's not multiphasics, so I'm guessing short-range… which means they either had a damned good idea where we were going to go down, or they're in the air and closing on us *now.*"

Kira was the least armored of the four mercenaries on the ground. Milani, Whittaker and the third trooper—Tsagadai Lovel, her headware reminded her—were all in combat armor.

She was in a more-armored-than-usual shipsuit under her dress uniform pants and jacket. The jacket wasn't going to make much difference if someone shot her, and she tossed it aside, drawing her blaster from its holster at the small of her back.

"Contact left, high!" Lovel snapped.

A moment later, an armored arm—Kira wasn't even sure *which* of her companions it belonged to—grabbed Kira and shoved her behind the crashed aircar as an airvan swept around one of the apartment buildings.

Whoever was flying the van was coming in low and fast, violating at least a dozen traffic regulations—but given that the van's side door was open and the antigrav vehicle was turning in the air to present three blaster rifles, Kira suspected traffic rules weren't on anybody's mind.

Plasma bolts walked across the park they'd crash-landed in as their assailants fired, then Whittaker's armored form blocked Kira's vision. The pilot was on one knee, taking careful aim and firing at the airvan as it sliced toward them.

Kira absently noted screaming in the distance, but it wasn't from any of her people or their attackers. Probably—*hopefully*—bystanders horrified to see the war come to their very doorsteps.

A nearer scream denoted the success of her own escorts. Kira didn't pick up the ugly underlying vibration to the sound for long enough that the airvan was almost on the ground before she registered that the antigrav coils had been shot out.

The craft had been low enough and fast enough that it *definitely* crashed, hammering into a thankfully now-empty street in a spray of debris and destruction.

"One down," Milani said grimly. "Whittaker, check on Lovel. Admiral...I need you."

That wasn't what Kira had expected, and she rose to her feet with a moment's aid from Whittaker. The pilot had covered her with her own body, but it didn't look like Whittaker had been hit.

Lovel, on the other hand, was on the ground with multiple blast marks across his armor. Even the heavy power armor Kira's ground troops wore was only rated to withstand one or two direct hits before the dispersal webs burned out—and he'd taken a lot more than that.

Her headware said he was still alive. Her experience suggested that situation wouldn't last much longer without medical attention—but Whittaker was already on it as Kira joined Milani at the back of the aircar.

The dragon-armored merc had managed to extract the long black box from the storage compartment, but they weren't moving right. Kira was used to watching Milani use every bit of speed and grace their power armor gave them, and to see them adjusting carefully was...strange.

"Took a hit to the hip actuators," they told her grimly. "I'm not hurt, but my entire left leg is frozen in place and parts of the suit network are flash-fried. Nothing's moving at speed, and I can't interface with the *fucking* launcher."

They managed to get an armored gauntlet into the box and pull away the top of the container. They might not have been able to exert their usual control and grace, but the exoskeletal muscles were clearly active, as the chunk of black-painted metal flew away and dug a dozen centimeters into the dirt.

"We're still jammed," Kira noted softly.

"Which means that was just the first strike—and even if they only *had* one strike team, the team with the laser is still in play. They won't have stayed with it," Milani warned. "We still have incoming."

Kira wasn't entirely familiar with the weapon in the case except in theory. Short-ranged and slow by space-combat standards, a hyper-velocity missile was a one-shot kill on most vehicles operating in atmosphere.

It consisted of a single overcharged Harrington coil that accelerated from nothing to about four percent of lightspeed in a fraction of a second—and then disintegrated into near-subatomic particles.

Inside the dozen or so kilometers the HVM *existed*, it was effectively instantaneous. Beyond that... Well, it wasn't *harmless*, but it wasn't the fist of an angry divinity it was inside that.

"Highlighting the shoulder and grips in your headware," Milani told her. "Goes over your shoulder, interfaces via the same hand-chip that links to your pistol."

Green highlights appeared on the weapon as Kira's subordinate spoke, and she followed the instructions, resting the curved and padded stock on her shoulder and sliding her hands in. Most the time, she forgot that she even *had* a short-range communication chip in her right palm, but it linked into the HVM launcher easily enough.

The weapon quite helpfully painted a three-dimensional red zone on her vision that showed what was going to be obliterated when she pressed the trigger—and calmly advised her that it was locked until her mental release.

"Still no coms," Milani murmured. "I don't see anything on sensors, but we're surrounded by dense-enough structures that they have cover."

"I'm a decent pistol shot, but this might be beyond me, Milani," Kira warned.

"Whittaker is keeping Lovel alive, and I can't move well enough to aim *or* interface with the launcher," Milani snapped. "It's you or it's nobody."

They paused, their helmet rotating slightly.

"What's the chance that Quaker City cops are here already?" they asked.

"Low," Kira murmured.

"Then the aircraft coming from *that* direction is the bad guys," Milani told her, pointing. "And boss?"

"Yes?" Kira asked, leaning into her own enhanced hearing to try to locate the incoming hostiles.

"If you have to miss, don't hit the buildings. That thing *will* obliterate a dozen apartments and as many innocents."

"Thanks." She'd got *that* from the red line in her vision. The weapon, at least, seemed to think that everything in that zone was going to cease to exist when she pulled the trigger.

She lifted the launcher slightly, adjusting the course to go past the building she was watching and above the one behind it. Then she released the safety, grimacing as she realized she was now a one-woman weapon of mass destruction.

"Ready," Milani barked.

"Ready," she confirmed.

"There!"

It was another unmarked airvan with the side panel open—but *this* one had a proper assault cannon hanging out the door! There was no cover or armor that would protect Kira's people from a weapon *designed* to suppress assaults by entire platoons of power-armored soldiers.

And there was no armor in the world that would allow an airvan to survive the impact of a hyper-velocity missile. There wasn't even a blip of recoil as Kira pressed the double trigger—but there wasn't even enough lag for her to think the weapon had failed to fire.

A shock wave rippled out from the space in front of the weapon, a sonic boom unlike anything she'd ever heard in her life, and the red zone the launcher's software had highlighted turned into a pillar of white fire.

As her implants and nanite systems cleared the afterimage from her sight, Kira looked for any sign of the airvan she'd aimed at.

There was nothing. She'd lined it up perfectly, and *nothing* in the path of the HVM had survived.

"Clear," Milani said quietly. "You can put the launcher down, boss. It only has one shot."

"What happens if they have a third wave?" she asked, lowering the weapon.

"Then it's a race to see if they can kill us before reinforcements get here," Milani told her. "And even if *Huntress*'s people had missed everything *up* to this moment, I guaran-fucking-*tee* you my people dropped assault shuttles when they saw an HVM fired!"

30

THE QUAKER CITY peace officers were the first to arrive of all the potential reinforcements, a pair of distinctly recognizable brightly colored aircars whipping through the air over the scene at a speed that said they had *definitely* seen some of what was going on.

They returned to settle down around Kira's crashed car a few seconds later, but they had—quite sensibly, in her opinion—been aware that their patrol units were far from equipped for the situation that had unfolded in that apartment's park.

An SDC fast mover was there shortly afterward, the armored antigrav craft landing long enough to disgorge two dozen armored troopers before lifting off to hang over the area like a floating citadel.

Kira simply waited for the locals to feel in control of the situation and checked her link to *Huntress*. The jamming had finally dropped as the peace force cars arrived, which meant that somebody had walked away.

"Lovel should make it," Whittaker told her and Milani. "He's stable, and the armor is in sustain mode. A hospital would be better."

Even as the pilot spoke, the first actual *siren* cut through the air as an air ambulance blazed out of the night.

"Admiral, are any of your people injured?" one of the peace officers asked as they stepped closer. "I'm Officer Tofa Kristiansen of the Quaker City Peace Service."

"One of my troopers took several bad hits," Kira told Kristiansen. "That ambulance sounds very helpful."

"We'll ping a second vehicle for the dead," the QCPS officer told her. "This is...rather outside our experience; I apologize."

"I don't expect many people to be experienced with assassination attempts at this level," she murmured. "*I'm* certainly not."

"I...do have to note that hyper-velocity weaponry is utterly illegal for private possession on Bennet," Kristiansen said slowly. "And your special permissions do not cover weaponry of that scale."

"Funny," Kira replied. "I was under the impression that anti-aircraft laser weapons and heavy assault cannon were *also* utterly 'illegal for private possession on Bennet.' Were the ones turned on my people in the possession of the SDC?"

"No," the peace officer replied. "And the decision on any of that will be far above my level, Admiral, though I suspect I know where it will end."

She gave a decent-enough salute.

"But I did have to mention it. I will need statements and, if you're prepared to consent, implant downloads from you and your people," Kristiansen continued. "I don't know if it will be enough to track the attackers down. We..."

She sighed.

"We are not generally required to track down murderers," she admitted. "My job is mostly mediating domestic disputes, Admiral, not dealing with this kind of...*event*."

Somehow, Kristiansen managed to pack the force of multiple four-letter words into a single five-letter one.

"I understand, Officer," Kira replied. "But three of my people are dead. We will provide any assistance we can, but we need to find the bastards behind this."

"Excuse me, Officer Kristiansen, Admiral Demirci?" One of the armored SDC soldiers had arrived. "From what I've been told, Admiral Demirci may be able to make sense of something we just found."

"What kind of something?" Kira asked carefully. "Soldier...?"

"Captain Chaha Paudel," the woman replied instantly. "SDC Ground Forces. We've got an intact body, and the gear is...weird. You know a bit more about the galaxy than we do, so..."

Kira glanced away to see the emergency medtechs working with Whittaker to get Lovel out of his armor and into the ambulance. They seemed unfamiliar with power armor but otherwise competent.

"All right, Captain Paudel, Officer Kristiansen," she told the two local officers. "These people took a serious shot at me and killed three of my people. Any help I can be, I will be."

FROM THE FIRST attack to the destruction of the second airvan, Kira had never paused long enough to take a good look at her attackers. She'd saved the recording to review later, and she would identify anything that stood out to her then, but she hadn't registered even the most obvious identifiers on the enemy.

As she followed Captain Paudel across the urban neighborhood that had turned into a battlefield, she could see that recording was probably going to be the best data they had on the assassins. The wreckage of the crashed airvan was spread across at least twenty meters of street, and she suspected the bodies were in a similar state.

"Here," Paudel told her, reaching a spot where the cops and SDC troops had spread a tarp over something on the ground. "One of your bodyguards landed a lucky shot, and their victim fell from the airvan before it went down.

"Probably the best chance we'll have for IDing them, but..."

"But what?" Kira asked.

"You'll see. Pull the tarp off, Corporal," Paudel ordered the soldier standing guard.

The canvas was whisked away, and Kira swallowed a curse as she recognized the hologram wrapped around her attacker. There was no way to tell how intact the body was after being shot with a blaster rifle and falling a dozen or so meters, because it was still covered in a very familiar hologram.

The Brisingr Shadows were perfectly *capable* of being subtle, but when the Kaiser's spies wanted to send a message, they had a specific style. When they came to kill and be *known* to have killed, they wore a standard holographic cover that concealed their identity from any security recordings...while making it quite clear *who* had ordered a death.

Even slumped dead on the ground, the masked and hooded figure was familiar to Kira. The Shadows that had come for her on Apollo had rarely worn the hoods, but other assassins she'd encountered elsewhere had.

"You recognize the hologram," Paudel said.

"They almost certainly aren't local," Kira told her. "Some might be, it's possible, but the hologram is used by the Kaiser of Brisingr's covert operatives when they're ordered to make an *example* of somebody.

"Kaiser Reinhardt, at least, wants people to know why they're dying when he orders them killed."

And if Brisingr's assassins were there on Samuels, she at least understood why they'd passed on the rich target of the entire party. They weren't going to try to win the war for Colossus...they were *just* there for Kira Demirci.

31

The next morning, Captain Paudel looked uncomfortable as she was escorted into the sitting room of the main penthouse suite of the Quaker City Pahilō Hōṭala. The dark-skinned local officer had shed her full power armor for a more subdued gray uniform, identical to the one worn by the slightly older man walking by her side.

The three mercenaries escorting them into the sitting room had given up any concept of "subdued" after a major attack on their superiors. Milani had doubled the number of ground troops in the hotel, taken over the *entire* top floor and put their soldiers in full power armor.

"Captain Paudel, welcome. I'm not familiar with your companion," Kira noted, "but you did meet Commander Milani."

The ground commander's armor had been repaired and the dragon was currently sitting cross-legged on their chest, eyeing the two SDC officers warily.

"This is Commander Bueller, my senior engineer," Kira continued. "He's on the surface, working with your people, but I wanted to keep my people together until we had a better idea of what's going on."

She was confident that the Shadows had come for her—and they had no evidence that Brisingr had put out any kind of termination order on Bueller—but given that Bueller was unquestionably guilty of treason against the Kaiserreich...

"I'm not sure we have any good news on that point," Paudel admitted. "But I'm only here for introductions. This is Colonel Tyag Sharma, the SDC's head of Intelligence."

Sharma was even taller than Paudel. Even with the dark coloring and lanky builds Kira was starting to associate with Samuels's Nepali-extract population, he towered over his fellows.

The towering Colonel bowed over his hands to Kira.

"May I sit, Admiral Demirci?"

"Of course. Is the peace service still involved in this affair?" Kira asked carefully.

"They are," Sharma confirmed. "But the decision was made that SDCI would take lead on this investigation, and I am coordinating a combined military and civil investigation."

The two local officers took a seat and Sharma leaned forward.

"My best estimate," he began slowly, "is that the attack on you involved between fourteen and sixteen individuals. We have retrieved two mostly intact bodies and achieved genetic identification of six individuals, all told.

"Thanks to the scan data and headware downloads you provided, we *believe* there were another six individuals in the airvan hit by your HVM," Sharma continued. "The decision has been made, unsurprisingly, not to prosecute anyone for the possession of that weapon."

"The jamming was still up after the second airvan was destroyed," Bueller pointed out. "That implies there was a third vehicle, or that the jamming was far more expansive than Commander Milani estimated."

"The jamming zone was approximately two point four kilometers across," Sharma said quietly. "While your crash was in the zone, it did move closer to you, and then moved away before being disabled. There was unquestionably a third vehicle.

"We believe it was a ground vehicle, but there was enough traffic in the area, we have failed to identify it," he admitted.

"What about the laser?" Milani asked. "That's relatively easy to backtrack."

"Indeed," Sharma conceded. He laid a holoprojector disk on the solid wood table in the middle of the luxuriously furnished sitting area, and an image of an apartment building roof appeared.

It only took Kira a moment to identify what was out of place, and she swallowed a curse as she recognized it. It was spindly and fragile for what it was, but that was because it was supposed to be carried by human beings.

"It appears to have been fired by remote control, but we're attempting to resolve the frequency to identify the source of the weapon," Sharma said.

"It's two point three six times ten to the power of sixteen hertz," Kira said quietly. "High ultraviolet."

"Admiral?" the SDC officer queried.

"That's a Centaur-Sixteen Hall Pass," Kira told him, then snorted at the ancient slang. "Or HPAAS," she explained, sounding out the individual letters. "Human-Portable Anti-Aircraft System.

"It breaks down into two cases, each the size of a large personal suitcase," she continued. "It can be completely automated or fired semi-manually."

She shivered.

"In fully automatic mode, it requires *extremely* specific targeting instructions to keep the human hand in the loop," she noted. Very few people liked automatic weapon systems of any kind, and most star systems and interstellar treaties included some verbiage around "hand in the loop" rules with regards to weapons.

Not least because AI warships given multiphasic jammers tended to never turn the jammers off to receive shutdown orders.

"So this a..." Sharma trailed off.

"It's an Apollon weapon system," Kira told him. "The Hoplites usually set them up around major events to reinforce no-fly zones.

They're not really designed to shoot down combat aircraft, but they're more than sufficient to handle anything short of that."

"That's...useful to know, I suppose," the SDC Intelligence officer conceded. "And consistent with the main issue we're facing: nothing these people used came from Samuels except the airvans. The blasters we've retrieved are from the Sabuko System. The holoprojectors, as expected, are from Brisingr, but...body armor, sensors, everything is from somewhere different."

It took Kira a few seconds to even locate the Sabuko System. It was a system sixty light-years around the Rim from the outer edge of the Samuels-Colossus Corridor, in the opposite direction from just about everywhere Kira had ever been.

"And the people themselves?" she asked.

"First-pass scans suggested locals," Sharma noted. "Further digging, however, revealed all of the identities we located are false. Inserted into our databases via assorted cyberattacks. Our civilian identification systems are...not as secure as I would like."

The Intelligence officer shrugged.

"My job is to be exceptionally paranoid," he admitted. "Nothing in my system is as secure as I would like. But with false identities, even linked to their genetics, I can't validate where the attackers were from.

"I'm guessing that, like with their equipment, they aren't from Samuels. But..." He spread his hands.

"So, we know very little, is what I'm hearing," Kira noted. "That doesn't make me overly comfortable about letting my people swan around in Quaker City, Colonel."

"Speaking for SDC Intelligence and the Quaker City Peace Service..." Sharma sighed. "I can't blame you, Admiral. We have clearly demonstrated that we can't support your security to the level that we feel is necessary.

"I would *like* to tell you that there is no way there is another cell of Brisingr Shadows on Bennet preparing to hunt you down," he noted. "I would *love* to say that only two or three people survived the attempt on your life and they won't have the resources to try again.

"I cannot, in good faith, say any of that," he admitted. "In your place, Admiral Demirci, I would retreat to my carrier, where I was in full control of the situation."

"That, Colonel, may not be an option," Kira told him. "But it appears I will need to be far more careful what parties I attend."

"And how we attend them," Milani said grimly. "They almost certainly scanned our aircars as we came in. They knew which vehicles were ours, they knew our route, and they knew you weren't in the first vehicle to head back.

"There was a fifty-fifty chance that they took you out with their first shot, Admiral. They guessed wrong—next time, they might not."

"What are the alternatives?" Kira asked.

"Assault shuttle," the ground commander said flatly. "You don't fly in local aircars anymore. I understand that the job means you have to attend these parties, but I think we *do* fall back to *Huntress* and attend any further events by shuttle from orbit.

"Our shuttles wouldn't even notice a light UV laser," Milani said, gesturing at the hologram of the Centaur-16 HPAAS. "And they carry their own defensive weaponry that can vaporize a unit like that before it can hurt them."

"I'm guessing the Shadows destroyed the AA unit?" Kira asked.

"It was rigged with explosives, detonated as soon as your car went down," Sharma confirmed. "In general, the QCPS strongly prefers to have spacecraft come to the spaceport and have people move from there to their destination.

"Given the circumstances, though, I think I can convince the First Minister to order an exception," he continued. "So long as you promise us one thing."

"And what's that, Colonel?" Kira asked.

"Please don't bring any more weapons of mass destruction onto our planet!"

32

THE ARRIVAL of the first freighters several days later marked the biggest measure of victory Kira could hope for. For civilian ships to once again be visiting Haven and Sanctuary for static discharge and fuel meant the news of the broken blockade had reached the ends of the Corridor.

Kira watched the relayed report from Haven's fortresses in her quarters aboard *Huntress*. The rooms weren't as personalized as her space on *Deception,* but they served well enough. The light carrier had never been intended to act as a flagship in the usual sense of the word, which was part of why Kira lived on *Deception* by preference.

As Haven's orbitals and service ships began to buzz with activity again, her main attention was focused on a single shuttle rising from the surface toward the carrier. Konrad Bueller was finally done with his two-week contract with the local design team, and the downside of being back aboard ship when he wasn't was that she wasn't spending the nights with her boyfriend.

Intellectually, Kira had anticipated the theoretical issue of missing Bueller, but they hadn't spent much time apart since the blockade of Redward almost two years earlier. It was surprisingly easy for her to justify keeping the most senior and capable engineer in her fleet in her back pocket for almost any mission.

Until she'd spent five days away from him, even *she* had believed her own justifications. Now, though, she was realizing how painfully she missed his solid presence and assured knowledge. He was reliable, he was capable and he *listened.*

Now he was on his way back to her, and Kira was finding herself engaged in a level of self-reflection regarding their relationship that she didn't normally bother with. It was...a surprisingly comfortable thing to put under a microscope and poke at the contours of.

It wasn't that the contours of the longest-standing relationship in her life were expected, per se, just that the surprises were quite...agreeable.

Kira wasn't sure what to make of those surprises and the realization that this particular relationship was perhaps even more serious than she'd thought. It didn't matter, truly. She wasn't under the impression that Konrad was planning on going anywhere, after all.

But it *would* be a factor when the time came to shift her flag to *Fortitude. Deception*'s flag facilities might be better than *Huntress*'s, but they still paled in comparison to a supercarrier half again the heavy cruiser's size.

And Kira couldn't justify operating from the smaller ship just to have her boyfriend in her bed each night...not unless she admitted that as a criterion in advance and made changes.

FROM THE FIERCENESS of his embrace when he joined Kira in their shared space on *Huntress*, Konrad had been feeling much the same as she had. Their daily calls had suggested as much to her, but it was still nice to feel loved.

"How was your internship as a design engineer?" she asked him once he released her.

"If there's an intern in the galaxy getting paid what we charge for my design services, they might single-handedly force us to redefine *intern,*" Konrad pointed out as he took a seat on the couch.

He winced a moment later.

"I know these quarters are so far down our priority list, they don't even *register*, but couldn't we have found actually *comfortable* couches for them?" he asked plaintively.

"I...haven't sat on the couches yet," Kira admitted. "The chairs are the same as every other standard chair in all of Memorial Force."

They'd got a deal from a furniture manufacturer on Redward to buy spaceship-style chairs with magnetized wheels in bulk. She was still, over a year later, impressed with Vaduva and Dirix, her purser and ground operations manager respectively, for managing *that* deal.

They were comfortable, practical and served in almost all settings perfectly well. The *couches* in people's quarters on the ships, though, were a far more eclectic mix.

"I believe the couch may be the end result of what happens when the Captain gets a new couch and offers the XO their old one, and a cascade of hand-me-downs occurs until the quarters no one is using get the last couch standing," she observed.

"Well, I've sat on more comfortable benches," Konrad told her. "Ones carved from stone."

"I'll keep that in mind the next time Davidović comes around with a request for a furniture budget," she promised. "Though we lost the original question."

He chuckled as he shifted on the couch to get more comfortable.

"Design engineering is always an entertaining vacation," he said. "I wouldn't want to do it as my main task—I got *so* bored when I lived behind a desk—but a few days or weeks is a nice change."

A few months, Kira remembered, had been too much. Though that had probably been as much the nature of the emergency construction program Konrad Bueller had helped lead during the blockade of Redward.

Her partner would never forgive himself for the workers who'd died building those cruisers. Those workers had *known* the compromises that had been made to accelerate the construction. There'd been no uninformed consent on the risks that had killed them, and with the fate of their star system in the balance, those workers had taken up the tasks freely.

But Konrad Bueller had been one of the people in charge, and he would always bear the weight of those deaths. If they hadn't worn on him, he wouldn't have been the man Kira loved.

"When do they lay keels?" she asked.

"Apparently, a lot of it is riding on the legislation going to popular vote tomorrow," he warned. "If I'm reading what I saw correctly, the SDC only has the authorization to assemble the military yards and build a single five-escort carrier group."

He shook his head.

"*Those* keels are explicitly restricted to the military yards, too," he observed. "A carrier, two cruisers and three destroyers. That authorization let them spend the time and money to draft designs for all three classes, but if the general vote blocks them building a real fleet..."

Kira grimaced.

"Everyone I've spoken to has presented that as a near-guaranteed thing," she noted. "But any vote is a risk, I suppose."

"Always," Konrad confirmed. "*If* the Nova Fleet Construction Bill passes the populace tomorrow, they're authorized to construct a two-million-cubic fleet anchored on five fleet carriers and associated escort groups."

Kira ran through the numbers in her hundred.

"So, at four hundred kilocubics a carrier group, I'm guessing thirty-ish-kilocubic destroyers and hundred-kilocubic capital ships?" she asked.

"Bingo," he told her. "Everything is built around twelve-X class one drives, but they're planning hundred-ten-kilocubic carriers, hundred-kilocubic cruisers, and thirty-kilocubic destroyers.

"Some obvious mistakes in their initial designs, some less obvious," he continued. "The biggest problem is one I can't fix in two weeks of flagging issues in the schematics, though."

"Oh?" Kira asked, then paused thoughtfully. "The nova fighters."

"The nova fighters," he confirmed. "Their current plan is to load the *Regiment*-class fleet carriers with a hundred Guardian heavy fighters each. It's not the worst plan, but the Guardians are jacks-of-all-trades."

A multirole heavy fighter like the Guardian—or the Colossus Nova Wing's Liberator or the Hussar-Sevens of Memorial Force—served a very necessary purpose. It was *useful* to have a nova fighter that could take on any role from carrier defense to torpedo strike competently. The problem was that an interceptor or a bomber of a comparable tech level did the specialty job *better* and for less money.

Plus, Kira could easily fit sixty interceptors in the same space occupied by fifty heavy fighters.

"But if the vote passes, they lay more keels in the civilian yards?" she asked.

"The plan is that they lay down ten destroyers in the Lagrange-point yards over the next three weeks if the bill passes," Konrad confirmed. "And when the military yards come online in two months, they'll focus on building the carriers and cruisers. Fifteen capital ships and fifteen destroyers to finish the fleet."

"That's a huge expansion, and they don't even have monitors to draw crews from," Kira noted. "But once two or three of those carrier groups are online, we'll be able to take our money and head home without any worries."

"Agreed."

Her boyfriend's gaze drifted to the display she'd been watching, showing the ships clustering around Haven.

"I wonder what news is coming from home," he murmured. "And, well, home."

Kira chuckled as she understood his point.

"Redward should be fine," she told him. "I can't speak to Apollo or Brisingr. I've had no idea what was going on at 'home' for a long time."

"Me either," Konrad admitted. "This is the closest I've been since Equilibrium sent us out to *fix* the Syntactic Cluster."

"Still far enough that none of it should impact us," Kira murmured. "And it's not like any of us are ever planning on going back, is it?"

"No," he agreed. "Especially when my Kaiser appears to *really* want you dead."

She shivered.

"A listed death mark was one thing," she admitted. "Most of the Rim knows Memorial Force too well for random bounty hunters to try shit anymore. Random Shadow cells trying to check off the Mark in the Crest's space... That was bad.

"But this... They passed up a chance to turn an entire war in favor of an ally to take a better shot at me. I don't like it."

"Neither do I," her boyfriend agreed. "I'm not sure what to do about it—and the fact that my Kaiser has assassins this far out does not fill me with warm fuzzy feelings about *home*."

33

"THE VOTE PASSED."

That was the result Kira had been expecting, but from First Minister Buxton's relieved tone as the mercenary Admiral took a seat at the conference table, it hadn't felt as sure as everyone had been saying.

"It was...somewhat less narrow than the polling suggested," Doretta Macey noted.

After almost a month in Samuels, Kira *still* wasn't entirely clear on what Mrs. Macey's formal role in the Ministries was. She wasn't one of the Ministers, the designated politicians in charge of the civil government's components, yet she was in almost all of the meetings Kira had with the Ministers.

Macey wasn't Buxton's right-hand operative, but Kira judged her to be the First Minister's *left*-hand woman.

Their right hand was their husband, and Batsal Tapadia was also at the table. He looked equally relieved as his partner—though it probably helped that he and his company stood to make a *vast* amount of money from the new fleet.

"Fifty-nine percent in favor, thirty-eight opposed, three percent abstained," Buxton confirmed, leaning back in their chair and surveying the table.

Kira had brought Davidović with her today, and the SDC had sent Commodore Bachchan, bringing the small meeting to a total of six people gathered around the table in the Rouge House.

"So, you begin construction of the fleet now?" Kira asked. "But still no idea on timeline for commissioning, of course. Not when you're building your first capital ships."

"That's why we engaged your full fleet, Admiral," Buxton noted. "Speaking of ideas on timelines?"

"The courier will reach Obsidian in about three days," she told them. "Depending on what, exactly, the contract there is currently involving, Commodore Zoric may be out of the system. Even once she's received the communique, there will still be components of the Obsidian contract that will need to be completed."

Kira spread her hands in a shrug.

"It may be as much as another three or four weeks before *Fortitude* and her escorts can commence their trip here," she warned. "That trip will take six weeks. I would not *count* on having *Fortitude*'s battle group in the Samuels System for at least ten weeks."

"That was what Mrs. Macey warned me," Buxton said. "I wanted to hear it from you, however, to be certain. Bachchan."

"Minister." The Commodore turned her gaze on Buxton and arched an eyebrow.

"Don't play innocent," Buxton warned. "There is exactly zero chance you don't know what finally landed on my desk this morning. Everyone with half a brain knew you were going to be the SDC's new CO a while ago, but unanimity takes time."

The First Minister extended a heavily muscled arm and indicated Commodore Mahinder Bachchan with an index finger.

"You are now *Admiral* Bachchan, commanding officer of the Samuels Defense Command. Ceremonies and insignia will follow, but if you're half the commander I'm told you are, you've collated an intelligence brief from the civilians arriving."

"I have," Bachchan confirmed. "I was expecting to need to present it regardless of how quickly we moved on the promotion."

Buxton made a clear "get on with it" gesture, and the newly promoted Admiral smiled.

The massive table they were seated around appeared to be carved from a single slice of the trunk of one immense tree. Despite its unmarred surface, it still clearly concealed holoprojectors somewhere, as a map of the Samuels-Colossus Corridor popped silently into existence amidst the small group.

"We've now seen ships from most of the usual entry points to the Corridor," Bachchan told them. "SDC Intelligence officers have talked to most of their captains, and I know that the Ministry of Commerce has had their own discussions. The Ministry was kind enough to provide recordings of their interviews to the SDC Intelligence team as well.

"Basically the same pattern is taking shape in all of the entry systems," the Admiral continued. "We have updated our local attaché offices with the situation and are advising people that the blockade has been broken and we expect to *keep* it broken. Our message, which our people are relaying loud and clear, is that Samuels is open for business as usual.

"Of course, Colossus *also* has people in all of those systems, and they are determinedly sticking to their party line. Samuels is under blockade by the Colossus Nova Wing, and any attempt to reach the system is at risk of seizure or destruction.

"There is an implicit threat of a more aggressive blockade strategy on their part," Bachchan warned. "If they are to begin a course of commerce raiding along the Corridor, it would be difficult for us to maintain the security of the trade routes."

"That is...basically how this kind of war is fought, I'm afraid," Kira warned her employers. "It requires a particularly dominant hand to impose a full blockade as the CNW attempted. Moving through the regions outside your immediate perimeter and destroying or capturing ships headed to Samuels is the logical next step."

"There has to be something we can do," Buxton replied. "I do not wish to stand by while Colossus strangles the economic lifeblood of our star system and murders innocents!"

"There are options," she told them. "None of them are good. With Admiral Bachchan's permission, I can lay them out."

"I have no illusions about which of us has more experience at this, Admiral Demirci," Bachchan pointed out. "Please, let us know what you are thinking."

Kira nodded her thanks to the Samuels officer and considered the holographic map hanging above the table.

The Corridor wasn't really a true geographic feature. There weren't *many* other star systems in the area around Samuels and Colossus, but they did exist. But they lacked habitable planets—and the two systems with habitable planets were in the rough center of the region, creating an easy stopover point for shipping through a significant volume of otherwise-empty space.

The biggest problem that any freighter captain heading through the Samuels-Colossus Corridor faced was the maps. Because those easy stopover points at the center of the region existed, the mapped trade routes led to them. Kira wasn't even sure that any of the other stars in the Corridor were within six light-years of the mapped nova points—let alone if those stars had planets for easy discharge.

"The first option would be to aggressively patrol the Corridor ourselves," she began. "But..." She gestured at the map. "Once we're past the initial surroundings of the Samuels and Colossus systems, the routes diverge quickly. We're looking at around sixty different mapped nova stops.

"To guarantee full security along those routes, you would need... well, at a *minimum*, sixty nova ships," she told them. "And they would need to be of sufficient weight to take down their most likely challengers."

Kira let that sink in for a moment, then shook her head.

"No one actually maintains security at that level," she continued.

"A level of acceptable risk has to be decided, but the truth is that we don't have the ships to maintain any level of security."

Bachchan had clearly anticipated that, though the civilians looked unhappier.

"*Deception* is due back in a day," Kira reminded them. "When she arrives, *Huntress* will leave to commence the same patrol of the nova points near Samuels. So long as there are only two ships available, securing the immediate area of this star system is honestly the limit of our ability."

"We cannot simply leave the Colossus Nova Wing to ravage shipping through the Corridor," Buxton said grimly.

"There are other options, First Minister," Kira told them. "But you have to realize that the CNW only has three ships at the moment. While they can *threaten* the entirety of the Corridor, they can only actively interdict one or two trade-route stops.

"That danger is not negligible, but it *is* one that will be acceptable to many freighter captains and shipping lines," she continued. "Especially so long as the CNW restricts themselves to forcing the ships they catch to discharge at Colossus.

"That will still swing the balance in the Corridor against you, not least by earning *them* goodwill, but it will keep the passage through Samuels open."

"And what are our options if they become more aggressive?" Macey asked quietly.

"Four of them," Kira laid out. "No. Five."

"Five?" Buxton asked. "That's about six more than I was expecting."

That got a bitter chuckle from the room's occupants, and Kira smiled thinly.

"First two are variations of the same thing. Turnabout," she told them. "We send the message to all of the systems at the ends of the Corridor that *Colossus* is under blockade. Then we either invest Colossus, as they did Samuels, or engage in the same kind of hopefully genteel commerce raiding we're worried they're planning.

"With only two capital ships, a close investment of Colossus itself is...hard," Kira warned. "Our blockade is going to leak like a sieve either way. The only real advantage of a close blockade over a commerce-raiding campaign is the likelihood that we can lure *N45-K* out into a carrier action."

"Even with the plan being to take ships intact and accept surrenders, a campaign of piracy is unacceptable," Buxton told her firmly. "I will not abandon the values our ancestors built our society on and lower ourselves that far."

"Fair enough," Kira told him. "Suffice to say there are versions of that campaign that *I* would refuse to take the contract for."

A campaign of true commerce raiding, where her fleet fired on any ship that was headed for Colossus with no regard for human life, would certainly be effective. It would also destroy the reputations of both Samuels and Memorial Force, even putting aside Kira's stringent moral objections to the idea.

"The other options," Macey demanded. "You said you had five. That's two."

"Three leads on from the close blockade," Kira replied. "In a close blockade of Colossus, we would be at least partially hoping to lure their remaining active warships out into an open engagement. Option three makes that the sole objective: a pure counter-force strike.

"But we don't *just* engage their active ships," she continued. "With a decent amount of scouting, we can make a hard run into Colossus itself. While we couldn't risk capital ships under the guns of the fortresses, I would be able to send bombers and heavy fighters into the military shipyards where they are refitting the rest of the Brisingr hand-me-downs."

Both Bachchan and Tapadia could clearly envisage the equivalent strike in Samuels and looked faintly sick. There were countermeasures to what Kira was suggesting, though she doubted Colossus had fully implemented them—and even if went perfectly, she would lose a lot of the planes she committed.

"Civilian losses would be horrific," Tapadia said softly. "I can intellectually concede that the yards are legitimate military targets, but the people working on those ships aren't soldiers."

"There are ways to minimize it, but yes," Kira confirmed. "I can promise you that those losses would be as few as possible, that we would launch as clean a strike as we can, but we would be novaing into the system, popping multiphasic jammers and then hitting the under-refit ships with torpedoes.

"Even if our strike were perfect—and we would only have a *minute*," she warned, "we would vaporize anyone working aboard the ships in question."

"I cannot, in the face of a threat that I do not believe to be utterly existential, accept a course of action I know will inflict mass civilian casualties," Buxton told her, his voice calm but firm. "I do not and cannot accept that the ends justify the means. I do not believe that even a negotiated surrender to Colossus will see such a complete loss of who and what we are that it requires a *sacrifice* of who and what we are to avoid.

"So, I believe, Admiral, that negates all of your first three options," the First Minister told her.

"I...admire your certainty, Minister," Kira said. She was even telling the truth, though she could tell that Davidović wasn't as sure.

From a lot of perspectives, the counter-force strike was the best option. It wasn't the best option to *Kira*, but that was because it called for the knowing sacrifice of a significant portion of her fighter wings to complete. Her first responsibility was to her people, and she didn't want to lose any of them she didn't have to.

But she also had the obligation to tell her employers what the options were.

"My recommendation would, in all honestly, be for a partial close blockade," she told Buxton. "But I am your contractor, Minister Buxton, not even the commander of your military. I can and will only do what you pay me for."

"You said you had two more options for us," Taparia said.

"I do, but both are...more passive than I suspect is the true best option," she warned. "The fourth option is to seek allies."

She gestured at the map, where a dozen systems served as the entry points to the Corridor.

"Right now, the systems people come here from have chosen to remain neutral in this conflict," she told them. "But those systems have between five and fifteen hundred thousand cubic meters of nova warships apiece, over ten million cubic meters of combatant starships, all told, per the last data I have."

Given how most star systems reported their military strength to even their own populaces, she figured that total could be off by as much as a million cubic meters—a dozen capital ships or multiple carrier groups—either way.

The only ones she was *certain* of were the ones on the Apollo-Brisingr side that were covered by the blandly named Agreement on Nova Lane Security—the peace treaty that restricted Apollo's former allies to five hundred thousand cubic meters of nova warships apiece.

"They have their own priorities and objectives," she warned, "but right now, the Colossus Nova Wing fields barely a hundred and fifty kilocubics of true warships, all told. It wouldn't take many allies to tip the balance against Colossus."

"The moment we start signing military alliances with non-Corridor systems, Colossus will do the same," Macey cautioned. "We could turn a relatively contained conflict between us and our nearest neighbor into a region-wide conflagration."

"The last option I see would avoid that, I think," Kira said. "But it's not one that's easy for anyone to swallow."

"The last option is to do nothing," Bachchan said grimly, "isn't it?"

"Exactly," she confirmed. "Right now, we have superior firepower to the deployable assets of the Colossus Nova Wing, but we don't have the hulls to provide security across the entire Corridor.

"Without some idea of where *N45-K* is going to be, I can't force a fleet battle. That means our best options are either almost purely defensive or extremely aggressive." She shrugged. "There is no question that we can prevent Colossus from imposing a close blockade, even once the rest of their hand-me-downs come online."

She couldn't fight a fleet battle against two carriers and a cruiser, plus escorts, but *Deception* and *Huntress* between them meant that the CNW had to *keep* the three capital ships together to keep Kira from taking them down in isolation.

"So, we just...wait," Buxton said slowly. "We let them raid the ships heading toward us and do nothing?"

"So long as Colossus continues to attempt to run a relatively clean war, the death toll should be minimal to nonexistent," Kira told them. "Once *Fortitude* arrives, I will have the force to push them back and impose a full closed blockade of Colossus. At that point, I can nearly guarantee the prevention of civilian casualties.

"We are currently in a state of strategic stalemate, barring a change in the priorities you want to bring to this conflict," she concluded. "They are waiting to finish their refits. We are waiting for the rest of Memorial Force to arrive."

"So, it's a race, then," Tapadia said.

"No," Bachchan told her civilian counterpart. "Because *Fortitude* will swing the balance of force so thoroughly in our favor that Colossus won't be able to wage war against us without an entire new generation of construction—a wave of construction we will match."

"From where I sit, Minister Buxton, Colossus has not yet lost... but from the moment Memorial Force arrived, they no longer had the ability to *win* this war," Kira told them. "Which worries me."

"That sounds like good news, Admiral," the First Minister replied. "Why does it worry you?"

"Because half the damn Rim knows that Memorial Force has *Fortitude*," she explained. "So, they almost certainly *know* that she's coming—but they haven't tried to negotiate yet, have they?"

"They have not," Buxton admitted. "They respected diplomatic immunity sufficiently to permit our courier to leave after they arrived in Colossus, but they were not prepared to let the envoy land."

"So, they know everything I know," Kira said. "And can, presumably, do the same math I can. I have bigger ships and better starfighters here already. Once *Fortitude* arrives, I will have just as many ships as them, including a supercarrier larger and more modern than anything they can build.

"That math tells *me* they can't win this unless they somehow convince you to surrender before *Fortitude* gets here," she continued. "So, if they're unwilling to talk, that means *they* know something I don't.

"Or at least they think they do."

34

"HAVE you seen the news from home?"

Kira looked up from her desk at Abdullah Colombera's question.

"I feel this is a silly question," she admitted, "but let's specify *which* home. The only thing I saw out of the Syntactic Cluster was a big announcement about a new university on Wilhelm."

Wilhelm was a barely inhabitable hellhole, but it was also the only inhabitable piece of real estate in the four systems known as the Costar Systems—once home to the group of raiders called the Costar Clans and now rapidly growing dependencies of the Kingdom of Redward.

Like the industrial nodes, agriculture stations and new habitation platforms in all four systems, the University of Wilhelm was being underwritten almost entirely by the Kingdom's government, an investment that King Larry and Queen Sonia expected to pay immense financial dividends in the future...but were making because it was changing the lives of a hundred million people and removing the *need* for them to be pirates at all.

"Well, I saw that," Colombera conceded, "and having *fought* the

Costar Clans, I'm a fan of everything that convinces the next generation to be engineers instead of pirates!"

He chuckled and took a cross-legged seat across from Kira.

"I meant *home* home. The Apollo-Brisingr Sector, if not necessarily Apollo itself."

"I glanced at the news," she admitted. "But I kind of…intentionally tune out most stuff about the area."

"I don't," Colombera said flatly. "Especially as the Kaiser starts pushing the limits of the peace treaty. He's testing to see what the Council will give up now."

"I hadn't picked that up," Kira said slowly. Which made sense to her, at least. She wasn't paying enough attention to notice that kind of slow provocation. "But…not really our problem, Scimitar, not unless someone back home wants to hire us."

"You care more than that," he countered. "We all still have family there, even if we're distant from them."

"I think my brother has sent me *one* message since I left," Kira noted. "I told him where I was and how to get in touch with me, and I got a thank-you and a picture of the latest round of lambs in return."

She chuckled.

"That wasn't really unwelcome," she said. "I love space, but I'll always have a soft spot for sheep. But I sent him a response to that and never heard from him again."

"I keep up an exchange with my mother," Colombera told her. "Things are…complex on Apollo. Politics are worse than usual, and no one is quite sure where things are going. But a lot of people think Brisingr is going to keep pushing."

"And enough are willing to let them that we gave up the damn war," Kira replied bitterly. If she was being honest, Apollo and her allies had probably been reaching the end of their ability to *fight* the war, but they hadn't lost yet when the treaty was signed.

"Yeah. And that makes me twitchy when *odd* things come up in the news from home," *Huntress*'s CNG said quietly.

Kira sighed and checked her reports. *Deception* was due in about an hour, at which point she'd swap back to her usual quarters and office—and wouldn't be nearly as accessible to Colombera, even with the extra access that being one of her old Apollo hands gave the man.

"Lay it out, Scimitar," she instructed. "You've clearly seen the pieces yourself, so fill me in on the puzzle I'm missing."

"Are you familiar with the Corosec System?" Colombera asked.

Kira had to pull up a datafile on the system—but once she did, she recognized it. She'd even been there once during the war, a short stopover while her carrier had been discharging static mid-op.

"Corosec is a backwater without a habitable planet," she noted. "Like the Costar Systems, rich enough in assorted resources to be worth exploiting, but it sucks to live there."

"About the only extraterritorial possession Apollo had left after the war," Colombera said. "Three million or so souls, working away for the greater glory of assorted corporate masters."

The Costar Clans had been born out of assorted workers left behind in those star systems after failed attempts to exploit the resources there. Given how Redward was handling them now... Well, Corosec was a reminder that things could have ended worse for them.

"Wait," Kira raised a hand, catching part of what he'd said. "The only possession Apollo *had*?"

"Past tense, yes," he said quietly. "Somebody hit the colony a month ago. It's gone."

"That's not possible," she argued. "I mean, it wasn't anybody's core system, but the ASDF had a proper asteroid fort there to watch over the corp stations."

"And it's gone too," Colombera replied. "I don't know details. Apollo isn't releasing much, but it sounds like somebody sabotaged the asteroid fort and then overran the defensive squadron."

"*Somebody*?" Kira countered. "Entire star systems don't get taken over by anonymous movers."

"No one is sure who," he told her. "Packed up everything of value and abandoned the system, leaving behind a couple of hundred nukes to cover their trails. If any of the workers survived, the raiders took them, too."

"Fuck." Kira stared into space for a moment. Three million people didn't move easily—but they could be moved *quickly* with the right kind of resources. "There shouldn't be any pirate forces with that kind of strength in the Sector," she murmured. "It has to be Brisingr."

"What little evidence I can find from here is pretty definitive that it *wasn't*; that's the weird part," Colombera replied. "But I can't see anyone else with the motive and the firepower to take down even *one* asteroid fort.

"I just wish I could guess what was in Corosec that was worth it. Only good news is that a joint expedition from a bunch of the old Friends of Apollo is helping the ASDF sift through the wreckage for survivors."

"There just aren't any," Kira guessed grimly. "No one who went that far was going to leave anything behind. They would have made damn sure."

"That's my guess." Colombera shook his head. "Whoever did this, everyone is looking to Brisingr to solve the problem. That's what the kind of treaty they signed with Apollo means...which seems to have thrown a wrench in their other plans."

"If they can't secure the trade routes and protect the systems in the sector, then their claim of supremacy starts looking real thin, doesn't it," Kira agreed. "But they're also the most likely culprit, too, whatever the sensor data says."

"I don't know if it's going to impact us, boss, but I wanted to make sure you took a look at the mess before *Huntress* and I head out on patrol," Colombera told her. "Maybe you'll see something I missed."

"I'll take a look, Scimitar," she promised. "But I suspect you've already found the bits that matter."

She sighed and shook her head.

"It's still not our problem," she reminded him. "But you're right. It's something we should be paying attention to."

"ADMIRAL, ARE YOU WITH US?"

Kira blinked away the report she'd been looking at and glanced over at Bueller.

"Sorry, what?"

Her boyfriend was rarely that formal in private, and the only other person in the passenger compartment of the shuttle carrying them back to *Deception* was Milani—and while the armored merc was a subordinate, they were also a trusted friend.

"I don't mean to interrupt work, but you were even more absorbed than usual and missed my asking what you wanted for dinner," Konrad teased. "Once I take a run through Engineering, I figured I could cook something up."

"Ah, fair," she allowed. "Um. I..."

He snorted and leaned back in his chair.

"All right, mutton burgers it is," he promised. "*If* you tell me what's bothering you."

Kira met his gaze and he smiled at her reassuringly.

Sighing, she flipped the report to him with a small gesture.

"Corosec System, in our home sector. You know it?" she asked.

"Vaguely," he admitted. "Extra-stellar territory of Apollo, right? Transuranics mining, among other things?"

"Exactly. Someone wiped them out."

Her boyfriend was suddenly very stiff and still.

"There were...several million people there," he murmured.

"Three, per the news reports on the incident," she confirmed. "And an asteroid fort. Parties unknown appear to have disabled the fort and overrun the system. They stole everything that wasn't nailed down and kidnapped anyone they didn't kill."

"And then nuked everything to cover their trails," Konrad whispered. "Gods."

"I'm trying to see if I can find anything in the publicly available data to work out who did it." She sighed. "I know wiser heads with more information are working on the same thing back on Apollo, but I can't help but feel I have some perspective they don't."

"You think it was Equilibrium," he concluded. His eyes were flickering back and forth as he reviewed the same data she'd been reading. "This report seems pretty definitive it wasn't Brisingr."

"And that report was from an Attacan destroyer, not an Apollo or Brisingr ship," Kira noted. "The Attaca System is part of the old Friends of Apollo and they are *pissed* about our surrender. The Agreement forced them to scrap two practically complete battle carriers."

"So, they hate both Apollo *and* Brisingr," Konrad said drily. "That does make them a somewhat trustworthy source. And the old-light data seems...clean enough."

"The fortress never even fired. It just sat there until they rigged everything in the system with nukes and vaporized it with the mining stations," Kira told him. "But the ships...I don't recognize them."

"Neither do I," her boyfriend admitted. "Not from Brisingr service, not from Equilibrium service, either. I'd say they're mostly... armed transports, not even warships. They knew the fort was going to be out of commission."

"Whoever they are, they killed or kidnapped three million people," she said. "If we can find a clue, that's a contract I'll take at a bloody discount."

"And the whole damn fleet will line up behind you to do it," Konrad promised.

"Without question," Milani added. "Very few people end up as mercenaries without having *some* kind of encounter with piracy. On this scale... Memorial Force will follow you into hell to find any of those poor bastards who are left."

"Thanks, Milani," Kira told her subordinate. "Fortunately, dealing with a pirate fleet willing to do something like this... That might be the only thing in the galaxy even *I* think the Brisingr Kaiserreich Navy might be good for!"

35

Huntress completed her patrol sweep. *Deception* completed a patrol sweep, then the carrier went out again. It was a simple cycle, one that put one of the two capital ships in every system near Samuels every five days.

Throughout, Kira remained in the Samuels System, rotating between ships to remain available to their employer as questions, concerns and problems arose. None of them were critical, but all of them were best served by her remaining in the system.

"Contact at the Bennet perimeter," Soler's assistant announced on the bridge. "Signature makes it twelve kilocubics."

Kira could have easily been on the flag deck or, really, *anywhere* on the cruiser at this point. Outside of combat, all she needed was access to the command net and the critical updates.

But she was bored and frustrated. The Colossus Nova Wing had done exactly what she was afraid of, and while two destroyers couldn't cut *that* wide a swathe through the shipping in the Corridor, they were doing enough.

And Kira couldn't do anything about it without uncovering Samuels itself.

So, she was on the bridge, sitting in the observer seat at the back of the U-shaped room and listening to Akuchi Mwangi's team competently go about their jobs.

"SDC has interrogated the IFF," Ronaldo reported, the assistant com officer sounding only slightly less bored than Kira felt. "Wait... it's *Harvest of Hopes*."

"On schedule," Kira said aloud. "That's not a great sign."

"Got to love when a courier returning on schedule is a bad sign," Mwangi said drily. "But yeah. If Colossus was willing to talk, *Harvest* would have been in-system for a while."

"On schedule" in this case meant that *Harvest of Hopes* had transited from Samuels to Colossus, transmitted her request for diplomatic clearance to talk to the Colossus government—and then been rejected and novaed right back.

It said something about the determination of Kira's employer that *Harvest* was making the same trip roughly every ten days right now. So far, Colossus had respected the courier's diplomatic papers, but they had also refused to even consider any discussions with the envoy aboard while the woman was stuck in their system for twenty hours.

"She should have passed through the same trade-route stop as *Huntress*," Mwangi pointed out. "Ronaldo, ping them and ask if they have any updates from Captain Davidović."

"Yes, sir."

Kira had been about to make the same request, but now she simply needed to wait. Her people knew their jobs—especially *Deception*'s crew, who'd been together the longest out of any of her ships now.

Davidović would have sent an update along with the courier if they had crossed paths, but it wasn't likely to be anything critical. The Nova Wing had settled on the strategy of trying to make it too risky for shippers to fly through Samuels. They certainly hadn't made any attempt to reimpose the blockade or even get within a single nova of the Samuels System.

"Any word from our Watchtowers?" Kira asked. That was a

collection of freighters under contract to the SDC to act as an early-warning net. At least one was sitting in each nova point within one jump from Samuels, ready to nova home, at all times.

If there was any word, it would have gone straight to the top of everyone's priority queue.

"Rotation is in twelve hours," Mwangi pointed out. "We'll get updates when the ships nova home in thirty-two. Nothing before then unless Colossus actually makes a move."

"I know," Kira conceded. "See if you can get the sensor data from *Harvest* for the Colossus System as well," she instructed. "Sooner we have that, sooner we can start looking for clues."

Deception's Captain turned far enough in his seat to give her a raised eyebrow—and sent a silent message to her headware.

Anything new in this cycle, boss, or are we just worrying out of habit now?

She shook her head silently at him. At least he wasn't calling her a mother hen out loud!

Nothing new, sorry, she sent back. *Just hate waiting for the other shoe to drop.*

"We'll forward everything to your office once it comes in," Mwangi promised aloud. "CIC will go over the Colossus data, too."

"They may be hiding the ships, but they only have so many yards, and if we have enough data samples..." Kira smiled, as much at her own twitchiness as anything else. "Sooner or later, we *will* locate them."

She didn't need to know where the ships were being refitted to launch a counter-force strike—if she launched that kind of op, it would open with her spreading nova fighters across the perimeter of the system for a *very* detailed look at her targets—but the more she knew about the CNW's refit program, the better she could anticipate when they were going to feel ready to attack.

AFTER REVIEWING the data from multiple diplomatic couriers, as well as the SDC's maps, Kira was now almost as familiar with the Colossus System as she was with the Samuels System—and she'd been in the Samuels System for over a month now.

There was a general standard to most inhabited systems, a pattern that seemed to help create habitable conditions. At least one gas giant in the outer system to sweep up debris and keep the worst of the meteors and comets away from the liquid-water zone. Usually an asteroid belt, formed in the gravity "dip" created by that gas giant. Then, of course, a planet in the liquid-water zone, often with a moon of some size.

Colossus checked off all of those boxes. Unusually, the habitable planet, Colossus itself, was the first actual *planet* of the system, with an inner system asteroid belt filling the orbit that the math would have put another planet into.

A couple of other rocky worlds, a large mid-system asteroid belt and a single gas giant with the wrong proportions to be easily processed into fuel made up the rest of the system. Artificial constellations of captured asteroids hung over both Colossus and Lindos, the gas giant.

All of this was lit by Helios, one of the larger G-type stars Kira had seen. And somewhere in the mess—she had her guesses, but they didn't have enough data to nail it down—was a brand-spanking-new military shipyard refitting the warships Colossus had bought from Brisingr.

CIC—both the combat information center and the tactical-analysis team that lived there—was doing their own analysis of the latest data as she stared at the holographic map she'd conjured above her desk, but she figured it never hurt to have multiple different perspectives on the data.

It had been extremely easy to confirm that the refits weren't taking place at the civilian yards in orbit of Colossus or at the planet's Lagrange points. Those yards were active and busy, but even at the distance that *Harvest of Hopes* took her scans from, it was straightforward enough to confirm that none of them appeared to be warships.

"Huh."

Kira exhaled thoughtfully as she looked at a missing data point.

N45-K had been present in orbit of Colossus in every previous data set. The two D9C-class destroyers had occasionally been with her, but mostly the CNW's single active carrier had orbited close to what Kira guessed was the command station for Colossus's defenses.

Now that orbit was empty. For the first time in the four trips *Harvest of Hopes* had made to the Colossus System as Samuels tried to negotiate peace, the carrier was missing from her position under the defense constellation's guns.

Mental commands highlighted several sections of the system she'd been keeping a careful eye on. *Harvest* had been too far out, and her sensors didn't have high-enough resolution to be certain, but those sections were where *Kira* would have put capital-ship yards.

The data they had from *Harvest* suggested that there were, at least, space stations at each of the locations. Now, though...

"Mwangi, I need your eyes and the analysis team to focus somewhere in the Colossus data," she ordered.

"If it's Colossus orbit, we already know that *N45-K* has moved. That's a problem, isn't it?" the Captain asked.

"It is, yes," Kira agreed. "But I want you to take a look at the map location I'm sending you now. It's hard to be sure with the resolutions we've got, but I've been watching this zone as one of the places *I* would have put a concealed military shipyard."

It was anchored on a larger-than-average asteroid that didn't quite qualify as a dwarf planet, one that orbited near the outer edge of the inner asteroid belt and was easily accessed from Colossus for at least half of the habitable planet's year.

"I'm flipping it to Analysis, but what am I looking for, Admiral?" Mwangi asked.

Kira was suddenly *very* aware that, experienced as her people were at this point, the vast majority of her officers and crew were from the Syntactic Cluster, a region only now being dragged kicking and screaming into military and economic technology parity with her home sector.

"That large asteroid creates a lee zone that's shielded from debris but has the asteroid belt to protect it," she told him. "My analysis of the previous scans suggested refined metals, power signatures, the works for a midsized complex."

There was a pause as *Deception*'s Captain ran through the same data.

"Okay, I can kind of see it," he conceded. "It looks like a mining outpost or something, though, nothing major."

"Compare it to the same location on the last scan, Akuchi," Kira ordered.

The pause was longer.

"Kuso," Mwangi swore. That was, she suspected, his *only* Japanese—but it was enough.

"There was a lot more activity there ten days ago, wasn't there?" she asked. "Am I right?"

"I'll let Tactical look at the map point themselves," her flag captain replied. "See if they hit the same pattern—but you're right. Whatever was under construction there is gone."

"Which means they've finished refitting at least one ship," Kira concluded.

ADMIRAL BACHCHAN LISTENED to the analysis report silently, her face impassive as she waited for Commander Soler to finish laying out what Kira's people knew.

"That's not much," she finally said. "Just enough to panic, not enough to action."

Kira, Mwangi and Soler were linked to the SDC's commander by hologram. She'd been expecting Bachchan to include other officers, but instead they were only speaking to the Admiral.

"Unfortunately, yes," Kira agreed. "Worst-case scenario, they've finished the entire refit ahead of schedule."

"How likely is that?" the Samuels officer asked.

"Possible, not likely," Kira estimated. "I mean, *Brisingr* could have finished bringing those ships up to speed in the time they've had, but Brisingr knows those classes inside and out. My guess is that they've focused their efforts on getting a portion of them online—as they did with the first wave from the Secondary Service Reserve."

Bachchan looked like she'd eaten something sour as she considered.

"So, it depends on their strategy and how they'd decided to work with it a month or more ago," she said grimly. "If they are sticking with the commerce raiding, they may have focused on getting the escorts online. If they've done *that*..."

"They may well have enough hulls to run a blockade across an end of the Corridor," Kira replied. "Leave merchants with no choice but to discharge at Colossus.

"That would be unlikely to be looked on positively by the systems on the edge of the Corridor," she noted. "And it would be a thin blockade, a fragile one. Fragile enough that even armed merchant ships would be able to breach it in places.

"But it would serve their strategic purposes quite well—until we decided we were prepared to risk uncovering Samuels and sent my ships after the blockade." She shrugged.

"There is no single ship in the flotilla that Brisingr sold Colossus that I am not confident in the ability of either of my ships to handily defeat," she reminded Bachchan. "While a blockade with their escorts would be a temporary inconvenience to your trade, it would spread out their ships and expose them to defeat in detail."

"Which they know," Bachchan concluded. "So. They will have commissioned as many of the heavy ships as possible and will attempt to force a fleet action. What is our countermeasure?"

"*Huntress* will have just novaed to her last trade-route stop," Kira said. "She'll return here in a bit over twenty hours.

"My recommendation at this point is that you see if we can reasonably configure the Watchtower volunteers to act as depot ships for your Guardians—and finish getting the depot ships we *have* online," she told the Samuels woman. "If we hold both of my ships at the ready, the Watchtower ships can bring us out from Samuels as soon as the Nova Wing makes their move."

"If they've commissioned the full strength that they purchased, that *is* more than you can handle," Bachchan pointed out. "What happens *then*?"

"They cannot both blockade Samuels *and* maintain sufficient force concentration to fight *Deception* and *Huntress*," Kira replied. "If they bring the full flotilla, we see what they do. If they attempt a new blockade, we defeat them in deta—"

"Contact! Unscheduled contact!"

Bachchan was receiving the alert from a different source than Kira and *Deception*'s officers, but she was clearly getting a notice from someone.

"It's *Shenzhen*," Bachchan told them. "Watchtower unit...from the nova-route stop *Huntress* should be at."

"Get the data from them, Admiral," Kira told her employer. "Mwangi, take *Deception* to battle stations."

"Demirci?" Bachchan demanded.

"We're not the only ones who can attempt a defeat in detail, Admiral!"

36

By the time Kira made it to her flag deck and linked up to the bridge, *Shenzhen* had finished transferring most of her data over to the warship. The crew of civilian volunteers had, quite reasonably, erred on the side of safety when the Nova Wing had jumped into the region.

That meant she didn't have a lot of data—but she had *some*. She knew that Colossus had achieved basically her worst-case scenario: both N45s and the surviving I50 had arrived together, with four destroyers in escort array.

That was the worst news. The slightly-less-bad news was that at least some of the merchants who'd been coming through Samuels had clearly been feeding intelligence to Colossus. Kira wasn't entirely surprised by that, but she was kicking herself for not varying the patrol routes more.

The CNW had known exactly which trade-route stop to find *Huntress* at. What they *hadn't* known, and this was the only good news she could see, was where to find the carrier inside a mapped zone roughly a light-hour across.

And they'd got it wrong. The seven-ship strike group had

emerged closer to *Shenzhen* than to *Huntress*, several light-minutes from the mercenary carrier. That meant their capital ships weren't in play and that there was a small but measurable warning to Captain Davidović's people.

"Wallis," Kira addressed the navigator. "We have their location. I want us to nova in right on top of the bastards."

"That's...risky," Lyssa Wallis replied calmly. "I can do it, but if we interpenetrate, it will be a *very* short engagement."

"Then don't interpenetrate," Kira told her. The best-case scenario for a six-light-year nova was a thirty-thousand-kilometer error radius. That could put *Deception* in plasma-cannon range of the enemy carriers, but it also meant that Wallis *couldn't* guarantee a safe emergence.

On the other hand, the odds of an unsafe nova were so low as to be almost irrelevant. But the navigator had to give the warning.

"Running the calcs. I need two minutes," Wallis warned.

"I need to talk to the locals," Kira replied. Adjusting her channels, she relinked to Admiral Bachchan.

The SDC chief was waiting patiently enough, to her surprise.

"*Huntress* is in trouble," Bachchan noted. "Distance gives her a chance, but it also risks her not seeing them coming. And the N-Forty-Fives have more fighters than she does."

"Scimitar has better planes and better pilots than Colossus does," Kira said firmly. "The odds are more even than you think."

"Still, I feel that we need to do *something* to help," Bachchan told her. "I have nova fighters scrambling as we speak; I can send them with you."

"Where they will be lambs to the slaughter with their drives on cooldown," Kira replied. "No, Admiral, we have this. Without carriers, your people are only set up to deal with pirates and troublemakers.

"Not a fleet battle."

She shook her head.

"If the depot ships we'd sold you were ready, we'd have your fighters *at* the trade-route stops, but they're not," she admitted. "So long as your fighters can't hit the battlespace ready to nova, they only have one punch in them before Colossus tears them apart.

"I won't sacrifice your people when I don't need them."

"I appreciate that, Admiral, but this is our star system and our fight," Bachchan reminded her.

"And you're paying me to fight it for you," Kira replied. "And I won't ask you to send your people to unnecessary deaths when I have the situation under control."

"Nova plotted," Wallis reported. "Orders?"

"That's my cue, Admiral Bachchan," Kira told the local commander. "I have a plan; I have the firepower. I *wanted* these people to court a fleet battle, and they've played right into my hands."

She smiled predatorily.

"I'll see you on the other side."

Dropping that link, she turned back to the virtual mirror of the bridge.

"Captain Mwangi, is *Deception* ready?" she asked.

"In all aspects," Mwangi confirmed. "We await your order."

"Then stand by jammers, cannon and fighters. You may nova when ready."

THEIR DATA from *Shenzhen* was eight minutes old. A lot could change in eight minutes—but with nova drives in cooldown, the location of a spaceship could only change so much.

There was no immediate need for *Deception*'s jammers. They emerged into the battlespace in the middle of the Colossus ships' multiphasic jamming field, barely a hundred thousand kilometers from the enemy carriers.

Kira spent a fraction of a second processing the entire scene, riding the digital speed of her headware to allow her to make mistakes faster and with more surety.

The CNW had split their forces. The two N45 light carriers had barely moved and were still roughly where *Shenzhen* had seen them. They had kept the two smaller destroyers—the newly refitted D5D-class ships—with them, but they had *no* carrier space patrol.

I50-Q6 had taken the larger destroyers from the SSR and headed straight for *Huntress* at full thrust. In eight minutes, they'd crossed a third of the distance to Davidović's ship and taken themselves entirely out of support range for the carriers.

Without data on the enemy course, Wallis had split the difference and dropped *Deception* almost exactly in the middle of the two Colossus forces. They were closer to the carriers, but *Deception* could easily catch up to the older I50 cruiser.

"Fighters up," Cartman's voice echoed in Kira's ear. "What's the target?"

That was the last decision *Kira* would make before this entire battle devolved onto her subordinates...and it depended entirely on what she thought her *other* subordinates had done.

"The cruisers are Scimitar's problem," she told Cartman and Mwangi. "We go for the carriers."

The whole analysis, discussion and decision had taken less than twenty seconds—the time necessary for *Deception* to fling all twenty of her active starfighters into space. It was enough time that the Colossus ships knew they were there too, and the two destroyers guarding the carriers were now charging toward the heavy cruiser.

"Clear the road," Mwangi ordered. "Soler? Get those destroyers out of my sky!"

Deception shivered as her turrets spun and opened fire. The destroyers fired first, but their lighter cannon simply didn't have the cohesion to reach the heavy cruiser at that range.

Mwangi and Soler, however, knew the K70-class cruiser's capabilities to a fine art. Fourteen heavy guns aligned themselves on their targets and spat plasma into the void.

The jamming made a mess of sensors and targeting, especially long-range targeting like this, but Soler's gunners knew their jobs.

Each destroyer was targeted by a shotgun-spread pattern of seven shots, the turrets cycling as they worked their way through the space the destroyers had to be in.

There was no guarantee that they'd see the results of a hit, let alone a miss. False negatives were far more likely than false positives, though, and Kira watched in silence as her people mapped the results onto the holographic displays around them.

The destroyers were doing the same, but the two older ships only had twelve main cannon between them, organized in dual turrets. When they hit *Deception*, it hurt—but they didn't land enough hits.

Damage reports flickered across Kira's displays, but none of it was severe. They were still in sections of ablative armor expended and energy-dispersal webs burned out, defensive systems doing what they were supposed to do and dying to protect the ship and crew.

One destroyer came apart moments before the other, but the conclusion of the uneven duel had never been in question. *Deception*'s guns began to track the carriers—but where the destroyers had charged, the carriers had retreated. They weren't in range yet.

And they didn't need to be. Cartman knew her trade as well as any fighter pilot ever born, and the Colossus Nova Wing were still amateurs at carrier combat. They'd assumed that the destroyers were a reasonable substitute for a carrier space patrol.

The twenty nova fighters appearing on the far side of the carriers were a lesson that the CNW's carrier captains wouldn't live long enough to process. Kira couldn't make out which fighters were which through the jamming, but she knew how *she'd* have coordinated the strike.

The eight Hussar-Seven heavy fighters would have carried the weight of the strike, with the Wolverines playing decoy to draw the fire from the N45s' defensive anti-fighter cannon. Sixteen torpedoes, launched at close range, would have gutted *Deception*.

The N45 carrier on the receiving end of *Deception*-Charlie's torpedo strike simply ceased to exist.

The other found itself the sole target of Mwangi's guns as *Deception* closed and the nova fighters vanished back to safety. The N45 design paid for its large fighter capacity by having extremely limited onboard defenses, and the carrier's light cannon were even less of a threat to the cruiser than the destroyers' guns had been.

There were ways to signal surrender even in the chaotic mess of a multiphasic jamming battlespace, and Kira half-expected to see them all. Instead, the Colossus carrier grimly plunged toward *Deception*, trying to bring her handful of guns into play.

She failed, breaking apart under the hammering of *Deception*'s own guns while still over fifty thousand kilometers away.

As the second carrier died, Kira's attention turned back to the enemy cruiser—in time to watch Scimitar's bomber strike go in.

Colombera clearly hadn't known if Kira was going to make it in time and hadn't seen her through *Huntress*'s own jamming when he'd put together his plan. Determined to clear the board and protect their carrier at any costs, *Huntress*'s Avalanche Flight Group, her two squadrons of bombers, went in with only a single squadron of fighters for cover.

That was Kira's *guess*, at least, since she only saw eighteen signatures appear out of nova for the run on the cruiser and her destroyer escorts. Again without nova-fighter protection, the destroyers tried to interpose themselves—but the Avalanches ignored them, evading around the lighter warships to clear their lines of fire.

It was a calculated risk, one that Kira knew had to come at a price—but it also fooled the destroyers into focusing on the bombers. It didn't matter whether the escorting fighters were Wolverines or Hussars at that point. The Hussar-Sevens had two torpedoes each to the Wolverines' one...but salvoed at point-blank range at a distracted enemy, the difference between three torpedoes and six per destroyer was irrelevant.

Kira *guessed* the escorts were Wolverines, though, because the destroyers *survived* the hammering. Crippled and suddenly focused on their own survival, they couldn't stop the bombers.

With the destroyers out of commission and the fighters either elsewhere or just gone, the cruiser could perhaps have stood off *some* bombers. She was far from defenseless, after all.

Against twelve bombers easily two decades more modern than the cruiser herself, she never stood a chance. Kira couldn't see how many torpedoes were launched through the jamming, but she saw the result: the cruiser, like the carriers a few moments earlier, simply ceased to exist.

"Set a course for *Huntress*," she ordered Mwangi as she saw the battlespace clear. "Drop our jammers and make full speed to the rendezvous.

"If you get a link to Cartman, send our fighters ahead to support her."

Deception's Captain chuckled softly.

"Do you think, for even one moment, that you need to give Nightmare that order?" he asked.

37

WITH *DECEPTION*'S JAMMING DOWN, at least, Kira was able to get a clearer view of the situation in the overall trade-route stop. While the computers on *Deception* were generally decent at picking out what was near the cruiser in the jamming fields, seeing *beyond* the jamming fields was impossible.

Now she could see the bubble, several light-minutes away, marking where *Huntress* had been fighting for her life. Kira didn't know, yet, how that battle had ended. She knew Cartman had taken another twenty fighters into it and that the capital ships supporting the enemy fighters were gone.

The Liberators' pilots might not know it, but they'd already lost the battle. For that matter, they might know it—the battle around *Huntress* could already be over, but Kira wouldn't see that for several minutes.

"We're about fifty-five minutes from rendezvous," Wallis reported. "Neither we nor *Huntress* will be able to nova to speed that up."

Kira nodded silently. The nova fighters would flit back and forth between the two capital ships, but that was why the parasite ships with their fast-cooling short-range FTL drives existed.

"We have to trust that Davidović and our fighter wings have the situation under control," she murmured. A hundred and twenty Liberators versus sixty Wolverines and Hussar-Sevens—and Scimitar had sent six of the Hussars away with his bombers, turning the odds even further against his people.

Kira trusted Colombera's judgment. The fact that he'd sent any escorts at all with the bombers told her that the battle had been more even than her worst fears. Now those escorts were presumably back in the fray—and Cartman's planes were reinforcing them, bringing the numbers to eighty on one-twenty.

Memorial Force's fighters were the latest designs from the Navy of the Royal Crest, a peer power to Apollo or Brisingr. She figured they were at least a generation ahead of the Liberators, and the Wolverines were specialized interceptors.

She suspected that the Colossus Nova Wing was getting a harsh education in why, sometimes, a master of one was better than a jack of all trades.

"Outside *Huntress*'s jamming bubble, nova zone is clear," Solar reported. "I've got three clusters of civilian ships, all making a run for it away from all types of battle zones."

"Good," Kira replied. "We want the civilians well clear." She paused. "Are there any Watchtower ships left?"

"Not that I have ID files for," Soler told her. "Might be someone we can talk into carrying a message to Samuels, but I suspect anyone who *can* nova has."

"I would," Kira conceded. She eyed the nearest cluster of ships. Some of the ships looked familiar, but her brain was still riding an adrenaline high. Whatever was familiar about the ships wasn't a threat, at least.

"Group one," she said slowly. "Soler, can you run IDs on those ships for me?"

"Standard sixty-kilocubic freighters, mostly," the Tactical officer replied. "Couple of tramps, few others of assorted sizes. I'll start a closer analysis if you want, but we were focusing on the area around *Huntress.*"

"Are any of them *missing* since we jumped in?" Kira asked softly.

There was a long pause.

"No... Wait... No... Huh."

"Commander?" Mwangi demanded a moment before Kira could.

"We have the same *number* of ships, but they're *different* ships," Soler said. "Two new sixty-kilocubic ships since we arrived, but two similarly sized ships have left, too."

In a perfect world, they'd have gone to Samuels and updated the SDC on what had happened. But the chill rippling down Kira's spine suggested another option. A much uglier option.

"Mwangi, pull the repair teams back inside," she ordered softly.

"We still need to replace damaged dispersal webs and plating," the cruiser captain complained. "The faster the teams get to work, the sooner—"

"Get them back inside *now*," she snapped. "And stand by for incoming!"

She was too late. Even as she barked the order, she knew she was too late—even before the nova flares flashed across the screen, someone *else* was doing what she'd done to the Colossus Nova Wing and emerging barely outside heavy-cannon range.

But where she'd done it with one capital ship, the newcomers did it with three. And escorts. She barely needed to reference her headware to identify them, either. In the stark light of their own emergences, her memories were more than sufficient to identify two K-90-series heavy cruisers and one HC-10 series battle carrier of the Brisingr Kaiserreich Navy.

The six D12-class destroyers arrayed around the carrier and cruisers were just the icing on the cake, even though the escorts alone out-cubed *Deception* two to one.

"Evasive maneuvers," Mwangi snapped. "Jammers up!"

"Hold off the jammers for a moment," Kira ordered. "Maintain evasives and get us clear...but if *they're* not jamming, they want to talk."

The first confirmation was that the carrier group didn't immediately attempt to close, though the Weltraumpanzer heavy fighters and other starfighters spilling out of the three capital ships were hardly a pleasant greeting.

A moment later, a chirping sound on several consoles confirmed her suspicions.

"Incoming transmission from the carrier," Smolak said in a small, very tired, voice.

"Link me," Kira ordered. "Time lag?"

"Third of a second each way," the coms officer told her. "Practically real-time."

Kira nodded and set the channel carefully. She'd see everything the BKN was sending—and they'd only see her. Hopefully, that would give the impression she had a full flag bridge and be a tad more intimidating than the empty space around her.

She received the same thing from the Brisingr ship as she was sending: a holographic image of a single person, standing stiff-backed at attention as they appeared in front of her.

"I am Vice Admiral Maxi Bueller," the stranger said grimly. Their basic headware beacon information came through on the transmission, informing Kira that the androgynous gray-haired officer was nonbinary...and a member of "*those* Buellers," as Macey had asked Konrad Bueller when they'd met.

This officer, like Kira's boyfriend, could theoretically stand for election to Kaiser.

"I am Admiral Kira Demirci," Kira replied. "I am not certain, Admiral Bueller, why your ships are present here. You have no conflict with Samuels or Colossus. That said, I have no contract to engage you and will not interfere with your passage through the Corridor."

"I am not one to cut fancy words and lies from whole cloth, Admiral Demirci," Bueller told her. "We both know how to play the political games, but I do not feel that deception or prevarication will serve us here, will they?"

"Perhaps not," Kira admitted. "I am aware, after all, that Brisingr provided Colossus with the ships that attacked Samuels."

"The ships you have handily dispatched," Bueller said, with clear admiration in their voice. "The argument over how much firepower was necessary to bring you in was heated, Admiral, but I saw Heller's Hellions in action at the end of the war.

"I had no illusions about the ability of an officer trained in *that* school."

Kira had to swallow a wince of both concern and surprise. She hadn't expected that the BKN carrier group was just passing through —the *timing* was suspicious enough, but the fact they'd been backing Colossus had made it likely they were making a play.

She just hadn't expected it to be that explicitly about Memorial Force.

"Neither I nor my employer are currently at war with Brisingr," she said softly. "I am...not certain what you mean by 'bring me in.'"

"You are a complicating factor, Admiral Demirci," Admiral Bueller told her. "One my Kaiser has decided we can no longer afford.

"Out of recognition of the situation, professional respect for your achievements and a desire not to have to kill a fellow member of the Succession in Commander Konrad Bueller, I have an offer to make."

"There will be consequences for this," Kira warned.

"Samuels is years from being even a *threat* to the Kaiserreich," Admiral Bueller replied. "Redward is too distant to ever be a real concern. Your friends are weak or distant, Admiral. There is only one way out of this."

"Then state your offer."

"Surrender. Yourself, *K79-L*, Commander Bueller, any other survivors of the Three Hundred and Third Nova Combat Group, and the Brisingr traitors from *K79* will enter my custody," the Brisingr Admiral told her. "We will permit any Syntactic Cluster crew members of *K79-L* to return to the Cluster aboard *Huntress*, but *K79-L* is our ship.

"I am authorized by my Kaiser to guarantee the lives of the Apollon and Brisingrian personnel surrendered to us," they continued. "You will all be placed under house arrest on one of the Kaiser's personal estates, where you will remain in a state of comfort and luxury until such time as Kaiser Reinhardt decides you are no longer a threat to the Kaiserreich."

As demands for total surrender went, the offer was surprisingly generous. The BKN *did* have a legitimate claim on *Deception*, not that Kira would acknowledge it, and there was a real argument that the forty-odd Brisingr members of *Deception*'s crew, like Konrad, had committed treason.

There was no legitimate claim on Kira, Colombera and Cartman, the only three members of the ASDF's 303 Nova Combat Group aboard *Deception* or *Huntress*, but sheer firepower made a lot of laws. Kira couldn't deliver Dinesha Patel or Evgenia Michel, the last two Three Oh Three survivors, into the Kaiserreich's hands—Patel commanded *Fortitude*'s fighter group, and Michel commanded one of the escort destroyers—but she had to admit that Admiral Bueller's carrier group could take the two ships she had.

Jamming is down around Huntress*; they're updating us*, Mwangi informed her by silent headware message. *Scimitar's people were hurt bad. They've got tracks on a lot of ejector pods, but all told, we're down thirty-five fighters.*

In Kira's experience, there was about a seventy percent chance that the ejector pods had worked properly, blasting the fighter crews out at the last possible second. That meant she'd likely *only* lost twelve to fifteen people, including copilots, so far today.

Those were names and faces she'd have to register later. Right now, the cold numbers that came along with Mwangi's message were critically important.

Memorial Force had twenty-seven Wolverines, twenty-two

Hussar-Sevens, and eight Wildcat-Fours left. Fifty-seven nova fighters.

Vice Admiral Bueller had three squadrons of Weltraumdachs-Fünf bombers, four of Weltraumfuchs-Sechs Interceptors, and eight Weltraumpanzer-Fünf heavy fighters. A hundred and fifty nova fighters, all told.

Plus the two K90 cruisers, slightly smaller than *Deception* but twenty years newer, and the D12 destroyers, half the size of the cruisers but still newer than *Deception*. And it wasn't like the carrier was unarmed either—and with the entire carrier group hanging just outside cannon range, that was *far* too relevant.

Your orders? Mwangi asked silently.

"My patience is not infinite, Admiral Demirci," the Brisingr officer said quietly. "I know your reputation, and I'm disinclined to let you come up with a clever solution. These terms are generous, but they are not negotiable.

"If you have not powered down *K79-L*'s engines and cannon in ninety seconds, I will assume you do not intend to accept my offer."

"Your terms *are* generous," Kira conceded, trying to play for time to think, searching through the scanner feeds of the trade-route stop for some kind of answer. *Huntress* could send the nova fighters back, but with the communication lag, *Deception* could be gone by the time her fighters made it.

The only nova fighter available, in fact, was Kira's own spare Wolverine. Kira was good—she knew it. Even rusty, she could fly circles around all but a handful of her own pilots.

But the Brisingr nova-fighter wings would have pilots forged in the same cauldron that had shaped her. Her Wolverine still had a *slight* edge over even a Weltraumfuchs-Sechs in speed and firepower, and she figured she could take the average BKN pilot at two-to-one odds.

Not at *a hundred and fifty to one*.

"You understand, Admiral, that surrender does not come easily to any of us, especially in the face of what is frankly an *illegal* demand,"

Kira said. "And you ask me to surrender people who have placed their lives and trust in my hands, not merely myself."

"Legality in interstellar affairs is a question of tradition and firepower," Admiral Bueller told her. "I have the firepower...and my Kaiser's order says damn the tradition. Your clock is ticking, Admiral."

Konrad. Maxi Bueller. You know them? She silently messaged her lover.

Her headware conversations were passing between the blink of an eye, but she knew that Maxi Bueller figured she was having them. The Brisingr Admiral could afford to be patient, and they'd already stated the limits of their patience.

Kira had forty-eight seconds left.

I know them, Konrad told her. *Not well. We're about as distantly related as we could be and still both stand in the Succession. They have a reputation as a straight shooter—but when you* are *the hammer, all problems are* definitely *nails.*

And that description sent a harsh chill down her back, and her gaze snapped back up to meet Maxi Bueller's gaze.

"This whole war between Colossus and Samuels," she said slowly. "Was it just to set this up?"

Bueller shrugged.

"Outside my area," they admitted. "But from my conversations with my counterpart in the Shadows...yes."

Straight shooter, indeed. Kira would almost have preferred they *not* be that honest. She perhaps could have surrendered if she'd thought this had been an opportunistic strike. As it was...

Admiral, we just received a transmission from Group One, Smolak told Kira.

What? Kira asked. *One of the freighters? What did they say?*

I think so, yes. Message was two words: "standing by."

Kira flipped her data feed to the collection of civilian transports, and a suspicion struck her. They were clustered in a strange fashion, one that made no sense for civilian freighters trying to evade a hostile fleet...but one that made a *lot* of sense for freighters trying to hide something.

"You started a war," Kira told Maxi Bueller softly. "Memorial Force has destroyed ten nova ships. Best guess...we've killed over fifteen thousand human beings. Ignoring the *civilian* losses that were inevitable in the commerce raiding and blockades that Colossus engaged in.

"So, what, twenty thousand or so people died to set up this ambush?"

"I won't pretend I like it, Admiral Demirci, but it doesn't change my objectives or my orders," Admiral Bueller told her. "You're just about out of time. I don't want to kill you. I really don't want to kill my cousin, but I have my orders.

"Surrender, Admiral Demirci, or die."

Kira swallowed and placed her faith in her friends.

"My contract with the Ministries of Samuels requires me to secure these trade-route stops against any and all threats to the Samuels System," she told the Brisingr officer. "By your own admission, you have effectively allied yourselves with the Colossus System in their war against Samuels.

"By the authority of my contract and the general acceptance of the exclusive security zone around a settled star system, I am ordering you to withdraw or be fired upon."

"That is an answer, isn't it?" Admiral Bueller said flatly. "I'm sorry, Admiral Demirci."

"So am I. When you get to hell, tell them your path was paved with your Kaiser's orders!"

38

"Accelerating evasive maneuvers; jammers online," Mwangi reported grimly. "Three minutes until *Huntress* knows what's happening." He paused. "Seventy-two seconds before their cruisers range on us. Their fighters could be here anytime.

"Your orders?"

"Vector toward Freighter Group One, maximum thrust," Kira ordered levelly. "Time until they see what's going on?"

"The freighters?" *Deception*'s Captain asked.

"The freighters," Kira confirmed.

"Twenty seconds left," Soler replied. "Their nova strike can arrive anytime after that."

Mwangi stared at his Tactical officer for a moment, then swore under his breath.

"The depot ships?"

"They need ten times as long as a carrier to launch fighters, but they can deliver them to the nova stop," Kira reminded him. "It seems Bachchan wasn't willing to leave things entirely up to us."

"We still have no fighter cover, and they're about to be on top of us," Mwangi warned. "This is going to hurt, boss."

For a single glorious moment, Kira was about to charge down to her nova fighter and take to space. Practicality shot that down far too quickly—if nothing else, the odds were that Dilshad Tamboli, *Deception*'s deck boss, hadn't even prepped Wolverine Thirteen for action.

And the math wasn't in Kira's favor, anyway.

"My faith is in your gunners, Captain," Kira murmured. "Fight your ship."

She met his gaze for a long second, then he nodded firmly and turned away to snap more orders.

Kira's own focus was on trying to pierce the jamming fields around all of the involved ships. It was *unlikely* the Brisingr fighters were going to make a sub-light-second nova—the cooldown was still a full minute at that distance, so they were more likely to nova out and nova back in.

Or they would come in with the capital ships, only lunging ahead when the cruisers started pounding *Deception*. There was a solid logic to that, especially when they *knew* there'd be no fighter cover until well after their strike.

There was no point in risking bombers to *Deception*'s turrets when they could get cruisers to cover them. With everything *known*, it was the right call.

And Kira desperately hoped she'd guessed right and that it was going to be the *wrong* call. Because if she'd guessed wrong...she should have surrendered.

"No contacts," Mwangi murmured on a private channel. "We... may be in real trouble here. Cruiser range in thirty seconds."

"Our job right now, Akuchi, is to stay alive," Kira told him.

Testing shots began to sparkle on the display. *Deception* was running away from the enemy as fast as she could, but the sad truth was that the Brisingr ships were newer and faster. Even the hundred-and-ten-thousand-cubic-meter HC-10 carrier had an acceleration edge on Mwangi's ship, and the entire carrier group was slowly closing the range.

The irony was that the K-90s had basically the same armament as

Deception. Fourteen heavy guns and twenty heavy fighters. The newer ships were faster and better protected, but their offensive capabilities were near-identical.

The carrier had the same guns but was hanging ever so slightly back from the cruisers, letting them take the long-range potshots that were slowly narrowing the target zone.

"Here they come," Kira said aloud as the movement she'd been watching for appeared on her display. She couldn't pick out individual nova fighters through the jamming, but she could see when over a hundred of them lunged forward.

Unlike Colossus, the Brisingr Kaiserreich Navy knew their game. They *also* knew that Memorial Force still had almost sixty fighters left, including enough bombers to easily take out a carrier if given a chance. Kira couldn't tell how many fighters Admiral Bueller had held back to protect their ships, but she assumed it was at least three ten-ship squadrons of heavy fighters.

"Their cruisers are being careful to avoid hitting their fighters, but we have to keep the heavy turrets on the big guys," Mwangi warned. "We've got *nothing* to keep them fro—"

"Nova flares!" Soler snapped. "Multiple nova flares... The hell? Jianhong radiation suggests full six-light-year novas!"

The jamming field would make it difficult for *Deception*'s sensors to even identify *how many* ships had just novaed in, but the difference in radiation between a light-minute nova and a multi-light-year nova was still discernible.

And somewhere over eighty Guardian heavy fighters had just appeared between *Deception* and the oncoming Brisingr fighter strike. Their position wasn't perfect, but given that they'd novaed all the way from Samuels based on data one of the fleeing freighters had brought them, Kira was impressed by how close they *had* managed it.

"Watch the SDC fighters," Mwangi ordered. "Let's not shoot our rescuers in the back, shall we? Pick a destroyer and focus her down; leave the fighters to the fighters."

Bueller's destroyers were advancing behind the nova-fighter

squadrons, but they weren't nearly as tough as the cruisers behind them in turn. It took only a handful of salvos for *Deception*'s gunners to get the rhythm of the lead destroyer—and only two more to reduce the forty-two-kilocubic ship to spinning debris.

Meanwhile, the entire zone in front of *Deception* was turning into a free-for-all dogfight, as the SDC's pilots threw themselves into the chaos of the fight. Kira saluted her allies mentally, but she *knew* the odds were against them. The BKN fighters had a wider edge over the SDC planes than her own craft had over the Brisingr ones—and there were more BKN nova fighters in space than SDC ones.

And then a *second* series of nova flares announced the arrival of Memorial Force's fighters, and Kira bit back a moment of hope. The same observer who'd sent a call for reinforcements across the light-years back to Samuels had *also* sent one across a handful of light-minutes to *Huntress*—and Mel Cartman and Abdullah Colombera were every bit as good as Kira was in a starfighter.

Chaos swirled across the battlespace, fighters intermingling in the radiation haze of the multiphasic jammers. Kira had no coms with her allies, only with the crew of *Deception*. She didn't have full visibility—she didn't even know how many fighters her allies and her subordinates had thrown into the growing dogfight around her cruiser.

Not *everything* was guesswork. *Deception* had incredible optics and powerful computers analyzing the imagery they picked up. Multiphasic jammers rendered even optical imagery messy, but it gave her a concept of what was going on.

But she had to guess what the SDC was thinking—and the main clue she had was that the only SDC fighters she'd seen had come all the way from Samuels. That was workable for a defensive formation like they were currently holding, but it didn't work for *offensive* strikes.

"Akuchi, we have to go after the cruisers," she told *Deception*'s Captain. "Leave the destroyers to the SDC heavies. We need to fix the capital ships' attention on us and kick the shit out of them.

"Bring us about, take us over the dogfight and ram our cannon down those bastards' throats."

Akuchi Mwangi had been a mercenary for far longer than Kira, and she could *feel* his urge to object, to point out *Deception* was their irreplaceable asset there...

But all he did was nod and turn to his crew.

"Wallis, bring us about," he ordered, repeating Kira's instructions. "Full thrust at the Brisingr cruisers! Soler, focus your fire on the cruiser to port. Let's show Junior that having the shiniest toys isn't everything!"

The cruiser shivered around Kira as she flipped in space. Their timing had been *almost* perfect—the moment before they turned was the moment the Brisingr carrier group finally dialed them in.

Half a dozen plasma blasts, each as powerful as a bomber's torpedo, hammered into *Deception* as the mercenary ship flipped in space. Damage alerts flashed red across Kira's displays, but none of it slowed the maneuver.

But when her ship finished the flip, only twelve heavy guns opened fire on the enemy cruiser. Two turrets were flashing red on the internal displays, a problem Kira needed to leave to her boyfriend and her flag captain.

Her focus had to be on the battle, judging the openings. Mwangi had to fight his ship—Kira had to fight the battle and tell him where his ship should be. There'd been an opening to get around the fighters and she'd taken it, but that had exposed the cruiser to the full fire of all three Brisingr capital ships.

Over thirty cannon blazed a pattern through the void around *Deception*. Soler's gunners were better. They got a lock on their target cruiser faster, hammering her with plasma blast after plasma blast, but the enemy had too many guns firing too many shots for the mercenary ship to go untouched.

"Come *on*," Kira hissed as damage alerts flared on the display again. "I *know* you, Scimitar. *Use the opening*."

People were dying on her flagship. She *knew* that. But she also knew, given everything that she believed Colombera had known when his fighters had novaed into the battle, what *she* would have done...and she'd trained Abdullah Colombera from the moment the man had left the flight academy.

"Nova flares!" Soler snapped. "Multiple flares on the far side of the carrier!"

"And there we go," Kira whispered.

Rearming the bombers took longer than any other type of nova fighter, and bombers were ineffective at best without their torpedoes. But the eight surviving bombers could carry *sixty-four* torpedoes—and Vice Admiral Maxi Bueller's ships' focus was entirely on the cruiser making a suicide charge on them.

The fighters tasked to protect the carrier and the cruisers had managed to remain focused on their mission—but sixty Guardians came with *Huntress*'s Flight Group Avalanche. Outnumbered three to two and taken by surprise, there was no chance for the Weltraumpanzer pilots to get in the bombers' way.

Maxi Bueller would be talking to the devil rather sooner than they'd anticipated, though it had been a long time since Kira could take pleasure in the destruction of a starship. At least five thousand people died aboard the HC-10 carrier as dozens of torpedoes slammed into the warship.

The Guardians had saved their own torpedoes while keeping the defenders off the bombers. Now they swung around and salvoed the weapons at the cruiser *Deception* wasn't hammering, following the opening Kira had ordered Mwangi to make.

Even through the jamming, Kira could see the Brisingr cruiser reel as her Harrington coils went wild. The destroyers and starfighters were torn, some trying to turn in space, some trying to win their close-range dogfights.

Then one of Isidora Soler's shots hit something critical and a gout of flame the size of a corvette blazed out the side of the still-fighting cruiser. Vacuum smothered the flame in moments, but even in the chaos of the battlespace, *that* got everyone's attention.

And then both cruisers brought every exterior light they had online, white and bright. A second later, engines and cannon shut down, the badly damaged ships drifting away from the battle while glowing with a stark brilliance.

It took ten seconds for the most-damaged destroyer to follow suit, but the domino effect was clear from there. First the destroyers, then the remaining fighters. Light after light came on and turned to a brilliant white, until the shattered survivors of a Brisingr Kaiserreich Navy carrier group resembled nothing so much as a scattered handful of pearls across the void.

"Cease fire," Mwangi ordered softly. "They're surrendering."

"That they are," Kira confirmed after a moment. "Cut the jamming; link up with our fighters and the SDC birds."

She smiled sadly.

"The rest of this is up to Milani's people, I think."

39

The advantage, Kira supposed, of having a planet that was technically going through an ice age was that it wasn't difficult to find an inhospitable chunk of land to put people on. While most of Bennet delighted in warm equatorial temperatures and gentle seasons due to the minimal axial tilt, the planet's orbit had slipped enough that the higher latitudes could get quite chilly.

The Ministries had found a region of permafrost that *looked* incredible, a vast, sweeping expanse of rough scrub, snow and native wildlife that was mostly inedible to humans.

The last was an important point, Kira knew, as she watched the first shuttles touch down at the temporary camp on the frozen plain beneath her hilltop perch.

"Two cruisers, four destroyers, forty-two starfighters," Milani listed off from where they stood just behind her. "Including the survivors from the ships we destroyed, seventy-five hundred prisoners."

And probably around as many dead. Kira wasn't going to forget that. The ships weren't a small matter, though. She could argue that, per her contract, all of them belonged to Memorial Force and Samuels had to buy them out.

"SDC got hammered, but they only sent in fighters," she noted. "Two hundred and twenty-six dead doesn't leave enough people clamoring for vengeance to be a problem."

She waved at the prison camp.

"Keeping them separated from the locals is still a good plan. I'm not sure BKN personnel would go easy on a police force used to a majority pacifist population."

"Probably not," Milani agreed. "We'll be needed to backup security for the camp for a while."

"Three months for you to train up the SDC ground team," Kira confirmed. "Though I suspect they're hoping to sort things out with Brisingr by then."

"They might be optimistic," Milani replied.

"And they might not," Konrad Bueller said, stepping up and taking Kira's hand to warm her fingers. "The Kaiser was after something very specific out here. He didn't get it—and while he's not one to cut his losses on his *goals*, Samuels is apparently irrelevant to them."

Kira shivered.

"The thought of being the target of this kind of operation is terrifying," she murmured. "Your cousin thought that *everything* here was to lure us into an ambush."

"I know Kaiser Reinhardt better than I knew Maxi Bueller," her boyfriend noted. "That doesn't mean much, though. I've met him five times. But..." He shook his head as he rubbed her fingers. "I can see it, I suppose. You've tweaked his nose via his Equilibrium friends a lot. He's gone this far... I'm not sure what he *won't* do to get at you, if he's willing to start a war and send a *carrier group*."

"I know," Kira agreed. "I *think* Samuels is safe from him if we're not here, but the contract has us sticking around for a while to back up their security. Setting up the deal for Milani to help run security here..."

She studied the prison camp again. The shelters were standard prefabricated structures that could be found anywhere in the galaxy. They'd run basically forever on solar power and provide just about everything the prisoners needed—except food.

Bennet's southernmost continent was almost completely uninhabited and had zero Terran crops or animal life. Nothing around the camp was edible to humans, and the nearest settlement, a scientific observation post keeping an eye on the ice age, was a five-hundred-kilometer hike across permafrost.

There were guard towers around the prefab barracks for the prisoners and a separate fenced base for the guards, but no one was really worried about the prisoners escaping.

They'd probably freeze to death before they starved, if they ran. Probably.

"Well, my people and I are successfully dropped off," Milani noted wryly. "I hope the locals picked a *nice* prefab barracks for us."

"If they didn't, we'll send you down a better one from *Deception*'s stores," Kira promised. "It's not like she's going anywhere else anytime soon."

Deception was less damaged than the two captured Brisingr cruisers. *Barely.*

"Either way, you two have places to be," Milani reminded her, gesturing to a pair of their troopers. "And while I appreciate the ride, Lovel and Carter are going to stick to you two like glue."

Kira chuckled as she glanced at the two mercs standing between her and the shuttle. They'd landed three shuttles and sixty armored mercenaries. Two of the shuttles would stay—and apparently two of the mercs were going to come with her when she left.

"We're not even going to Quaker City, Milani," she reminded her security chief. "There's apparently a few ski resorts on this continent, near the north coasts. The Ministries have taken one over for a 'strategic planning summit.'"

By which, so far as Kira could tell, Buxton meant a "We're at war with the biggest bully in the neighborhood now; what do we *do*?" summit.

"I've met what the locals regard as solid security," Milani pointed out. "Be glad I'm not telling Whittaker to take off and orbit over the resort with cannon and missiles pointedly aimed."

"Behave, Milani. We *like* these people." She chuckled. "I also like their money, and they owe us a lot of it."

FOR ALL OF Milani's complaints, there were at least two companies of the Samuels Defense Command Ground Forces encamped around the ski resort. That Kira could *see* the mobile anti-air units spoke poorly to their experience, but the units and troops were out and deployed.

The resort itself was built into the side of a large hill, with sprawling chalet-style structures laid out in parallel to the ski slopes. Her headware told her there was *always* snow at the resort, but the grounds of the chalets, at least, were clear.

It was evident from the air that the resort wasn't operating, either. There was no one on the ski slopes, and the visible pathways and gardens and restaurants were all sparsely populated. There were politicians and military officers there, key leaders of the Ministries and the Quorum, but none of the general tourists who would normally use the place.

Her pilot touched the shuttle down on the runway and followed an invisible guide into a designated spot, alongside SDC shuttles and civilian suborbitals.

One of the last bore a familiar marking that made Kira grimace. She wasn't entirely *surprised* to see the flaming sword and gauntlet of the Brisingr Kaiserreich there, but it wasn't an icon she was ever going to be happy to see.

"That's got to be the embassy transport," Konrad murmured as he saw the same logo. "Why do I have the feeling there's only one person from the embassy that Buxton would invite to *this* affair?"

"Might explain why I just got a ping from whoever is running air control, *suggesting* I get you two moving ASAP," Whittaker said from the cockpit. "Something is going down in short order, and the locals want you there.

"Flipping directions to your headware, but there should be a guide as well."

"Thanks, Juliet," Kira replied. "Come on, Konrad. Let's go see what trap Buxton has laid."

"Can I at least hope it isn't for us?" her boyfriend said drily. "Only Lovel and Koch get to be in armor."

"My dear, in all of the time you have known me, do you think I've *ever* gone to a diplomatic function without armor and a blaster?" she asked. "If *you've* been coming without guns and gear, we may need to fix that!"

THERE WAS, in fact, a guide waiting for them. The young woman in a black suit was trying to conceal her agitation when Kira and Konrad reached her, but she swiftly took them to what appeared to be hotel's conference center.

The room they were led into had clearly been set up for a press conference, with three dozen reporters lined up along one wall with cameras and microphones.

The opposite wall had neatly organized chairs for the people who were here to be reported on, Kira figured, and she and Konrad were ushered to seats that had been left open for them, between Doretta Macey and Admiral Mahinder Bachchan.

Their two armored escorts threw their bureaucratic guide off a bit, but they calmly took up positions against the wall behind Kira, looming decoratively at the rest of the room.

"What's going on?" Kira whispered to the officer next to her. Bachchan made a small shushing gesture.

"Patience," she whispered back. "The Brisingr ambassador should be here any moment now."

There was no lectern, Kira realized. Instead, roughly where she would have expected the lectern to be for a press conference, there were two large dark blue chairs facing each other.

The first chair was occupied a moment later when Buxton and Tapadia entered the room from deeper in the hotel. The First Minister took their seat in front of the reporters' cameras, carefully angled to give them a good shot of their muscular frame and carefully made-up face, while their husband joined the row of observers.

Then the doors from the outside swung open, letting a blast of cold air in as a tall Black woman regally walked into the room.

Kira wasn't familiar with the ambassador, though she suspected that the Brisingr ambassador to Samuels was about as far down the list of "people who deserve ambassadorial appointments" as you could be and still *get* an embassy.

Still, she had to appreciate the woman's style. She stood in the door, framed in sunlight, for several seconds as the wind whipped a ceremonial black cloak around her.

Even when the doors slid closed behind her and the single aide-slash-bodyguard she'd brought, she still effortlessly *oozed* grace and elegance as she walked across the conference room. Kira doubted she'd been warned that the meeting with Buxton would have an audience, but she took it perfectly in stride.

The only hint of a break in the ambassador's ironclad façade was when she saw the Memorial Force mercenaries. Kira met her gaze and *saw* the lines around the woman's face tighten as she recognized Kira.

"First Minister Buxton," she greeted the planet's elected leader.

"Ambassador Kristina Schirmer," Buxton replied, rising from the chair to offer her their hand for a brief handshake.

Schirmer did not sit or take the proffered hand. She stood next to the chair meant for her, giving the reporters the benefit of her stern profile as she proffered a formal envelope. It would, in Kira's experience, contain both a physical letter and a datachip.

"I have a formal note to deliver," she announced. "I was surprised to be told to deliver it here."

"The situation has grown complex," Buxton said. "I, Ambassador, serve at the pleasure of a direct democracy. The people of Samuels deserve for these matters to be handled in the light of day."

He took the envelope and laid it aside.

"Summarize the note for me, if you will, Ambassador," they instructed.

"Are you certain you would not prefer to do this in private?" Schirmer asked.

"Summarize the note, Ambassador." Buxton's tone was cold iron.

"Very well." She somehow straightened even further, resembling nothing so much as a statue carved from black ice.

"I have been advised that six Brisingr Kaiserreich Navy vessels and seventy-five hundred and twenty-seven Brisingr Kaiserreich Navy personnel have been illegally detained by the Samuels Defense Command," she continued. "Combined with the illegal and unprovoked attack on our personnel and vessels in the trade-route stop nearby, this represents an unacceptable level of aggression on the part of the Samuels System.

"But Brisingr has no hostility toward Samuels, and I wish to bring this to a peaceful resolution as quickly as possible," she continued. "Therefore, I am using my full authority to render an offer to head off this crisis immediately."

Buxton made a "go ahead" gesture...and if it looked like someone playing out rope, that was *probably* just in Kira's head.

"Brisingr requires the return of all of our warships and personnel," Schirmer said flatly. "We require the detainment and surrender of all members of the criminal organization calling itself Memorial Force to Brisingr authority, as well as the stolen Brisingr warship in their possession.

"If these terms are met, we will not seek reparations for the involvement of Samuels Defense Command nova fighters in the attack on our ships," she continued. "We understand that your personnel were acting in support of your contractors, even if they misunderstood the situation."

Kira could hear the inhalations of the people surrounding her. The single row of chairs she'd been seated in included key members of the Ministries and Defense Command. The people around her knew *exactly* what had gone down in the void around Samuels.

"Curious," Buxton said calmly. "I suggest you sit down, Em Schirmer."

Kira wasn't sure if the ambassador was married...but from the First Minister's tone, she doubted they would have extended Schirmer any honorific that suggested respect in Samuels's culture.

"I do not require an immediate response," the ambassador replied. "You have twenty-four hours."

"I don't need them," Buxton told her. "Sit down, Em Schirmer. We are not done here."

"I will stand," she said calmly.

"As you wish." Buxton placed their hands on their knees and leaned forward. Tall as Schirmer was, Buxton was a big-enough person that, even sitting, they barely had had to crane their neck to look at her.

"It appears we have a fundamental disagreement on the nature of what occurred at trade-route stop Y-Six-Three-Five-Seven-Seven-D-R-Six-W-S-Nine-A-Three-K," the First Minister of Samuels said, their voice still ice-cold.

"Memorial Force was and remains contracted to secure the trade-route stops around the Samuels System," they stated. "When challenged by a Brisingr Kaiserreich Navy carrier group under Vice Admiral Maxi Bueller, Admiral Demirci did *exactly* as she was contracted to.

"*Your* officer, Ambassador, opened the engagement. *Your* officer attacked Memorial Force after being explicitly advised of their contract. By the standards of interstellar law, Ambassador, *that* was an act of war against the Samuels System."

"That is no—"

"Shut. Up."

Kira could hear the *reporters'* breathing now as the room stilled at Buxton's harsh words.

"You can tell whatever story you want to the Kaiserreich's people," they told Schirmer. "But the people of Samuels will not be lied to. The Brisingr Kaiserreich Navy has committed unprovoked acts of aggression against us.

"This will not be tolerated and will not be covered up. The seizure of the remaining warships of Admiral Bueller's battle group is a necessary *tactical* action. It does not begin to cover the compensation owed for the deaths of our personnel and the betrayal of our trust.

"It is the judgment of the Quorum of the People of Samuels that Brisingr has engaged in open and covert warfare against us, both directly and using the Republic of Colossus as a proxy," Buxton continued.

"Your *terms* are rejected. These are *our* terms," they stated. "All civilian Brisingr personnel are now under house arrest. You will leave the embassy only under armed guard.

"Your courier ship will be *immediately* dispatched to Brisingr, bearing a formal note of our displeasure to Kaiser Reinhardt. We will patiently await the Kaiser's response...but until such time as we have a satisfactory response from him, the Samuels-Colossus Corridor is closed to Brisingr military and civilian traffic."

Even Kira was stunned by that, but Schirmer adapted quickly, glaring down at the First Minister.

"You have neither the authority nor the firepower to impose such a closure," she snapped.

"I have more authority to close the Corridor than your Admiral Bueller did to attempt to detain my mercenaries," Buxton replied.

"And as for firepower...we appear to have four brand-new nova destroyers, and a contracted supercarrier on its way.

"This is not a discussion, Ambassador Schirmer. This is not even *my* decision," they noted. "This is the will of the Quorum of the People of Samuels. We are not a belligerent people. We do not choose confrontation as a first recourse.

"But equally, we will not be attacked, bullied or walked over. Colonel Skenandoa!"

An SDC Ground Forces Colonel seemed to materialize out of nowhere, with four armored soldiers in tow.

"First Minister!" the soldier answered crisply.

"Please escort Ambassador Schirmer and her aide to their aircraft and see them safely to their embassy," Buxton ordered.

"Yes, First Minister!"

The five soldiers closed on the elegant ambassador, and for a moment, Kira half-expected Schirmer or her bodyguard to do something truly stupid.

Then the tension released and Schirmer allowed herself to be escorted from the room in silence.

That quiet lasted just long enough for the doors to close behind the ambassador before the reporters exploded into a thousand questions.

40

WHEN THE PRESS conference finally died down, Bachchan gestured for Kira to follow her. She and Macey fell in around the two mercenaries, clearly following a preplanned maneuver that swept them down the halls of the resort.

The SDC's commander finally led them into a small lounge area appointed in dark hardwood and a selection of chairs of assorted styles.

"Have a seat," Macey told them. "Tapadia and Buxton will be with us momentarily."

Kira obeyed and was surprised when one of the hardwood panels unfolded, revealing itself to be a wood-sided artificial stupid wet bar. It rolled over to her, and her headware received a request for a drink order.

She and Konrad both took coffees from the machine. Bachchan took the thick black tea the SDC favored—and Kira could *not* stand—where Macey laid out three beers before the door opened again.

"I collected your escorts," Tapadia said drily as he stepped in. "They're happily looming in the corridor outside, but I think they got lost in the reporters."

Kira cursed.

"I was taken aback enough by the whole display that I didn't think of them," she admitted. If she'd thought about it, she would have expected Koch and her ground-force trooper companion to follow her—and Milani would probably have *words* for the two escorts if they learned that their people had even temporarily lost track of the Admiral.

"It was quite the display, wasn't it?" Tapadia murmured. He grabbed one of the beers Macey had laid out with a nod to the older woman. "I honestly did not think we were going to take Schirmer by surprise like that, not when we needed a unanimous vote out of the Quorum in advance."

"We got the vote," Macey noted.

Kira had to wonder how much the First Minister's hatchet woman had been involved in that. Her lack of formal title concealed an impressive amount of informal power.

"We did," Tapadia confirmed. "Though if it comes to war, that goes to the general vote. Blockading the Corridor is only *arguably* in the authority of the Ministries, but the unanimity of the Quorum covers a multitude of sins."

"Democracy is a wonderful thing," Buxton told them as they stepped into the room, closing the door firmly behind them. "It may not move quickly, and it may not move with certainty, but when it moves, it moves with the force of an avalanche.

"The people of Samuels are with us in this. There will be no question, no hesitation. Brisingr came to the wrong neighborhood if they expected us to take this lying down."

"I appreciate the support, First Minister," Kira said as Buxton took their beer and sat down. "Many systems would be more willing to cut loose a mercenary company than challenge Brisingr."

"I am not intimidated by Brisingr," Buxton replied. "Now, to be honest, much of that is recognizing that we are at the far limit of the Kaiserreich's ability to project force and they have problems closer to home."

"But there is also the realization that we were played and far too easily," Macey said grimly. "From your conversation with Bueller—Admiral Bueller, apologies, *Commander* Bueller—I am looking at the sources that made us consider Memorial Force as our first choice with suspicion."

"Starting a war between us and Colossus wasn't enough to guarantee you were here for them to move against," Tapadia agreed. "They had to make sure *we* knew you were out there and thought of you as our first option.

"As Doretta says, we were played...and you very nearly paid for it."

"Speaking of paid..." Kira murmured.

Buxton laughed.

"Full combat and risk pay have already been transferred to your local accounts," they promised. "Death benefits for your people will follow shortly."

"I don't want to seem...rude," Konrad said slowly, "but I was under the impression that those destroyers you were waving at Schirmer were, ah, ours?"

Kira had been going to let that simmer for a bit longer, but it had *definitely* been on her list.

"Per the contract, you own ships taken in actions where Memorial Force is the sole or primary combatant," Admiral Bachchan observed. "So, the depot ships that we purchased from you, for example, had unquestioned ownership.

"The contract did not specify exactly what ownership took shape when a *joint* operation between Memorial Force and the SDC took place."

"We could argue back and forth around exactly how to divvy things up, but we have an offer to make," Tapadia told them before Kira could say anything. "*Deception* requires significant repairs, yes?"

"Yes," Konrad said grimly. Kira had barely managed to tear him away from the damage surveys sufficiently in advance of the meeting for him to *shower*. "We lost thirty-seven people, even putting aside fighter-crew losses, and one of our heavy cannon is straight-up gone."

"The cruisers we captured are in similar or worse shape," the Samuels businessman told them. "The destroyers, on the other hand, are in decent condition. Some repairs and refit required—replacing all of their software as a precaution at a minimum—but we could get all four destroyers into space inside a month.

"My engineers estimate it will take us at least two months, likely three, to repair either of the BKN cruisers," he continued. "My gut feeling is that *Deception* will take about the same—and we will have three cruiser-scale yards online at the new shipyards inside two weeks."

"A logical split would be for each of us to take half of the cubage captured," Buxton suggested, meeting their husband's gaze. "But frankly, we need all of those destroyers if we're going to even *begin* to enforce the blockade I've announced."

"The cruisers are conveniently twice the size of the destroyers, aren't they?" Kira noted.

"That was exactly my thought," Bachchan agreed. "Mr. Tapadia?"

The industrialist nodded and leaned forward.

"As I said, the full military shipyards are almost online," he told them all. "My suggestion—*our* suggestion—is that we take the four destroyers and Memorial Force takes both cruisers. We will also cover the full costs of repairs to all three ships."

"Since we're planning on hanging on to you for at least six months, we get the benefits of those cruisers for some time *anyway*," Buxton observed. "And I feel that two modern cruisers are a sufficient augmentation to your forces to be worth some patience?"

"You could certainly say that," Kira agreed drily. She could argue that all six ships belonged to her under the contract—there were certainly grounds to support that—but that would require a legal fight. Plus, a six-month contract for the entirety of Memorial Force was *more* than enough to buy four destroyers from most systems that would sell them—and while everything was going smoothly with Samuels so far, fighting them in court over the destroyers could easily ruin that.

"We can live with that agreement," she continued. The repairs on the three damaged cruisers wouldn't be cheap, either. "And, of course, Commander Bueller is available to contract to assist with the repairs and refits of the destroyers."

She winked at her boyfriend, who simply smiled and nodded gently.

"I can think of a few precautions you'll want to take above and beyond removing the software," he warned. "How much of that I can provide for free is, of course, up to the Admiral."

"There'll be no need," Tapadia said immediately. "If the SDC doesn't want to pay for your expertise, Commander Bueller, Samuels-Tata Technologies most definitely *does*."

"It is decided, then," Buxton concluded. "We, of course, await the arrival of *Fortitude* and your destroyers with bated breath, Admiral, but unless the Kaiserreich has a few spare carrier groups floating here at the extreme end of their logistics ability, I think we have time to sort things out."

"We should," Kira agreed. "And while *Deception* may be out of commission, *Huntress* is fully functional. We retrieved enough of our pilots to operate her full flight group, though it will take us a few more weeks to fabricate replacement fighters.

"Assuming, of course, that you are prepared to sell us class two drives?"

Operating in the Outer Rim as they did, Memorial Force's fighters were rigged to eject their class two drives as well as their crews. Priority was still given to the crew survival pods, though, so while Kira's people had saved forty of the fifty-nine people aboard the thirty-five lost fighters, they'd only salvaged eighteen drives.

"I will require explicit permission from the Ministries to do so," Tapadia observed wryly. "Somehow, I believe it will be forthcoming. Right, love?"

Tapadia's partner, the planetary head of state, could only laugh at that.

Kira smiled and leaned back in her own chair. The leaders of the Samuels System had played their part in luring her into a trap, but they hadn't *known* that was what they were doing—and they were trying to make it right.

She wasn't going to fly for *anyone* for free, but she was comfortable that she'd chosen the right side to take money from in this particular mess.

41

Even with the damage the cruiser had taken, *Deception* was still better suited to operate as Kira's home base than *Huntress*. The flag deck and Admiral's quarters were deep enough to be undamaged, which allowed her to continue to work from her usual spaces even as the engineering team under Bueller began to prepare the ship for the repairs.

Deception had moved under the guns of the Samuels fortresses now, orbiting only a few hundred kilometers from the yards that would shortly receive her and her two younger siblings, *K92E* and *K91A*.

Eventually, Kira and her people would come up with new names for the ships—she was more willing to risk the superstition that name changes were bad luck than she was to send people into battle aboard ships with only numbers.

A sort of calm watchfulness had descended over the Samuels System over the last few days. It felt like everyone in the star system was watching to see what happened next.

For Kira's own part, her focus was mainly on the yards. The four ex-BKN destroyers were being refitted in the civilian yards—and the keels of six new Samuels-designed destroyers had been laid alongside them. That was fully half of the nova-ship yards available until the new military yards came online.

Samuels's population might not want war. They might actively hate the concept—but they clearly hated being pushed around even more. The SDC's new recruiting programs were having no problems filling their quotas now.

Kira wasn't sure where *she* was going to find crews for her new cruisers, but she was prepared to wait for *Fortitude* and Kavitha Zoric to arrive to sort that out. Once she had her full fleet, it would be a lot easier to send a destroyer or a logistics ship to the Outer Rim end of the Corridor to recruit new crew and pilots.

Everything seemed in order, progressing as expected. It would still be almost two weeks before they heard from Brisingr. And yet.

Somehow, she understood the feeling in the star system. Everyone was waiting for the other shoe to drop. Kira wasn't sure what it was, but she could definitely sense it out there, lurking.

A new nova flare drew her attention, and it took her a second to realize why. With the Corridor reopened—to everyone except Brisingr, at least—a minimum of twenty ships came through Samuels each day.

But they stopped at Haven and Sanctuary to discharge static. Only a handful of ships novaed in near Bennet itself, as this ship had done. And the ones that did...didn't come with an escort of Kira's own nova fighters, clearly deployed from *Huntress*'s patrol to make sure that *this* ship made it in safely.

Marija Davidović and Abdullah Colombera had clearly felt that this particular ship needed to be kept safe, no matter what—and with *that* thought, Kira finally recognized the Core-built freighter already vectoring toward *Deception*.

Baile Fantasma spent most of her time pretending to a regular merchant transport. For her captain to have requested an escort from Davidović and to be coming toward *Deception* that directly was out of character.

Kira didn't know Captain Tomas Zamorano well, but she *did* know that he was a senior officer in the Interstellar Intelligence Service of the Solar Federation, the government that encompassed Earth and the surrounding star systems.

If he was risking his cover, something major was going down.

"THANK you for seeing me without notice," Zamorano told Kira as he stepped into the meeting room. Battered as *Deception* was, the room attached to the flight deck had a visible patch applied over the bulkhead.

Eventually, the bulkhead would be replaced. Right now, a rough-welded sheet of steel covered the hole where a plasma burst had run the full length of the landing bay.

"Take a seat, Captain," Kira told him.

Zamorano nodded calmly and obeyed, glancing around the mostly empty room. Konrad Bueller was the only other person she'd brought in—but they'd both met the scrawny Spanish spy when they'd been operating in the Crest.

"As for seeing you without notice, you certainly got our attention," she continued. "When I gave you code words to get help from my people, I honestly didn't expect to see you again."

"I expected to see you again," Zamorano said drily. "That's the nature of the universe, though. I suspected fate would bring you back to the Apollo-Brisingr Sector. Now, of course, I know that the Kaiser made it happen for his own reasons."

"His ambush failed," Bueller noted. "He underestimated us."

"He also perhaps did not have the resources to spare he might have preferred," the spy told them. "He's been busy."

"Busy?" Kira asked. She studied the Terran. "You're dodging around something already, Zamorano."

"I am," he admitted. "I *watched it happen* and I still can't believe it. Brisingr has done the impossible, Admiral Demirci."

"There are many things in this universe people believe to be impossible that aren't," she said slowly. "What exactly has Brisingr done?"

"Apollo has fallen."

The words didn't even process for a moment, and even then, they didn't make any sense.

"What do you mean, 'fallen?'" Bueller demanded while Kira was still trying to register what had been said.

"When I fled the system, a hundred thousand Brisingr Weltraumsoldats were already on the surface, and the orbital defenses were either destroyed or in Brisingr hands," Zamorano said softly. "They had secured Athens itself and were deploying special operations teams to sweep up the members of the Council of Principals they'd missed.

"A second wave of over two hundred troop transports had just arrived in-system, to reinforce the armed transports that delivered the first wave," he continued. "They were still reorganizing the nova-fighter wings after the battle...but I also get the feeling that they *let* the civilian ships run."

"That isn't possible," Kira whispered. "There were fortresses... monitors...the ASDF..."

"Treachery and sabotage took out the fortresses," Zamorano said flatly. "They have to have been laying the groundwork for years—possibly since before the *last* war. A third of the fortresses just...blew up. Half of the remainder turned their weapons on the monitors and the other forts.

"A third of the nova fleet was gone before the BKN even *arrived.* The rest tried to fight, but they never expected to fight in Apollo without the fortresses for support. Maybe half a dozen carriers escaped."

"My god," Bueller said. "That's...madness."

"The impossible, as I said," Zamorano told them. "I knew where to find you, so I came here. I have other stops, other people to inform and, hopefully, connect."

Kira was silent in shock, trying to process a changed reality. Even as Apollo had conceded the war and accepted a secondary status versus Brisingr, they'd still remained a potent and major power in the region. Wealthy and technologically advanced by Rim standards, Apollo's fortifications had been impenetrable, insurmountable by anything except vastly superior technology.

Or treachery. She'd known since the day she'd fled her homeworld that the Brisingr Shadows had heavily infiltrated Apollon society, but she hadn't thought they were *that* powerful.

"What do you expect us to do?" she demanded.

"I don't know," the SolFed spy admitted. "All I can do is make sure the people who have the power and the will to potentially fight Brisingr know what happened and about each other."

Kira swallowed, looking at Konrad.

"The crews will follow you; you know that," her boyfriend told her. "*I'll* follow you, into the teeth of my Kaiser's anger. This is...new."

"This is dangerous," Zamorano said. "Even if no one else can likely repeat what Brisingr has done, I can count on the fingers of one hand how many times a star system has been successfully invaded and conquered."

"I know," Kira replied, swallowing again and marshaling her will. "Who else are you contacting?"

"Thanks to your reference, I have a drop point to make contact with Colonel Killinger," Zamorano told her. "I haven't spoken with the damn man except by dead drop, but I know he's *acquired* a few capital ships that used to belong to the Friends of Apollo that were supposed to be scrapped.

"I also *think* I picked up enough information on the way out here to know where Admiral Michelakis will have taken the carriers that followed her into retreat," the spy noted. "I have a few other levers to pull, but those are the names I know you know."

Fevronia Michelakis had been a Commodore during the war.

Kira didn't know her—but she knew James Heller had respected her. That was all she had...but it would have to be enough.

"It's going to take time to make contact," Konrad Bueller said softly. "Time the Kaiser's people will use to tighten their hold on Apollo."

"You can only tighten your hold so much over a world that never even anticipated they might kneel," Zamorano said. "There is time."

"That's good," Kira murmured, pulling up a virtual update on her ships. "Because I don't know how long it will be before *Fortitude* gets here, but I *know* it's going to be three months before I have cruisers ready to deploy."

"We make a war of it, then?" her lover asked.

"We reach out to everyone we can, at the very least," Kira promised. "To hell with your Kaiser, Konrad. I left my homeworld behind, but this... This can't stand."

"I'm with you," Konrad promised.

"There's not much else I can do," Zamorano warned. "I'm going to poke at resources and see what I can quietly move in this direction, but I won't even be able to swing Fringe tech. Don't expect much."

"I won't," Kira promised. She made a gesture, and the three cruisers—*Deception* and the new captures—appeared as holograms in the room. "But we'll fight," she continued. "And I guess that helps with one decision."

"Oh?" Both men looked at the holograms of the three warships.

"Names," she told them. "I wasn't sure what to name our two new cruisers, but now I know.

"This one will be *Harbinger*...and this one will be *Prodigal*."

She smiled thinly.

"Because I promise you, gentlemen, that Apollo's prodigal daughter is coming home...and I will be the harbinger of the Kaiser's destruction."

JOIN THE MAILING LIST

Love Glynn Stewart's books? To know as soon as new books are released, special announcements, and a chance to win free paperbacks, join the mailing list at:

glynnstewart.com/mailing-list/

ABOUT THE AUTHOR

Glynn Stewart is the author of *Starship's Mage*, a bestselling science fiction and fantasy series where faster-than-light travel is possible–but only because of magic. His other works include science fiction series *Duchy of Terra, Castle Federation* and *Vigilante,* as well as the urban fantasy series *ONSET* and *Changeling Blood*.

Writing managed to liberate Glynn from a bleak future as an accountant. With his personality and hope for a high-tech future intact, he lives in Southern Ontario with his partner, their cats, and an unstoppable writing habit.

VISIT GLYNNSTEWART.COM FOR NEW RELEASE UPDATES

CREDITS

The following people were involved in making this book:

Copyeditor: Richard Shealy
Proofreader: M Parker Editing
Cover art: Jeff Brown
Typography: Danika Challand
Typo Hunter Team
Faolan's Pen Publishing team: Jack, Kate, and Robin.

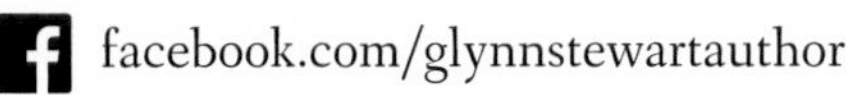

OTHER BOOKS BY GLYNN STEWART

For release announcements join the mailing list or visit **GlynnStewart.com**

STARSHIP'S MAGE

Starship's Mage
Hand of Mars
Voice of Mars
Alien Arcana
Judgment of Mars
UnArcana Stars
Sword of Mars
Mountain of Mars
The Service of Mars
A Darker Magic
Mage-Commander
Beyond the Eyes of Mars

Starship's Mage: Red Falcon
Interstellar Mage
Mage-Provocateur
Agents of Mars

Pulsar Race: A Starship's Mage Universe Novella

DUCHY OF TERRA

The Terran Privateer
Duchess of Terra
Terra and Imperium
Darkness Beyond
Shield of Terra
Imperium Defiant
Relics of Eternity
Shadows of the Fall
Eyes of Tomorrow

SCATTERED STARS

Scattered Stars: Conviction

Conviction
Deception
Equilibrium
Fortitude
Huntress
Prodigal *(upcoming)*

Scattered Stars: Evasion

Evasion
Discretion *(upcoming)*

PEACEKEEPERS OF SOL

Raven's Peace
The Peacekeeper Initiative
Raven's Course
Drifter's Folly
Remnant Faction *(upcoming)*

EXILE

Exile
Refuge
Crusade
Ashen Stars: An Exile Novella

CASTLE FEDERATION

Space Carrier Avalon
Stellar Fox
Battle Group Avalon
Q-Ship Chameleon
Rimward Stars
Operation Medusa
A Question of Faith: A Castle Federation Novella

Dakotan Confederacy

Admiral's Oath
To Stand Defiant *(upcoming)*

VIGILANTE
(WITH TERRY MIXON)
Heart of Vengeance
Oath of Vengeance

Bound By Stars: A Vigilante Series
(With Terry Mixon)
Bound By Law
Bound by Honor
Bound by Blood

TEER AND KARD
Wardtown
Blood Ward

CHANGELING BLOOD
Changeling's Fealty
Hunter's Oath
Noble's Honor
Fae, Flames & Fedoras: A Changeling Blood Novella

ONSET
ONSET: To Serve and Protect
ONSET: My Enemy's Enemy
ONSET: Blood of the Innocent
ONSET: Stay of Execution
Murder by Magic: An ONSET Novella

STAND ALONE NOVELS & NOVELLAS
Children of Prophecy
City in the Sky
Excalibur Lost: A Space Opera Novella
Balefire: A Dark Fantasy Novella

Made in United States
North Haven, CT
25 January 2024